Praise for *Learning Curves*

"A quirky, fast-paced and fun romp . . . *Learning Curves* is a fun ride and you'll chuckle all the while you're on it."
—Armchair Interviews

"A fascinating boardroom romance. Gemma Townley writes a strong tale."
—*Affaire de Coeur* magazine

"Bouncy . . . Jennifer Bell navigates corporate and family intrigue with a mix of pluck and naïveté. . . . Charming."
—*Publishers Weekly*

"This potboiler with a comic edge has an interesting central conflict so realistic that it could have been ripped directly from last year's headlines. . . . Jen is an appealing character who is sure to please readers."
—*Romantic Times*

"Townley shines at creating characters who are engaging and realistic. . . . Readers will be charmed . . . and intrigued by the family drama."
—*Booklist*

Also by Gemma Townley

LITTLE WHITE LIES
WHEN IN ROME . . .

Books published by The Random House Publishing Group
are available at quantity discounts on bulk purchases for
premium, educational, fund-raising, and special sales use.
For details, please call 1-800-733-3000.

Learning Curves

A Novel of Sex, Suits, and Secret Affairs

Gemma Townley

Core —
Rfs
Dec 2007

BALLANTINE BOOKS · NEW YORK

2007 Ballantine Books Mass Market Edition

Copyright © 2006 by Gemma Townley
Excerpt of *The Hopeless Romantic's Handbook* copyright © 2007 by Gemma Townley

Published in the United States by Ballantine Books, an imprint of The Random House Publishing Group, a division of Random House, Inc., New York.

BALLANTINE and colophon are registered trademarks of Random House, Inc.

This book contains an excerpt from the trade paperback edition of *The Hopeless Romantic's Handbook*. This excerpt has been set for this edition only and may not reflect the final content of the novel.

Originally published as a trade paperback in the United States by Ballantine Books, an imprint of The Random House Publishing Group, a division of Random House, Inc., in 2006.

ISBN 978-0-345-49601-0

Cover illustration: © Anne Keenan Higgins

Printed in the United States of America

www.ballantinebooks.com

OPM 9 8 7 6 5 4 3 2 1

To Abigail, who makes a little black suit look cool:
May your holiday allowance cup runneth over

ACKNOWLEDGMENTS

There are a lot of people who deserve a big thank-you for their help in getting this book started and finished. Mark, for hours (and hours) spent listening as I ummed and ahhed over the plot; my agent Dorie Simmonds for wise counsel, patience, and essential motivational pep talks; Allison Dickens, my editor, for patience (again . . . !), enthusiasm, and advice; and Maddy, for pointing out the obvious (and not so obvious) when I couldn't see the wood for the trees. But finally, big thanks and heartfelt congratulations to the Zone 2 team—Roger, Yvonne, Robin, Ross, and Charl. Who'd have thought that going back to school could be so much fun.

❧ PROLOGUE

My God, Jen, what the hell are you getting yourself into this time? Jennifer Bell thought to herself as she put down the phone and looked around her kitchen, trying desperately to make sense of what she'd just agreed to, trying to make it seem less ridiculous, less terrifying. *I'm doing an MBA,* she thought, rolling her eyes in incomprehension. *I hate business. I hate Bell Consulting even more. And yet I've just agreed to do an MBA at Bell Consulting.* She was already queasy at the thought.

How did it happen? she thought to herself. *Why on earth did I say yes?*

Only a few minutes before, she had been watching the news. Just sitting there, minding her own business, with no thoughts of any major changes to her life. But, as she'd learned over the years, a lot could change in a few minutes. Particularly when her mother was involved.

She frowned, trying to work out if she'd been totally suckered in to this little venture or whether she'd actually been involved in the decision. *Probably the former,* she thought with a sigh, as she turned the events of the past ten minutes over in her head. . . .

"And we've got more news of the latest earthquake in

Indonesia. More than five hundred families have lost their homes in this latest tragedy. Susan Mills reports."

"Thanks, Sandra. Well, scientists said it would happen, but none of us expected it quite so soon after the Boxing Day Tsunami. And what is really worrying people here is that some of the houses that were built after the tsunami, specifically to withstand that sort of disturbance, have crumpled to the ground, increasing speculation that building standards were not met by some of the contractors here. There's been talk of corruption and bribes being paid to secure contracts, but so far none of these allegations have stuck. Axiom, one of the big construction firms, is denying any involvement in shady dealings, and has issued writs against two newspapers . . ."

Okay, so she'd been watching television, getting depressed by the news, as usual. Wondering what kind of world she lived in, when tidal waves killed thousands of people one month, and a few months later they all lost their homes again? It was just too horrible.

"And we've got more news of the latest . . ."

She turned off the television impotently and made her way to the kitchen to pour herself a glass of wine. Not exactly helping, she'd acknowledged, but required nonetheless. She'd wanted to go to Sri Lanka when the tsunami hit, had wanted to physically help out by building houses or doing something to help the people there to rebuild their lives. Not that she knew anything about building houses—if anything, she'd probably just get in the way. But it would make her feel better. Anyway, she had a proper job now, she reminded herself, in a proper office, and while she was enjoying the security, it did mean that commuting was in and that ditching everything to fly to Sri Lanka was pretty much out. Fat lot it would have done anyway.

And that's when the phone rang, interrupting Jen's thoughts. She'd looked at her watch and realized that she should be ready to go out by now. She was meant to be going out with her friend Angel, and this would no doubt be her asking where she was.

Not that she felt much like partying. The news had stirred up feelings she'd been trying to ignore. Of wondering what the *point* was. Of her. Of everything. Until a year or so ago, everything had seemed pretty straightforward. She'd had a boyfriend and a purpose; she was an eco-warrior. She stood up for the little guy, for nature, for . . . for anything, really, and that had been the problem. The charity she'd worked for was full of people who were sure about what they were against—big business, most governments, consumers—but didn't seem to know what they were for. She'd started to think that she was doing it more to prove a point than to actually achieve anything. Of course, she'd jacked it all because she suspected her boyfriend Gavin of cheating on her, but that wasn't the real reason. The real reason was that she didn't know why she was doing it anymore.

Although the prospect of spending a week stuck up a tree with Gavin protesting about a new road scheme was also a pretty good reason to leave, too. Maybe she was just growing up, she thought to herself sadly.

"Hi!" she said distractedly. "Look, I'm running a bit late . . ."

"Aren't we all, darling. Aren't we all?"

Jen started. It wasn't Angel.

"Sorry, Mum. I thought you were someone else."

"Sometimes I wish I was someone else," Harriet said with a sigh.

"Are you okay?" Jen ventured, pulling up a chair and checking the clock again. Conversations with her mother were not known for their brevity.

"Oh, I'll be all right. I assume you've been watching the news? All those houses destroyed. Livelihoods wrecked. It's just too awful."

"Yeah, I know. I just turned it off, actually." Jen and her mother didn't have a huge amount in common, but there was nothing like a natural disaster or perceived political lethargy to get them talking. Or rather, to get Harriet talking. Jen didn't usually get to say much more than "I know. You're so right."

"Oh, darling, it's just so terrible. And to think of all that money going to waste. All those donations sent in by those kind people, and all for nothing."

"Not for nothing," Jen interjected. "The houses might have been flattened, but a lot of it went on aid . . ."

"Yes, well, we'll see about that."

Jen rolled her eyes and thought, "Here we go." Harriet loved nothing more than making insinuations, giving people knowing looks as if she were omnipotent, as if she knew more than what she'd heard on the radio or read in the papers. Once, when Jen had been working on a project for Greenpeace challenging an oil company in the North Sea that was dumping crude oil and killing a whole load of marine life, her mother had called her up to give her a lecture on environmental planning, based on a call-in she'd heard on Radio 5 Live. No doubt she had a theory on the Tsunami aid, too. There were plenty of stories doing the rounds about customs problems and corruption and it was exactly the sort of conspiracy theory that Harriet thrived on.

"Why," Jen said now, after a little pause, "are you suggesting that it didn't go on aid?"

"It might very well have gone on aid. But it's what's meant by *aid* that I'm worried about. Who might have got their hands into the pot before it was spent where it was needed. That's what concerns *me*."

Jen bit her lip, trying to suppress her irritation. Harriet always assumed that she was the only one who saw the seriousness of any given situation. It infuriated Jen the way her mother turned a crisis into her own little melodrama in which Harriet herself always seemed to play the leading role. But she wasn't going to let it show, she told herself. Now was not the time to snipe.

"I'm sure it does, Mum, but I'm actually on my way out," she said diplomatically. "Let's just hope that some money gets through to the right people, shall we?"

"Hope?" Harriet retorted immediately, then her voice lowered. "We need more than hope," she said darkly. "This is a very serious business, Jennifer. Very serious indeed."

Jen sighed. It looked like she was going to be late for Angel . . . again. "Do you have any facts to go on here," she asked carefully, "or are you just talking in general terms?"

She heard her mother give a little satisfied sigh.

"Well," Harriet said conspiratorially, her voice betraying her excitement at finally getting to the theory she'd obviously been desperately hoping Jen would "prise" out of her. "I'm not sure I should be telling you this, but I have it on very good information that some of the construction work out there is being run by a company who secured its contracts with bribes. And as soon as the government started looking into the situation, papers started to go missing and they drew a blank. It's completely corrupt. And I wouldn't be surprised if it doesn't come out soon that some companies rather close to home were involved. *Are* involved."

Jen felt her hackles rise at this injustice, and her irritation at her mother subside. "Are you serious? That's . . . well, it's outrageous."

"*Outrageous* doesn't come close," Harriet continued. "It's a travesty. It just shouldn't happen in this day and age . . ."

"But someone should do something." As soon as the words left her lips, she regretted it. This is Mum, she reminded herself quickly. It might not even be true. But, then again, Harriet did have good sources. It was rare for her to get things entirely wrong; she usually just exaggerated here and there to add a bit more spice.

"Of course they should, darling, but that's just it, isn't it. No one has the courage to. No one who can get access to the right information is willing to get involved."

"How do you know all this?" Jen asked suddenly, a little voice inside her reminding her that her mother could get carried away sometimes, could turn a hypothesis into fact with the mere turn of her head.

"Darling, you will have to trust me on this one," her mother said darkly. "I know things that I simply couldn't tell you. It wouldn't be fair."

"Wouldn't be fair? To whom?"

"To you."

Jen's face twisted in annoyance. Why couldn't her mother ever just come out with whatever it was she wanted to say?

"What do you mean? How would it not be fair to me?" She tried to keep the irritation out of her voice, but it wasn't easy. This was what happened when you spent too much time with a parent, she realized. Until six months ago, she'd got on brilliantly with her mother. They'd spoken on the phone about once a fortnight or thereabouts, and had seen each other about once every two months when Jen would pop round for tea. She and Harriet had always had plenty to talk about, and just when they were beginning to irritate each other, just when their conversations were beginning to turn into arguments, it would be time for Jen to go, time for her to go up to Scotland or down to Dorset, railing against a new supermarket development or fighting for the protection of dolphins. Jen had worked for Fighting for Survival, a group known for its advocacy on behalf of lost causes, and Harriet used to love hearing Jen's tales—and, more to the point, also used to love regaling her own colleagues with tales about her brave, committed daughter, exaggerating a bit here and embellishing a bit there.

And then everything had changed. Jen had split up with her boyfriend, Gavin, and since he was the reason she'd got involved in Fighting for Survival and was also the group's leader, Jen had decided that perhaps she should rethink her options. Harriet had stepped in right away with an invitation to come and work for her for a bit at her consultancy firm, Green Futures.

Jen had refused at first, naturally—working for a consultancy firm hadn't exactly been on her list of dream jobs; nor had working for her mother. But Harriet was a determined woman and she had approached Jen's dubiousness with her usual tactics of persuasion: bombarding her with facts, making her feel guilty, and creating a situation in which, if Jen turned the job down, she would be letting down not just Harriet, but the entire planet. Green Futures, she'd pointed out, helped companies to find socially and environmentally responsible solutions, and without Jen to help them find those solutions, the companies would go back to their bad habits. Jen had known deep down that her joining Green Futures would make no difference whatsoever, since they'd gotten along fine without her for nearly fifteen years, and she had been secretly worried that her mother's high hopes would be cruelly dashed when she discovered just how little Jen really knew about corporate behavior. She'd met Gavin at a rally she'd gone to with Angel, protesting against an oil company that just happened to be a client of her father's. That fact alone (apart from the incidental fact that she had just been fired from her job in marketing for arguing with a prospective client during a pitch) had made joining his charity seem like the best idea in the world, particularly when it turned out he was also a great kisser. And while she'd learned a lot (her main role had been "research" because no one else in the charity seemed interested in going to a library) what she really knew about organizing protests or business ethics could pretty much be written on the back of a matchbox.

Still, it would do for the time being, she'd decided. She didn't have any other job offers on the table, or any money in the bank, and while she may not be camping out in trees anymore, at least Green Futures had a worthwhile purpose.

Once there, she'd actually rather enjoyed settling into one spot and the luxury of having her own flat, complete with on-demand hot water. It was like "campaigning-lite"—she could feel good about doing good in the world without having to wear the same pair of combat trousers every day for a week. She was wearing lipstick again and buying shoes that weren't designed for walking through muddy fields. And the routine of going to the office and seeing the same people, developing relationships, had become quite soothing. It was a slippery slope toward complacency, but it felt quite nice slithering down it. Somehow, although she longed for something a bit more exciting, she wasn't sure she could give up her power shower or cable television now that she'd grown so fond of them. A little bit of complacency actually felt pretty good sometimes.

"So why wouldn't it be fair?" she demanded patiently. "Why would I care either way?"

Harriet sighed dramatically. "Darling, it's easier for me. I've known your father for years. I know who he really is, but I don't want to sully his name further for you. I know how hard it was when he deserted you."

"Dad?" Jen asked incredulously. "Now you've really lost it. Oh, and by the way, he deserted *us*, not *me*. And I don't give a shit about him. You know that." She paused, then frowned when she was met by silence from her mother. Silence only meant one thing—Harriet was serious. Jen looked at her watch, then asked cautiously, "So you think he's involved in this? I don't understand. He runs a management consultancy firm." She gave a half laugh as she said it, disguising her unease. She hated talking about her father. She generally convinced herself that she didn't have one. Talking about him just reinforced the fact that he was alive and well and utterly uninterested in her. But suggesting that he was involved in something like this was a whole new ball game. He stood for everything she hated—big business, huge profits, slick suits and fat wallets; he had also displayed next to no interest in his only daughter. She hated him, and had no interest in him at all. But he was still her father.

"Jennifer, as you well know, management consultants advise on all sorts of things, from strategy to . . . well, international development, if you know what I mean."

Jen frowned. "No, I don't know what you mean. But I imagine you're going to tell me."

There was a long silence, but eventually Harriet spoke. "You didn't hear this from me, but as I understand it, whoever masterminded this corruption, this awful system of bribes and dodgy dealings in Indonesia, well, they had to have a cover as a respectable business. An international business with offices in the region. A business that has many clients, that could easily be meeting with government officials one day and a construction client the next. And your father's name has come up . . ."

"I don't believe you," Jen said hotly. "He wouldn't . . . there's no way . . ."

"Darling, you really don't know your father that well," Harriet said quickly, and Jen bit her lip. It was true—she barely remembered him. Even when he'd been around he'd cared more about work than about her, and when he left her mother, he didn't even try to keep in touch.

"Your father would do anything to make money for his precious firm," Harriet continued, taking advantage of Jen's silence. "And believe me, I'm not the only one who thinks he's involved."

"Then why are you telling me?" Jen demanded. "You should be telling the police!" She waited for her mother's response. Talking about the police or the Environment Agency or any other official body was generally a good way of ascertaining whether Harriet was talking in terms of fact or fiction.

"Oh, it's far too early for that. They'd find no proof. The fact that Axiom is one of your father's clients might make you or me suspicious, but sadly not everyone knows him like we do. No one's found a shred of proof that Axiom has been paying bribes, but then, I suspect they might be looking in the wrong place. No one thinks to question the management consultants, you see . . ."

"Axiom? What's Axiom?"

Harriet tutted. "Darling, do keep up. Axiom is the construction company that's been winning all the contracts for all the building. If you can call it building."

Jen shook her head in disbelief. It was all too much to take in. Could her own father really be behind something like this? "Mum, look, this is all really interesting," she said cautiously, "but don't you think you should be talking to someone who can do something about it rather than me? Or, you know, get hold of some proof? Find something to incriminate him. You need someone to go undercover—I'd suggest Gavin, but we're not exactly on speaking terms right now . . ."

Harriet sighed, but suddenly the sigh seemed a bit calculated, and Jen's antennae quivered. "Oh, Jen, someone like Gavin would never get the better of your father—he's far too clever. No, to get the proof we'd need someone who works at Bell Consulting, and they'd never talk to us. Your father's firm and mine . . . well, can you see a Bell consultant telling me anything?"

Jen shook her head silently. Bell Consulting and Green Futures were very much the products of their leaders and the consultants shared the same animosity as Jen's parents.

Still, she wasn't entirely happy with her mother's liberal use of the word "we" as if this were now "their" problem. If it did have anything to do with her father, then she wanted nothing to do with it.

At least, she wanted nothing to do with him. She frowned. If he *was* involved, then he couldn't get away with it. Frankly, he'd got away with enough already.

Jen rolled her eyes as her mother continued to talk. Anyone else would be wondering why Harriet was talking as if she was the only person who could possibly find out the truth, but she knew her mother too well. If there was something untoward going on, Harriet had to get to the bottom of it—she didn't trust the police, the government, or anyone else for that matter—to do a better job than her. And the truth was that Jen was the same—they both rushed headlong into crises, determined to take on the problems, sort things out. The fact that her father could be involved in this particular situation was like waving a red flag at a bull. Of course Harriet was going to run at it.

"So you should get someone in there, like the guy who got a job in that fast food restaurant and wrote an article about the lack of hygiene procedures," Jen said cautiously. It was one thing for Harriet to get involved, but this conversation was giving Jen the uneasy feeling that there was going to be some big request for a favor from her. It wasn't that she didn't want to help, she thought to herself as she bit her lip apprehensively. It was just that she'd kind of had enough of trying to save the world lately, and anyway, she was always very dubious about getting involved in her mother's plans.

Another pause.

"Well, that does give me an idea . . . but no, no, you'd never agree. And it would be too much to ask."

Jen looked up at the ceiling and counted to three.

"Never agree to what?" she asked patiently.

"Well," Harriet said slowly, "it's just occurred to me that you're right—the only way we'll find out if Bell Consulting is involved is by having one of our own people in there. Someone who can dig around a bit, listen to people's conversations."

Jen frowned. "Exactly. So what's the big idea? They must have jobs that someone could apply for. The post room or something?"

"Too remote," Harriet said vaguely. "No, we need something more central. You know that Bell runs an MBA course?"

Jen breathed in sharply. She had a horrible idea that she knew why her mother had called her. This wasn't a favor—it was way bigger than that.

"Um, no, no I didn't. But you're not thinking about putting someone on it, are you?" she asked tentatively. "That's a *lot* to ask of one of your employees, isn't it?"

"You're right. But not because it's a lot to ask; it's because none of them would be up to the job. You would, of course, but then why should you be interested? It would be very demanding. . . ."

"Me?" Jen's eyes opened wide. Even though her mom couldn't see her, she felt she had to feign surprise.

"I couldn't trust anyone else, darling. But forget I said it. Really. We'll just have to think of something else. Anyway, I'm sure the . . . *authorities* are looking into it."

Harriet emphasized the word *authorities* in a way that suggested that they would be doing no such thing. Jen sat back, trying to gather her thoughts. Trying to remind herself that right now, she wanted a quiet life. That she was meant to be figuring out what she wanted out of life, not agreeing to one of her mother's crazy schemes. That this ridiculous feeling of excitement bubbling around her stomach should be ignored. It was insane, the whole idea. Do an MBA at Bell Consulting? Spy on her father, whom she hadn't seen for more than fifteen years? The man who was one of the most successful businessmen around and who hadn't even bothered to contact her once since he moved out of the family home? No. No way. Although it would be a pretty good way of paying him back.

"Don't you think that doing an MBA is a little extreme?" she asked gently. "I mean, those things last for a whole year. And there are exams and stuff. I think the post room idea's much better. I wouldn't mind doing that." Jen had seen a fly-on-the-wall documentary recently in which the post room staff of a big corporation whizzed around on roller skates and her inner teenager rather liked the idea.

"You think that it wouldn't look odd, a girl your age, with your talents, working in the post room? And you think the post boy or girl gets access to important meetings?"

Jen was about to say that the post room probably got more access to information than any other department except perhaps the IT department, but she didn't get a chance, because her mother was now in full steam. "Believe me, Jen," she said briskly, "I've thought it through and this is the only way."

"Funny, your way always seems to be the only way," Jen said, only half under her breath. "Anyway, I thought you'd only just had the idea? Look, I'd never get on the course," she said quickly. "And even if I did, Dad would recognize me immediately."

"Nonsense. You're a clever girl, Jen. Of course you'd get on. And with more than three thousand people working in Bell Towers I shouldn't think you'll be exactly running into him. . . ."

Harriet's voice was silky now, and Jen knew exactly what she was doing. You didn't start your own environmental management consultancy firm and build it into a three hundred-person-strong business without the ability to persuade people to do things they'd usually never dream of doing.

Don't be flattered into saying yes, Jen told herself.

"You'd be back in the action," Harriet continued. "You'd be really . . . achieving something."

"And what if it's nothing to do with him?" Jen asked, stalling for time. She was trying hard to overcome her tendency to jump straight into things before considering whether it was a good idea or not. Trying even harder to convince herself that this was a very bad way to get over her "what's the point of everything" issues.

"Then we'll be a step closer to finding out who really is behind it."

Jen sighed. She knew when she was defeated, and had known her mother long enough to know that she wouldn't give up until Jen agreed.

"You had all this planned, Mum, didn't you? I mean, you've had this idea for a while now, right?"

"Darling, what do you take me for?" Harriet asked, her voice incredulous. "Although I did take the precaution of sending off for the MBA prospectus, which you should get tomorrow. Who knows, you might even enjoy it."

Jen laughed. "Enjoy it? You really are mad. I've lived in a tree for a week, which, let me tell you, is pretty uncomfortable. But I'd rather move back there for a month than sit in a room full of bloody MBA students learning about . . . well, whatever it is they learn about."

"But you'll do it?"

Jen frowned. She looked around her cozy flat and thought of her desk at Green Futures. She did like the stability of her new job and home, but the truth was, she also missed the excitement, the passion of her old job. Hadn't she wanted a challenge like this? Wasn't this an opportunity to make a difference, and without even having to give up this place! But then again, this wasn't some exciting adventure—it was a business course and it would be full of boring geeks in suits. It would be hideous, beyond hideous, even. And if Gavin found out, she'd never live it down.

Unless she uncovered a huge scandal, she found herself thinking. She could be a hero . . .

"I'm not wearing a suit," she said flatly, playing for time. She didn't mind nice shoes and the odd pencil skirt, but she really hated suits, and Harriet knew it. Part of her strategy for getting Jen to work at Green Futures had been to emphasize the "casual" dress policy and to warn her that pretty much every other company in the whole of London insisted on their employees wearing suits, even Friends of the Earth.

Harriet laughed. "I'm sure you won't need to. But we'll need to think up a name for you, too. I think putting 'Jennifer Bell' on your application form might just raise a few eyebrows, don't you?"

"You're talking like I've agreed to do it."

"Haven't you?"

Jen shook her head resignedly. "It would appear that I have," she said with a little smile. "But I have one condition."

"Anything, darling."

"I don't want anyone to know. This is not going to become one of your stories, one of your dinner-party gossip fests."

"Oh, Jen." Harriet sounded hurt, but Jen knew that she was just disappointed.

"I don't want you telling anyone at Green Futures, none of your friends, no one. I'm really serious."

"Well of course, darling. What do you take me for?"

"Even Paul."

There was a silence.

"But I tell Paul everything . . ."

"Well, you tell him, and the whole thing is off."

Another silence, then a sigh. "Very well. I shan't breathe a word."

Jen raised her eyebrows, wondering whether her mother would be able to keep her promise, then shrugged. "Look, I've really got to go now, okay?"

"Of course. See you on Monday. And you've made the right decision, you know."

That was when Jen had put the phone down and realized the enormity of what she'd agreed to. The phone rang again, and she picked up quickly.

"What now?" she demanded.

"Okay, okay, don't bite my head off. I just wanted to know what time you were planning to be at my place. Only I thought we were meeting half an hour ago . . ."

It was Angel. Shit. They were meant to be going out to a glamorous new bar, and Jen hadn't even started to get ready. She looked down at her jeans-clad self and jumped up.

"Sorry, got caught up in something. You just won't believe what . . . I'll, um, be there soon. Give me twenty minutes?"

"Jen twenty minutes or a normal twenty minutes? Only yours always last twice as long as anyone else's . . ."

Jen grinned ruefully. "I'll be there as soon as I can, okay?"

She ran into the bedroom and scanned her wardrobe for something to wear.

I'm doing an MBA, she thought to herself again as she pulled out and then rejected various T-shirts and shoes. *I'm actually doing an MBA at Bell Consulting.*

It already felt like a terrible mistake.

1

Jen looked up at the large, gray building in front of her and tried to convince herself that she was doing the right thing.

Somehow it had seemed easier when it was just a matter of telling her mother she'd do the MBA. She'd had visions of herself spying on board meetings, eavesdropping on conversations as she walked down long corridors, compiling a dossier of information and bringing the perpetrators and their heinous crimes to justice. In her mind she'd been the heroine of her own little film in which she (pretty much single-handedly) saved the world and got a thank-you letter from the Queen. Even Angel's protestations that she had finally lost the plot completely hadn't deterred her. In many ways, they'd made her feel more of a rebel, made the whole idea more appealing.

And then she'd got the application form. She'd had to write essays, sit tests, and be interviewed by men in gray suits whom she'd had to convince that a career in business management was everything she'd ever dreamed of and more. But now she was actually about to walk right into the Bell Consulting offices and go to her first lecture. Somehow in her daydreams she'd skipped the bit where she actually had to do an MBA.

It can't be that hard, she told herself. Just boring. Like being back in a physics lesson at school. Or a Durkheim lecture at university. Jen had taken sociology for a term, thinking that she'd get an insight into people's motivations, thinking that she'd unlock the key to human happiness, but instead she'd spent weeks learning why people commit suicide less often in wartime. Apparently it had gotten more interesting later on; those who stuck with the course kept telling her how great it was. But Jen couldn't wait that long; she'd switched to philosophy and never looked back. Well, not until she'd had to endure lectures on Hegel, but by then it was too late to switch again.

Anyway, she reminded herself, the point was that she just had to get into a role. Everyone here would think she was a perfectly normal MBA student; all she had to do was to go along with it. Pretend she found it interesting. She shuddered. She'd read the brochure cover to cover, and they were going to be learning about things like "business process reengineering" and "managing the bottom line." It was too hideous to even bear.

Still, at least she was doing something worthwhile. The truth was that she'd been kind of wondering where her life was going recently. She had started to feel just a little that she was just killing time at a desk at Green Futures and had even started wondering whether she'd been right to split up with Gavin. It was as if she wasn't entirely sure if her place in the world was the one back in London, wasn't entirely sure who she was anymore.

She'd thought it would be different, somehow, working for Green Futures. When the firm had started up, her mother had been huge, talked about by everyone. Hers was the first consultancy firm to talk about corporate social responsibility, to suggest that businesses couldn't just go around doing what the hell they wanted just to make bigger and bigger profits. When Jen had been at school and university, everyone thought she had the coolest mum and she'd thought so too. She'd been really proud, which had been quite nice really bearing in mind that her father was a total bastard who advised companies to do the absolute opposite, focusing on profits alone and not giving a shit about anything so inconsequential as people or global warming.

And the media had loved it, too. Harriet had worked at Bell Consulting before launching out on her own, after all. Her split from George Bell, and subsequent launch of her own rival firm, filled column inches for weeks. Back then Harriet had appeared regularly on the front covers of *Newsweek, The Economist,* and *Time.* She was big news and she loved it.

But actually, Jen had discovered that Green Futures was just like any other office. Lots of desks and people sitting at them, furiously tapping away at computers and talking about their children/pets/hobbies over the (organic) coffee machine. Maybe it used to be a revolutionary firm once upon a time, but now it all seemed a bit . . . tired. And in truth, they didn't have anywhere near as many clients now as they used to have. Other firms had gotten in on the environmental act, and her mother didn't seem to realize that she wasn't the big name she used to be. In many ways it was a bit of a relief to be out of there.

Out of the frying pan and into the fire, Jen thought ruefully as she looked up again at the building in front of her. Bell Towers, built to intimidate and impress all those who crossed its threshold. Somehow she'd never seen herself working for either of her parents, and now it seemed she was going to end up working for both of them. *But not for long*, she told herself. *This is the means to an end only.*

Forcing a smile onto her face, Jen walked through the doors, and before she knew it, she was standing in the reception area, signing in.

"You in the MBA program?"

Jen looked up at the earnest-looking guy standing next to her in the lift.

"You're going to the seventh floor," he explained quickly. "I don't think there are any offices on that floor—just, you know, lecture halls."

She studied his face for a moment. Slightly chubby, face a bit rosy, glasses slightly steamed up. Your typical MBA student if ever there was one. He was appraising her too, she noticed, his eyebrows rising as he took in her jeans and Ugg boots. She'd meant to buy some smart clothes, had really and truly intended to dress the part, but she just hadn't gotten round to it yet. And anyway, it had said in the information packet that dress was "smart casual." She figured that fulfilling one of those descriptors was sufficient for now.

"Yes, I am," she said dismissively, then remembered that she was meant to be a typical MBA student too.

"Me too!" he said unnecessarily. He was carrying four textbooks and a binder stuffed full of notes and labeled very clearly BELL MBA PROGRAM, ALAN HINCHLIFFE. "My name's Alan, pleased to meet you. So have you done any of the pre-reading? I started on Strategy in Motion but

I'd covered most of it already in my business studies diploma, so I focused more on Strategic Business Management—this one . . ." He pointed to the larger of the four textbooks, and Jen looked at them incredulously, then checked herself. *I am an MBA student,* she repeated in her head. *I must pretend to be interested in this crap.*

"I . . . uh . . . you know, dipped in and out of them," she said carefully, hoping that Alan wouldn't ask her about any of them. "I'm Jen, by the way. Jennifer Bellman." She cringed as she said it, but choosing a new name wasn't as easy as it sounded. She'd left it until she filled in the application form and had spent a good half an hour looking around her flat for inspiration—Jennifer Television, Jennifer Lamp, Jennifer Wall. And then she'd turned to the telephone directory and tried some names in there, but she was terrified that she might choose one and then forget it. So in the end, she'd gone for Bellman, the most unimaginative adaptation of Bell as you could possibly imagine. But at least she could remember it.

Alan shifted his files carefully onto one arm and held out his hand. Jen stared at it for a moment, then realized that she was meant to be shaking it. She did so and smiled uncertainly at him.

"Shall we?" she suggested, looking into the lecture hall with trepidation.

"Oh, yes. Right ho."

They walked into the lecture hall and found two seats next to each other. The room was full—there were about fifty people, all in their late twenties or early thirties, and all looking very serious.

Jen took out her course agenda. Introduction, followed

by Strategy in Action, followed by lunch, followed by a meeting with your personal tutor, then an introduction to your team, followed by Strategy in Action recap, then close.

She looked around the room and waited.

"Is anyone sitting here?" Jen looked up to see a huge smiley face surrounded by blond hair. "You're the only other person here in jeans and the only other person who looks vaguely human, so if you don't mind . . ."

"I suppose," Jen said uncertainly. She wasn't sure she wanted to look human to an MBA student.

"I tell you," her new companion continued as she sat down and pulled out pads, pens, books, and folders, "there's a lot of reading in this course. Have you seen the list? Bloody nightmare." She looked around the room, frowning. "Not many lookers, are there?"

Jen raised her eyebrows. "Lookers?"

"Men. God, that's the only reason I'm here. I tell you, I've tried bars, I've tried Internet dating, I've tried buying a bloody dog, and nothing. There are no single men in London as far as I can tell. Not sane ones anyway, or ones that don't look like they're ax murderers in their spare time. Then I noticed that more and more people were putting 'MBA' as an attribute on dating Web sites. And I thought—why wait till they've done the course? Why not get in there at the beginning?"

Jen stared at her. "You're doing an MBA to meet men?"

"Of course. Why are you doing it?"

Jen grinned, relieved to have found a fellow impostor. "Oh, I just had some time to kill. My name's Jen, by the way. Jen . . . Bellman."

She smiled. "Lara. I'm Lara. Pleased to meet you."

*   *   *

A man walked into the lecture hall and stood at the front. Gradually everyone stopped talking and started to look at him instead. He had a very prominent jaw, Jen noticed, and white-blond hair.

"Good morning, folks," he said with a New York accent. "My name is Jay Gregory, and I'm the director of the Bell Consulting MBA program. I'm delighted to welcome you all aboard—I know you've faced stiff competition to come this far, so we've got a pretty good bunch of people sitting in this room."

There was a murmur around the room as everyone made little noises to both suggest modestly that they didn't think they were so great, and to also suggest that, if pushed, they would accent that they were pretty marvelous, actually.

"D'you think he dyes his hair?" hissed Lara. Jen wrinkled her nose.

"Would you actually dye your hair that color?" she hissed back.

"Andy Warhol did."

Jen shrugged and grinned at Lara.

"But what you've done so far is peanuts compared with this program," Jay continued. "This next year is going to be the toughest you've ever faced. You'll be expected to show your commitment, add value, and provide insights at every stage of the way. And you'll be working in teams so that you learn the value of teamwork, the need to work as one unit and not as individuals. You have till June, ladies and gentlemen—nine very exciting months—and I hope you will make the most of it."

Jen cringed as a couple of people said "we will," and Jay smiled appreciatively.

"And now," he continued, "I'm delighted to introduce your tutor for Strategy in Action, Professor Richard Turner. Many of you will have heard of Richard—he is one of the leading strategists in Europe and has written more books than most of us have read. I'm sure you are going to learn an awful lot from this guy—so, over to you, Richard."

A rather skinny gray-haired man stood up, and Jen noted appreciatively that he looked much more like an academic—he had those molelike features found on people who spent all their time reading books.

He surveyed the room for several minutes and everyone sat silently, waiting for him to begin.

"Coca-Cola," he said eventually. "Imagine that sales are down for some reason. Should it produce generic cola for supermarkets to make up for the drop in brand value that it faces?"

Everyone looked at one another hesitantly, then Jen saw a guy at the front of the room put his hand up. The professor motioned for him to speak.

"No, because then why will people buy the Real Thing?" he said and a lot of people started nodding.

"Kellogg's does it," Richard said. "Doesn't stop people buying Cornflakes, does it?"

"I think they should," a girl near Jen said quickly. "People are becoming less brand focused, and more supermarkets are pushing their own brand merchandise."

"But then Coca-Cola will lose their differentiator. What's more, they are beholden to the supermarkets, who can at any time choose a different, cheaper cola provider and no one would know from the packaging. That's not a situation I'd be comfortable with if I were on the Coca-Cola board."

Silence descended on the room and the girl went bright red.

"Welcome to strategy," said the professor with a little smile. "And if you take one thing—and one thing only—away from this session, it should be this: You can analyze external factors, you can analyze internal factors, and you can forecast whatever you want. But you can still screw things up because the world out there isn't interested in your strategy. It changes. Your customers change, your suppliers change. And unless you keep up, unless you are ready to change, to adapt and accept that strategy is a movable feast, then you will end up like the dodo. Do I make myself clear?"

Everyone nodded.

"Personally," the professor continued, "I think you're right." He was looking at the guy who said Coca-Cola shouldn't make cola for anyone else. "But that doesn't mean that tomorrow you couldn't be wrong."

The guy nodded earnestly, and Jen found herself tutting in irritation. Who cared whether Coca-Cola made cola for anyone else? It was a horrible, sugary drink that was bad for the teeth. And the fact that this lecture had made her want one really badly was, frankly, adding insult to injury.

ᕷ 2

Bloody stupid MBA. Jen dumped four huge textbooks and two binders on her kitchen table and shook her arms, which were trembling from having carried the load all the way on the tube. No one had warned her about the sheer amount of reading she would have to do on the course. Or carrying, for that matter. Sod interviews, they should do a fitness test of prospective students. Lugging *Foundations of Management* around was no easy matter.

She went straight for the bottle of wine she'd opened the night before and poured herself a glass, sitting down and staring furiously at the books in front of her. She'd had to endure five hours of lectures. Plus an hour and a half of "team building" which had involved her, Lara, and Alan having to go into a room and come back with three facts about one another that they hadn't known before. Jesus, it was just too soul destroying. What on earth was the point in knowing that Alan liked history books, was born in Hampshire, and spent his childhood holidays in Wales? And while discovering that Lara was a thirty-four double-D was quite interesting, she hadn't particularly enjoyed conveying this piece of information to her entire class. Especially since she herself was closer to a thirty-four B and just knew that they were all going to be making little comparisons in their heads.

Jen sighed. This was just day one, she told herself. It would get better.

But what if it didn't? What if it just got worse? What if she was stuck doing team building exercises all day and never got close to doing what she was there for—uncovering a conspiracy and showing her father to be the bastard she knew he was. She had no idea how she was even going to start fishing for information, and sitting in a lecture hall all day long wasn't helping at all.

Jen downed her wine and poured herself another glass. Maybe she'd turn into an alcoholic, she decided. Maybe if she was drunk all the time she wouldn't mind sitting through skull-numbing lectures about corporate strategy.

She frowned. Or maybe not.

Slowly, she got up and wandered out through her back door into the little area she called her back garden but which was really too small for such a grand name. It was ten feet by five feet, a teeny-tiny little area that over the past few months she'd managed to turn into somewhere worth sitting, complete with herbs and climbers growing all over the place.

Was she kidding herself, she wondered, thinking that being at Bell Consulting was actually achieving something? Was this really about corporate espionage and bringing her father to justice, or was it rather about her having something to prove? She knew she'd been right to split up with Gavin; knew she had to create a life of her own. But was this the right way to go about it? Wasn't she secretly deep-down inside doing this in the hope that he'd find out? Be impressed? Realize that he didn't have the copyright on heroic deeds?

Jen laughed at herself. Doing an MBA a heroic deed? She really was delusional.

She looked around her a little disconcertedly. Things were getting a bit out of control. The clematis was getting everywhere, the jasmine needed deadheading, the poor basil was wilting, and the rosemary was drying out. She wasn't surprised—they weren't exactly equipped to fend for themselves against the London grime and uncertain weather. Then again, she wasn't exactly convinced that she was either.

"What do you say, shall we run off to the south of France together?" she asked her plants conversationally as she put on her gardening gloves.

Slowly and methodically, Jen watered and pruned her plants, gently aerating the soil, adding compost and fertilizer, and imposing some order back into her little enclave. It was the only thing she ever took her time over, she thought to herself curiously. The only thing she did that she didn't rush, didn't cut corners. And one of the only things that she was really, truly proud of, too. It wasn't like it was some great feat; it was just a few square feet with some plants stuck in it, but she'd planted every single one of them herself. No one had had any influence or input—in fact no one else really knew it existed. It was her little sanctuary. And it came in rather handy when making a mozzarella, tomato, and basil salad, too.

She sat back and appraised her work. The herb garden was situated in the far left-hand corner, then to the right where her garden got most sun, she'd planted jasmine and clematis that covered the battered fence separating her garden from her neighbor's. And at the front, to the side of the little paved area onto which she'd squeezed a small table and two chairs, were pots and pots of heavenly smelling lavender.

All pretty hardy plants, she recognized. Nothing there that would vex the average amateur gardener. But still, an achievement. And nice smells, too.

Satisfied, she nipped inside to get her wine, then came back out and sat down on one of the rickety chairs. Life seemed so simple when she was out here, Jen thought to herself. So basic—life, renewal, and death were the only real principles. Plants didn't have to worry about ex-boyfriends, estranged parents, and strategic alignment. They just got on with living, growing up toward the sun, and burrowing down for water and nutrients. They were tough, too—Jen loved nothing more than the sight of a little weed growing through concrete, a small display of power that reminded her that in spite of all the buildings, roads, and computers humans had built, they were never going to be able to tame Mother Nature.

Jen sighed and took another gulp of wine. Taming her own mother was just as hard, she realized, as her eyes rested on the clematis for a moment and her brow furrowed a little. The plant had wrapped itself around the wires she had carefully positioned to support it, but was equally as wrapped around the jasmine next to it, which in turn had buried itself into the fence, taking advantage of every crack and hole. And there, at the base of both plants, was a small gardenia, its feeble attempts to grow being thwarted by the greedy climbers.

She hadn't even noticed the gardenia before—certainly didn't remember planting it. Quickly she took out her trowel and, feeling her way with her bare hands, gently

scooped out the roots and lifted the plant out of its rest-
ing place.

She frowned, wondering where to put it. The left hand
side of the garden was too shady and the right-hand side
would leave it at the mercy of the various climbers that
were ruthless in the pursuit of growth.

"Where would I want to go?" she asked herself out
loud. "Shade or sun? On my own or fighting for space?"

Finally, she decided on a little space about a foot away
from the clematis and dug a hole. Filling it with compost
and earth, she eased the little plant in, gave it a quick
blast of water, then sat back and let the last minutes of
the autumn sun warm her face before it disappeared behind the wall.

Just as she started to relax and let her mind drift far
away from thoughts of her mother and Gavin, the
phone rang, shattering her peaceful reverie. Jen reluctantly went inside to answer it.

"So how was it?" Jen heard her mother's voice and
half wished she'd left it after all. Maybe she could learn
something from the gardenia—if she'd ignored Harriet's
calls a bit more often she might not be doing the MBA
in the first place, which would mean no aching arms and
sore head.

"Oh, Mum. Hi. Yeah, it was . . . well, you know. It
was okay."

"Did you see your father? Did you find out anything?"

Jen sighed. "Mum, I've been there one day. No, I
didn't see him and no, I don't know anything yet. I've
been in bloody lectures all day. I'm knackered actually,
and I'm getting a real headache. . . ."

"Oh dear," Harriet said, rather unsympathetically in
Jen's opinion.

"So anyway, how are things with you? Anything happening at Green Futures?" Jen asked conversationally. She wanted to hear about something other than corporate strategy and was even prepared to listen to one of her mother's tall tales if that was all that was on offer.

"Oh, you know, the usual sort of thing. We're having a meeting next week that you might want to come along to—on the Sacred Feminine. You remember, it came out of our book club when we were reading *The Da Vinci Code*. We've got a meeting to work out strategies for building business success through empowering the Sacred Feminine in all of us—and in our clients. I think this could be really big for us."

Jen wrinkled her nose. This wasn't quite what she'd had in mind for conversation.

"The Sacred Feminine?" she asked, staring at her nails and wondering how Lara got hers so long and shiny. Jen had never really been the long-and-shiny nail type and she didn't particularly want to start now, but she was still curious. "I thought *The Da Vinci Code* was fiction."

Jen heard her mother snort contemptuously.

"Fiction? Is that what you thought? The greatest conspiracy of our time uncovered, and you think it's fiction?"

Jen smiled to herself as Harriet launched into a defense of the book and its theories.

"And you think it's going to help you get more business?" Jen asked eventually.

"I know it will. I had the idea when I was choosing crystals with Paul and it almost felt like a vision, it was so clear."

Jen groaned. Her mother's whims were one thing, but the whims of Paul bloody Song, feng shui expert and Harriet's latest guru, were quite another. Jen knew she should be more charitable, but anyone who walked around in long, flowing trousers talking about crystals and meditation just shouldn't be taken seriously in her book. Her mother had only known him for a few weeks and already she was dropping him into conversation like she'd known him all her life.

"You're choosing crystals with him now. How romantic," Jen said sarcastically. The tone wasn't lost on Harriet.

"I know you're at an age when everything seems to be about sex, darling, but some of us have moved beyond the physical to the spiritual," she said crossly. "I don't know why you don't like Paul, but I think it reflects badly on you. He's a wonderful support, really. And he understands me in a way that no one else does . . ."

"You mean he lets you talk for longer than anyone else will put up with," Jen said amiably. "Look, I'm sure your Sacred Feminine idea is a really great one, but I'm kind of tied up with this little MBA thing I've got going on. So you might have to leave me out, I'm afraid."

"Fine," Harriet said dismissively. "Oh, and did I mention that I've booked a table for the Tsunami appeal charity dinner? You are going to come, aren't you?"

"No, you didn't mention it," Jen said firmly. She'd been to charity dinners before and had no intention of going to another. They were full of people who thought that paying eighty pounds for a ticket made them the world's expert on the charity concerned, and anyway, there was never anyone there under the age of fifty.

"I'm sure I did, darling. It's on Friday. The tickets were very expensive."

"Well, you should have mentioned it, then. I'm going out on Friday, with Angel . . ."

And I think I'm a little bit old to be spending my Friday night out with my mother, she wanted to add, but thought better of it.

Harriet sighed dramatically. "I thought this was important to you, Jennifer. Honestly, I get you a ticket to a Tsunami dinner, knowing that Bell Consulting has a table, and you can't be bothered to—"

"Dad's going to be there?" Jen interrupted, her tone suddenly more serious.

"Not your father, no. I can't see him deigning to attend something that's for a good cause. But some of his consultants are going. I know the organizers, you see. And they kindly gave me a little peek at the guest list. But if your social life takes precedence, then I completely understand."

"I think I'm going to be seeing enough of Bell this week, don't you?" Jen said hesitantly. She could already hear a little voice in her head telling her that maybe she shouldn't rule it out altogether.

"And I thought you actually cared about those poor people who's lives have been destroyed," Harriet said, her voice catching slightly. "Do you not think that a dinner, with free-flowing wine and champagne, might not be a good opportunity to catch people off guard? To listen to conversations that they may not have walking down a corridor?"

Jen sighed. How did her mother do it every single time, she wondered? How did she make it almost impossible to say no?

"What time does it start?" she asked resignedly.

"Seven thirty P.M. or eight P.M. Oh, it'll be so much fun."

Somehow I doubt it, Jen thought as she put down the phone.

ॐ 3

Jen looked at herself disconcertedly in the mirror. It was a Friday night, and she should be going out dancing. But instead of hitting the town, she was being forced to put on a ridiculous dress and go to a dinner with her mother, Paul bloody Song, and a bunch of Green Futures cronies. She groaned. When she'd split up with Gavin and moved back to London, this wasn't quite how she'd imagined her life turning out.

Jen turned round to look at her back view. She was wearing a dress that she'd had for nearly eight years—she didn't usually have much call for a cocktail dress, and there was no way she was going to spend her hard-earned cash on something she'd probably never wear again—and where it had previously flattered her curves, it now seemed to cling to them in all the wrong places. Had she got bigger, Jen wondered, or did the dry cleaner shrink it?

Not wanting to face the more likely answer, Jen quickly dug out an old pashmina and wrapped it around herself, then put on the highest shoes she could find. It wasn't great, but it would do. It wasn't like this was really "going out" after all; this was a duty dinner. It didn't really matter what she looked like.

Grabbing her bag, she went out into the street and flagged down a taxi.

"What a pretty dress!" Harriet smiled beatifically at Jen and immediately turned to Paul. "Isn't it a pretty dress?"

"You look enchanting," Paul agreed, and Jen forced herself to smile. It was a horrible dress, but she was pretty much beyond caring. The dinner was being held at the Lanesborough Hotel on Hyde Park Corner and half of well-heeled London seemed to be here—at least the ones with gray hair, Jen noticed. She could smell pressed powder and sweet perfume everywhere.

Trying to forget the fact that right now she should be out somewhere in a proper bar with young people, she looked around the room. It was for a good cause, she told herself, even though she knew that Gavin would laugh his head off if he saw her now. "Yeah, dressing up in a little black dress is really going to help the planet," he'd say sarcastically. "Bunch of old gits filling their faces? Pur-lease . . ."

And he'd be right, Jen thought to herself with a sigh. Still, she was here now; she may as well make the most of it.

She saw a waiter walking around with trays of champagne and took one gratefully.

"Jen!"

She grinned. It was Tim, the finance manager at Green Futures. "Hi, Tim, how's things?"

He smiled awkwardly. His trousers had obviously been bought a few years before too, and his stomach was straining over the top of them, matching his neck, which was spilling out of his dress shirt. It made Jen worry about her own tightly fitting dress and she pulled her pashmina around her.

"Oh, you know, can't complain," he said affably. "Didn't know you were coming tonight. Then again, I haven't seen you around lately. You been off sick?"

Jen shrugged awkwardly. Evidently Harriet hadn't told anyone where Jen had been, which was good, but it also meant that she had to think up some other excuse for having disappeared. "No, just been, you know, doing stuff," she said vaguely. "And I didn't know I was coming here until Monday, but you know what Mum's like."

Tim grinned. "Do I ever. Been trying to pin her down for two weeks now to talk about our accounts and she's mad busy, can't find the time. But mention a charity ball and suddenly she's got all the time in the world . . ."

They both looked over at Harriet, who was holding forth, captivating a group of people with stories. She caught Jen's eye and motioned for her to come over, but Jen shook her head and waved instead.

"Not joining her ladyship?" Tim asked, raising an eyebrow.

Jen took a gulp of champagne. "Sometimes she seems to think I'm about twelve," she said with a little smile. "If I go over there I'm worried she might start telling everyone how well I did in my A Levels or something. . . ."

Tim called over a waiter who was proffering little sausages and blinis, and grabbed a couple of each, wolfing them down in two seconds.

"Wish you hadn't come to work for her, then?" he asked conversationally.

Jen thought for a moment. "Dunno, really. I knew it

wouldn't be ideal, but it was nice to have somewhere to go."

Tim nodded. "Well, if you do get a moment with her, let her know that she's got some cash flow issues, will you? I've tried e-mailing, but I think she sees my name and deletes them straightaway."

Jen grinned. "I'm sure it's not that bad, is it?"

Tim raised his eyebrows. "Your mother," he said, pausing to take a swig of champagne, "is the world's best networker, the world's best saleswoman, and a bloody great storyteller. But when it comes to figures . . . Well, anyway, you just tell her she needs to sit down with me so I can walk her through it, will you?"

Jen nodded, frowning slightly, as Tim wandered off in search of more food, then started as a gong sounded and everyone was asked to take their seats. She nipped over to the seating plan and her heart sank slightly when she saw that she was sitting between Paul Song and Geoffrey, one of the Green Futures consultants, who was known as "Beardy Weirdy" by everyone in the office.

"That's a very nice dress," Geoffrey said brightly as she sat down. "My mother's got one just the same."

Jen smiled thinly. Somehow, she thought to herself, this was going to be a very long night.

"So then I asked them whether they'd considered recruitment in the region. And do you know what they said?"

Jen noticed Geoffrey had stopped talking and realized that he must have asked her a question. She smiled, hoping that he'd carry on talking. This dinner had been an absolute joke and she was angry at herself for being suckered in to it. She wasn't going to find anything out about Bell, or Axiom, or anything else of any interest. Plus she felt like a frump in her dress, and was feeling bad that vanity had become so important to her. It shouldn't matter what she looked like, she knew that. But somehow, it just did.

"Well, do you?"

Shit. What was the question, Jen wondered desperately. She searched through her head, trying to recall what on earth Geoffrey had been droning on about for the past two hours, or however long it had taken them to get through three long courses.

"I bet you're going to tell me," she said eventually and was relieved to see a satisfied smile appear on his face.

"They said no!" he said triumphantly. "And just like that, they realized where they'd been going wrong. They couldn't thank me enough after that, of course, but I said to them 'don't thank me, thank yourselves for having the foresight for—' "

"You know, I'm just going to . . . get a drink," Jen interrupted with a little smile. "Can I . . . um . . . get you anything?"

Geoffrey shook his head. "Don't want to drink too much on a school night!" he said conspiratorially.

"It's Friday," Jen pointed out.

"Even so . . ."

Jen shrugged and wandered over to the bar, relieved to escape from his incessant talking. He wasn't a bad person, she knew that. And actually, she kind of liked him in a deep down sort of way. So long as he wasn't in the same room as her for too long.

"Vodka tonic, please," she said as a barman rounded on her. Then, drink in hand, she perched on a seat and turned around to look at the rest of the diners. There were about twenty tables, each with twelve people on it, which made . . . Jen frowned as she did a quick calculation . . . 240 people. And at least one table was made up of Bell Consultants. But which one?

She stared ahead, wondering for the millionth time that evening what she would be doing if she were out with Angel. Or anyone else she actually chose to spend her time with.

"So then she says that she doesn't want to see him anymore because she's been sleeping with his best friend for a year."

"No!"

Two men had approached the bar and were talking in animated voices. Jen looked at them briefly, then turned back to her drink.

"Yes. And he's standing there in his underpants, and he's looking at her, and . . . oh, 'scuse me . . ."

Jen heard a mobile phone ring, and the guy who had been speaking answered it and pressed it to his ear.

"Mr. Bell. Yes, I'm there now. No; not really. We're just . . . you know, networking . . . Right you are. Yup. Yup. Okay, then. 'Bye."

Jen froze and gripped her drink. They must be the Bell consultants. And they were right next to her! She allowed her hair to fall in front of her face, and tried to edge a little bit closer while staring resolutely ahead.

"Okay, so then, he goes round to see the friend," the man continued, putting his mobile back in his pocket.

"He goes round to see the friend? Seriously?"

"I'm serious. He decides to have it out with him."

"And his wife is there?"

"Yes. But not with the friend. She's with the friend's wife. Her girlfriend."

"No!"

Jen rolled her eyes. So much for finding out anything useful, she thought, telling herself that she had no interest whatsoever in the man in his underpants.

"I'm telling you. So he rocks up in his Mercedes. Locks the car. The front door of his friend's house opens, and he jumps. I mean, the guy is all nerves. Anyway, he drops his car keys. He bends down to pick them up, but they've fallen down into the drain."

"They've fallen down into the drain?"

"The God's honest truth."

"And he's still in his underpants?"

"Seriously. Look, I need a slash. You get the drinks in and I'll be back in a sec."

"I'll come with you. I wanted to ask you about that Axiom thing, by the way."

Jen's eyes darted toward the men, then back to her drink. Axiom? This she had to hear.

"Oh that. Yeah, bloody nightmare. Where's the men's?"

He directed his question at the barman, who pointed to the other side of the room. As they walked off, Jen looked around furtively, slipped off her stool, and followed them out of the ballroom and down a corridor. She watched them go into the men's room, then she opened the door slightly, trying to hear what they were saying.

"So anyway, he's lost his car keys . . ."

She rolled her eyes. What about Axiom, she wanted to ask. Sod the guy in his underpants.

". . . and he looks up and there in front of him is . . ."

"Hello."

Jen looked around, startled. There was someone right behind her, evidently trying to get into the men's room, and she was blocking his way. He was looking at her curiously and she wondered how long he'd been there.

"Hello!" she said falteringly. She knew she should move, but with him right next to her, it wasn't that easy—she couldn't go forward into the men's room, and now she couldn't go back either.

"Is this the . . . er . . . welcoming party?" he asked with a little smile. Jen reddened. This didn't look very good, she realized. She was standing right in the doorway to the gents and, to add insult to injury, her head had been pressed right up against the door.

She turned around to face him and cringed. Naturally, he was gorgeous. Had she been doing something that wasn't embarrassing, and wearing a dress that fit her properly, it probably would have been one of the old codgers who found her.

"Sorry. I was just . . . um . . . looking for someone," she said quickly, wrapping her pashmina more closely around herself and nearly spilling her drink all over him in the process.

"Can I help?"

"No!" Jen said, too quickly. "I mean, thank you. But no."

He was still looking at her curiously, and she figured that she'd better move to let him through. Otherwise he really would think she was weird.

"Sorry," she said again, moving too quickly and ending up with her face buried in his armpit. She stepped back again and as she did so, her face nearly brushed his, making her go even redder than before.

His eyes met hers and twinkled slightly. And just when she thought things couldn't get any worse, she saw Geoffrey coming down the corridor, his brown squishy shoes looking so utterly wrong with his dinner jacket and black trousers that it was almost comical.

"Hello, Jennifer," he said, seemingly oblivious to the oddness of finding her in the doorway to the men's room, tangled up with a stranger. "I was just looking for you at the bar, as it goes." Jen felt her heart sink as the stranger deftly moved away, freeing her up to pass.

"Well, it looks like you've found your someone," he said, and, with a little smile, he disappeared into the men's, Jen's eyes following after him. She turned to Geoffrey, who was smiling inanely.

"Looking for me?" he said brightly. "Well, there's a little mixup! I'll tell you what, let's go back to the table, shall we? Unless of course you want to stand around the men's room!"

He laughed at his joke and Jen smiled reluctantly. "Of course not," she said halfheartedly. "Why on earth would I?"

Jen returned to the table, accompanied by Geoffrey, and slumped on her chair. This had to go down as the worst night ever, she thought despondently, staring at her vodka tonic and taking a sip. She'd totally screwed up, missing out on the Axiom conversation, embarrassing herself in front of the only good-looking man in the entire room, and was now back where she started, next to Geoffrey.

"You okay?"

She looked up to see Paul gazing concernedly at her. *That's all I need,* she thought with a sigh. *Someone to tell me I should move a mirror in my flat and everything will suddenly be okay.*

"I'm fine," she said politely. "Just, you know, a bit tired."

"Maybe you need someone to talk to," he said.

She looked at him suspiciously. "Thanks, but I'm fine, really. I should have been out with my friends tonight, as it happens."

Paul nodded sympathetically. "But it is good that you support your mother, no?"

"I suppose." Jen shrugged despondently.

Paul frowned, and for a moment Jen thought that he was going to argue with her, tell her that she wasn't supportive enough, but then she saw him put his hand in his pocket and take out a pager. He smiled apologetically, bowed his head, and stood up.

"Please excuse me," he said, and Jen smiled back.

"Sure," she said vaguely. "Whatever . . ."

Geoffrey tried to catch her eye, and Jen looked away quickly, scanning the room to see if she could see the Bell consultants anywhere. Or the guy from the news. If she was completely honest, she was probably more interested in finding him than the Bell consultants, but she'd never have admitted that.

Anyway, it didn't matter because neither of them were there. Her eyes rested on each table, but they were nowhere to be seen.

As she turned back around, though, she suddenly saw him. Mr. gorgeous was heading for the exit, and she found herself fighting the urge to follow him.

Not the best idea, she told herself seriously, her eyes unable to leave his back. *He already thinks I'm a freak who hangs out around men's rooms.*

She forced herself to turn back to the table. Geoffrey smiled at her. "Jen, I was just telling Hannah here about a new type of recycled paper that a company we're working with has developed. Did you know that there are fifteen different ways of manipulating the dye in order to . . ."

"I'm just going to pop into the loo, actually," she said quickly, standing up before she could talk herself out of it. Darting around the room, she maneuvered herself around the tables, squeezing between chairs and making her way to the exit, but by the time she got there, the man had gone.

"Typical," she muttered under her breath, and leaned against the stone banister leading down the steps to the road, looking left and right to see if she could see him anywhere. Not that it mattered. It was probably a good thing he wasn't here. What could she have said to him even if he had been here? And at least she was out of that awful party.

The air was cool and she wrapped her pashmina around herself more closely, listening to the traffic around Hyde Park Corner and wondering whether she really needed to go back in to the dinner. She could feign a headache. Apologize the next day for not having said good-bye . . .

She noticed the doorman looking at her strangely, and she turned around, putting her elbows on the stone banister and trying to decide whether she could get away with leaving now. It was getting late, after all. And having failed to hear a single word of those consultants' conversation about Axiom, there didn't seem much point staying on.

She breathed in deeply, enjoying her inertia. And then she noticed something. Or, rather, someone. A man, down below, talking in an animated voice. Was it a lovers' tiff, she wondered? A falling-out of friends?

She narrowed her eyes, trying to pick out the figures,

and then they widened. The man she'd seen was Paul Song. And there was another man, too. *Maybe he's unhappy with Paul's choice of crystals,* Jen thought to herself, frowning. *Although he doesn't look like a crystal kind of a guy.*

She saw Paul passing what looked like a letter to the older man, and then they parted company. Which meant that Paul was on his way back in, Jen realized, and she'd be forced to go back with him.

Smiling at the doorman, Jen ran quickly down the steps, turned the corner, and disappeared into Hyde Park Corner's tube station.

ɛ 4

"You really shouldn't do that slumpy thing with your shoulders, Jen. Honestly, you'll end up with so much tension in your upper back. Look, do this stretch with me."

Jen grimaced as her best friend, Angel, deftly contorted her body with an arm movement that she couldn't hope to follow. It was all right for her, Jen thought to herself as she contemplated copying her and then decided against it. Angel had been doing yoga since she was about two. Her Indian mother had taught her the downward dog before she could even walk.

She took a sip of coffee and pushed away the Sunday newspapers in front of her. "I was born with slumpy shoulders," she said with a wry smile, not entirely sure what "slumpy" meant but assuming that it was Angel's way of telling her to sit up straight. "It's part of my Anglo-Saxon heritage."

Angel grinned. "You mean, like the missing link?" she asked playfully. "Did you English learn to stand tall later than the rest of us?"

Angel always sat up straight. She was one of those people with strength and grace and lovely skin and bright eyes and she could sit in the lotus position for hours. That's how she watched television, all taut and relaxed at the same time.

"So how's the yoga thing going?" Jen asked. Angel had just started teaching in a community hall around the corner.

"Really good. I mean, you know, okay. It's going to take some time to get people coming, right? I mean, I need to wait for word to spread. But it's wonderful. You should come down."

"I will, honestly," Jen said, taking another gulp of coffee and looking guiltily at Angel's herbal tea. "I'm just not sure I'm really a yoga person."

"Everyone's a yoga person!" Angel said, a little frown appearing on her otherwise unlined face. "Jen, it's so amazing for you. It'll stretch all your muscles and build your core strength and get the blood pumping . . ."

"I know, I know." Jen grinned at Angel. People like Angel didn't understand, she realized, that not everyone found it easy to twist their left leg around their body, stick their right arm up in the air, and stand on the tips of their toes. It wasn't that Jen didn't like yoga. It was just that every time she tried it she felt so clumsy, so unsupple, that she didn't dare go back. "But I'll need to practice first. Maybe I should get pre-yoga lessons," she said with a little smile.

Angel shook her head. "You always turn everything into a joke," she said seriously.

"What's wrong with that?"

"It's a cover-up! Life isn't always funny, you know. Sometimes it's painful. You deal with the pain, and then you move on."

Jen frowned. "I'm not in pain, Angel, I promise."

Angel shrugged. "I know. I'm just a bit pissed off. Only two people came to my class yesterday."

"Ah." Jen put her hand out and squeezed her friend's arm. "I'm sorry. They'll come soon, I know they will."

"Maybe they all need pre-yoga lessons," Angel said with a little sigh. "So how about you? How was your dinner on Friday? I missed you when I was dancing the night away surrounded by lots of very handsome men."

"All right for some," Jen said enviously. "Any of them get your number?"

Angel raised her eyebrows and shook her head. "Not that handsome," she said with a little smile. Angel loved the idea of going out and meeting men—particularly men who weren't Indian. The idea of being out dancing in the sort of place that would make her mother squeal with indignation was delightful to Angel, who'd been fighting off the prospect of an arranged marriage for the past five years. But that was as far as she ever went—to Jen's knowledge, she'd had never so much as gone out on a date with any of the men who followed her round the bars and clubs they frequented.

"So tell me about your dinner," Angel continued, deftly moving the conversation on. Her eyes were twinkling and Jen shook her head.

"Don't get me started," she said grimly. "I knew I shouldn't have gone."

"No nice young men at your charity dinner, then?" Angel, who still felt responsible for both Jen meeting Gavin and subsequently splitting up with him a couple of years later, was determined that she should meet someone and soon. Jen rolled her eyes.

"No, but that's not why I went. I stupidly thought I

might actually find something out about Axiom. Some chance."

"Ah, yes, the war on your father. I forgot."

Jen frowned. "It isn't a war on my father. I'm trying to get to the bottom of a corruption ring. It's serious."

"A corruption ring that might involve your father."

"And?" Jen could feel her defenses rising.

"And you think that by finding out the truth he might actually notice you."

Angel looked directly into Jen's eyes and Jen winced. *Why is it that Angel never skirts around an issue,* Jen found herself wondering. Most people were polite and evasive and agreed with you, even if they knew you were talking bullshit. Whereas Angel always looked straight past whatever you said and found the one thing you were ignoring as hard as you could. Trust her to find the only best friend in the world who didn't let you get away with anything, even subconsciously.

"No," she said, trying to convince herself as much as anything. "It's nothing to do with that."

Angel shrugged slightly. "I just hope you know what you're doing. I don't want to see you hurt, okay?"

Jen finished her coffee. "Of course I know what I'm doing. And I won't get hurt," she said defiantly.

"If you do, you can always joke about it, I suppose," Angel said thoughtfully. "Now, pass me the Style supplement. I want to do something new with my hair and I can't decide what."

The next morning, a fired-up Jen found herself in a small room, staring at a man in his early forties, wearing sandals over socks. She just had to get through this meeting with her private tutor, then a lecture on something boring, and then she was going to start her corporate espionage in earnest.

Somehow Angel had managed to get under her skin with those comments about her father the day before. She'd refused to admit it, of course; Angel had this theory that when you got agitated about something it was usually because there was a kernel of truth there that you didn't want to admit to or face, and there was no way she was going to let Angel think she'd struck a chord. But the fact was that she had, and the more Jen thought about it, the more determined she became to prove that this whole exercise had nothing to do with her father. Or Gavin, for that matter.

So as soon as she'd gotten back from brunch, she'd made a list of all the things she needed to do—find out where people gathered to talk, figure out where key people worked, find out who was on the Axiom account. Now all she had to do was get on with it. She was going to show everyone that she was serious.

"Okay, so, Jennifer Bellman. Right?"

Jen looked at the man impatiently. This wasn't quite what she'd expected. This was her first meeting with her personal tutor and she'd been expecting someone in a suit, someone who looked like a Bell consultant, who would quiz her on strategy and internal analysis and ask about her assignment results.

Instead, the man in front of her had long straggly hair that looked like it could do with a cut, and he was sitting crosslegged on his chair. *I wonder if he does yoga,* Jen found herself thinking idly. *I wonder if he'd be interested in Angel's classes.*

"Great. Well, I'm Bill. The official title is Dr. Williams,

but I'm happy with Bill if you are? I like to keep things informal if you know what I'm saying."

Jen realized that he actually wanted an answer, so she nodded again and said "Yes, that's fine," just for good measure. She was getting quite good at pretending to be an MBA student, she thought to herself confidently. Maybe next year she'd have a go at pretending to do a PhD. . . .

"Great. That's just great. So, Jennifer. What can I do for you?"

Jen gave him a sideways look. Why should he be able to do anything for her? It wasn't like she'd set this meeting up or anything. It was on her agenda, that's all.

Perhaps she should ask him about corporate greed, she thought to herself with a little smile. She could ask him whether he knew that his precious firm might be implicated in the corruption scandal in Indonesia.

Then again, perhaps not.

"Nothing. I mean, you know, I don't know what a personal tutor does, really," she ventured after a pause. Bill smiled.

"Anything and everything. Except supply you with drugs!" he said brightly. Jen managed a half smile.

"See these bookshelves?" he said, pointing to a row of fitted shelves. "These books are invaluable when you're doing an MBA. And you can borrow them from me so you don't have to go to the library. Which will save you a lot of time, believe me."

Jen surveyed the books. There were a few things like *Ten Ways to Improve Yourself and Your World* or *How to Be More Effective and Save the Planet,* but there were also some scary-looking books like *Economic Growth:*

An Epistemological Study and *The Strategy Focused Organization: How to Align Your Objectives to Drive Bottom-Line Performance*.

"I didn't think that Bell Consulting was particularly interested in improving the world," she said caustically as she reviewed the titles.

Bill frowned. "Oh, I wouldn't be so sure. Corporate social responsibility is big these days."

"Good for marketing, is it?" Jen asked sweetly.

Bill raised his eyebrows. "I guess so, although I happen to think it's a bit more important than that." He grinned again. "So, then, there's your workload," he said, moving over to his desk and sitting on the edge of it. "I've been a personal life coach for more than ten years," he continued, "and have psychology degrees, coaching accreditations, and a black belt in karate. You begin to find things getting on top of you, you come to me. Need an extension on a deadline, you let me know and I'll see if I can sort it for you. You dig?"

Jen smiled in spite of herself. *You dig?* Who actually spoke like that anymore?

"You have any personal issues you want to discuss, my door is open," Bill was saying, getting into his stride. His eyes were shining, and he looked as if he would not be satisfied until he had fought for something on Jen's behalf. "Not getting on with a lecturer or subject, come see me. And when you get your MBA and a great new job, you take me out and buy me a few beers. How does that sound?"

Jen relaxed and grinned back at him. "And if I get a crap job, do you buy me beers?"

"You won't," Bill said seriously. "You focus on your

goals and align your life around them, and you'll get where you want to be."

"Okay," Jen said quickly. Bill was right; she had to focus on her goals. Goal one: get the information she needed so she could get the hell out of this place. Goal two: work out what she was going to do next. She grimaced. Maybe one goal was enough for now.

"So what happens if I don't need an extension or experience any personal issues?" she asked curiously. "What if I don't have any problems?"

Bill looked disconcerted. "People always have problems," he said, frowning. "You get through this without any problems and that's me out of a job. You remember that."

Jen raised an eyebrow at him, and Bill slammed the desk with his fist.

"I'm kidding! I'm kidding you! No problems would be terrific. Just fab, you know?"

"Okay. Well, thanks. I mean, it's good to know you're here," Jen said as genuinely as she could manage, and Bill shrugged gauchely.

"Just doing my job," he said with a grin. "Feel free to swing by any time. Deal?"

"Deal," said Jen and stood up. *If only he knew,* she thought to herself as she left the room, realizing as she did so that she was late for her lecture.

Jen saw the elevator doors open and made a run for it, sticking her hand in before they could close again. She quickly perused the occupants, then stepped in with a relieved smile on her face. When she'd first arrived at Bell a few weeks ago she'd been terrified of taking the lift in case her father got in, but since she'd discovered

that George Bell rarely left the eighth floor when he was
in the building, and that he was only in the building
about half a day a week, she'd grown more confident.
Blasé even.

"Thank God for that." She sighed, ignoring the raised
eyebrows of the lift's occupants, three serious-looking
consultants. "I thought I was going to have to walk up
three flights of stairs!"

They looked at her curiously, then turned away as Jen
realized that she'd seen one of them before. He was one
of the guys from the charity dinner.

"Anyway," he was saying to one of the others, an
older man, "those bloody environmentalists are at it
again. Milton Supermarkets has had two planning appli-
cations turned down because of them—they've got
protests organized and vigils over the trees. It's a bloody
nightmare."

Jen watched silently as the older guy nodded.

"All right, Jack. Thanks for keeping me up to date.
What are you recommending?"

"A delay of a couple of months. Soon as it starts to get
cold again, the majority of them'll lose the enthusiasm
for it. Students will be back at university. They know
they're fighting a losing battle anyway. If Milton doesn't
move in, another supermarket will."

"And Milton is happy to wait?"

"Not really, no," said the young man. "But they don't
really have an option." He smirked, and Jen's hands
clenched into fists, as she felt her familiar temper flare.
Friends of hers and Gavin's were protesting against Milton. They kept building supermarkets and frankly, the
world did not need more supermarkets in her opinion.

Still, this was not the time for an argument. *Do not say anything,* she told herself firmly. *Just let it go.*

But before she could stop herself her mouth opened.

"I bet the protesters won't go away," she found herself saying. The lift went silent and everyone turned to stare at her.

The young man looked at her uncertainly. "Er, yes they will," he said in a patronizing tone. "Sorry, do I know you?"

Jen looked at the floor, telling herself to stay silent, then sighed and looked back up. It was no use—she always found it almost impossible to bite her tongue when she saw something wrong or heard something she disagreed with. It had gotten her into fights at school, ended two promising relationships at university, and earned her a reputation for being "difficult" at school. And now, if she wasn't careful, it was going to get her kicked out of Bell.

"No you don't," she said flatly. "But if you think that a bit of cold weather will put off the protesters, then I just think you're misguided." The young man looked at her incredulously.

Okay, this isn't good, she thought, annoyed with herself, but at the same time rather pleased at the reaction she was getting. *What bit of "keep a low profile" has my brain not understood?*

The older guy smiled slightly at the younger man, as if to say "Don't worry, it isn't worth it," which made Jen even more irritable, but since he hadn't actually said anything, she kept her mouth shut and the four of them stood in total silence until the doors pinged open on the seventh floor, Jen's cue to leave.

She walked out, but just as the doors were closing, put her hands up to stop them.

"Just so you know," she said quickly, "it might actually be an idea to talk to the protesters. They are human beings, and if you were to treat them with a bit of respect and demonstrate that you're not too arrogant, or too paranoid, to discuss your ideas, then you never know, you might actually work something out. If they want open space, Milton could offer to buy more land than it needs and to keep the remainder as a playground or park. Maybe they could try to understand that along with cut price milk and bread, communities like having places to run around in, too."

The four men were looking at her with open mouths, and she smiled sweetly. "But I'm sure you've already thought about all of that, haven't you," she added, her sarcasm only thinly veiled. "Delaying things and just hoping that the protesters will get bored of protesting sounds like a really good idea, too."

With that, Jen stepped back and watched the lift door close. She looked at her watch and groaned. *Bloody big mouth*, she chastised herself. But she couldn't help smiling at the look on the young guy's face, his mouth hanging open as the doors had shut.

"Who the hell was that?"

George looked up in surprise at the two men as they stepped out of the lift. "Problem, Jack?" he asked curiously.

"Some madwoman, talking about protesters like we should invite them in for tea or something," Jack said, his eyes flashing in irritation.

George laughed. "Sounds like my wife. Ex-wife, rather.

Now, have you got the notes from your meeting with Axiom?"

Jack nodded and the older consultant moved forward to greet George.

"Bit more complicated than we'd thought," he said quietly. "I'll fill you in later, shall I?"

5

"Welcome back, folks. Now, we're into week two of the course, and that means that for the next six to eight weeks we'll be taking a look at the internal workings of organizations. Today, we are very lucky to have a guest lecturer who really knows his stuff. . . ."

As Jay, the program director, introduced Daniel Peterson, their internal analysis lecturer, Jen nipped through the double doors and down the side of the lecture theater, squeezing in beside Lara, who looked at her curiously.

She sat down, but as she did so, she accidentally pushed Lara's pencil case off her desk, scattering pencils everywhere. Shooting an apologetic smile at Lara, Jen ducked down quickly to pick the pencils up, then sat back up, noticing as she did so that things had gone a bit quiet.

Nervously, she turned to the front of the room, where their new lecturer was looking right at her, at which point she dropped her own notepad on the floor, to the hilarity of everyone sitting around her. She went bright red and stared at him in disbelief. It was him. It was the man from the men's room at the dinner.

"Sorry, I was, um . . ."

He was staring at her too. He'd obviously remembered as well.

"Yes?" he asked.

He was sort of smiling at her now, and Jen felt herself going a deeper red. Oh, God, he was going to think that all she ever did was say sorry and blush. Still, at least this time she wasn't pressed up against the door of the men's loo. At least this time she was just dropping pencils and papers all over the floor.

"Sorry," she said again.

"Well, then." Daniel looked back at his notes, then briefly gazed at Jen again. She felt her heart quicken, and looked away, quickly picking up her pad and burying her head in her notes. So he was a Bell lecturer!

As he started talking again, she watched him, taking in his dark hair, his eyes—hazel or green, she couldn't tell at this distance—his animated expression. Not that she was interested, she told herself. She was just interested in the subject matter. Then she frowned. She couldn't be less interested in the subject matter. So maybe it was him after all.

"So, when undertaking an internal analysis, we start at the beginning, with a MOST analysis," he was saying. "For the uninitiated, that's Mission, Objectives, Strategy, and Tactics, and the four should be mutually supportive."

Jen shook herself and started making notes. *Mission,* she wrote down. *Objectives. Daniel Peterson. Daniel. Dan.*

"The mission statement can be as loose as you want it to be, but it needs to give direction," Daniel was saying. "Someone, give me an industry so that we can bring this to life a bit more."

No one said anything.

"How about you?" He was looking at her. Oh God, he was looking at her and she couldn't think of a single industry.

"How about condom manufacturers?" whispered Lara with a little giggle as she reviewed the notes Jen had made so far. "Or motels . . ."

Jen shot her a look and furtively covered up her notes. Her mind had just gone completely blank.

"Come on, any industry," Daniel said encouragingly.

"Um . . . ," Jen said desperately. She needed to say something. "Um . . . condom manufacturers?"

There was a ripple of laughter across the room, and Daniel looked slightly taken aback.

"Right," he said, slightly incredulously. "Right, well, condom manufacturers it is. So, er . . ."

He looked back at his notes, put his hands through his hair, then looked back up.

"Okay, then. So a condom company might choose to be the largest global supplier of condoms if it wants to focus on growth and market share, or it might opt for better sexual health if it wants to be considered the ethical, caring provider. The first statement would suggest aggressively targeting new markets; the second might mean partnering up with bodies like the World Health Organization to improve awareness of sexually transmitted infections and building the brand as the informed choice. Either way, the intended results would be more condom sales and better profit margins."

"Surely a condom manufacturer is looking for market penetration?" someone at the back shouted, and there was a murmur of laughter.

"And fighting off stiff competition," shouted someone on the other side of the room to rapturous applause.

Jen buried her head in her hands and wished that the ground would swallow her up.

Daniel Peterson forced himself to look anywhere but at the girl from the charity dinner. The girl he'd thought about on and off all week, smiling each time he did. He'd expected a boring dinner full of suits—hadn't even wanted to go, and wouldn't have either, if his chairman hadn't booked a table—and he'd been right, too. Except for her. She hadn't been boring at all.

Don't look at her, he said to himself like a mantra. *You're a lecturer. Focus on the task at hand.*

He didn't know why he found this lecturing lark so difficult. Sure, he wasn't an academic; he didn't have any teaching qualifications, but he managed to give presentations at work all the time without any problem. *But of all the places for her to turn up.*

He put his hands through his hair for the third time in five minutes, a reflex action that he did when he was nervous and that sometimes meant he had to wash his hair twice a day, particularly when he was stressed.

Okay, he told himself, *you'll just have to make the best of it.* He looked around the room and saw a rather overweight young man in the front row. Perfect, he told himself. Focus on the fat guy.

He shouldn't have asked her to pick an industry, he thought ruefully, but somehow he hadn't been able to stop himself. He'd been thinking about her all weekend, and now there she was, right in front of him, and he found himself utterly unable to look elsewhere. But Jesus, why did she have to choose a condom manufacturer?

Was it so bloody obvious that he was staring at her? Of course it was. She was taking the piss. It was her way of telling him to back off.

Or was she flirting with him?

The fat guy was looking at him. He looked like he'd just said something. Damn it.

"Great points, articulately presented," he said quickly. He had to move away from condoms and back to mission statements. He found his eyes wandering and pulled them back to the front row. "But what I'm really trying to explain here is that the mission statement isn't just a few words cobbled together to look good. It sets out the strategy. And if the mission statement says you're aiming at doing good in the world, and your tactics involve getting products manufactured in sweat shops, then there's an obvious problem there. Either the mission has to change or the tactics do."

"Surely business isn't there to do good in the world," the fat guy said. "Surely business is there to make money."

Daniel frowned and unconsciously put his hands through his hair again. "Yes, well," he said seriously, "ethics is a rather big subject for me to cover today. But there are businesses whose key selling point is that they are ethical or environmentally sound or whatever. Take the growth in organic food or fair-trade coffee. It can be quite a compelling offering to customers." He saw Jen stare at him furtively, then look away.

"But then the motivation is still making money; you're just doing it by being good," the fat guy continued. "If people stopped wanting fair-trade coffee, the company wouldn't go on selling it, would they? They'd switch to whatever customers were buying. Business needs to be profitable, otherwise it can't survive."

"Bollocks!"

Daniel looked up quickly. It was the girl. He arched his eyebrows.

"I'm sorry?" he asked, trying to keep his face even and normal—whatever normal looked like. Right now he couldn't remember.

"It's just that he's talking total rubbish," Jen continued, her voice full of passion and her lips dark red as the blood rushed to them. Daniel wondered what it would be like to kiss them, then shook himself. "Companies have to be responsible—they can't just operate like they don't have an impact on the world. Otherwise you'd say that corruption is fine so long as customers don't mind . . ."

"Well, it is," the fat guy said glibly. "Government protection schemes could be viewed as corrupt, depending which side of the fence you're on."

Daniel put his hand up. "Okay, guys, thank you for your input," he said quickly. *Think work,* he told himself forcefully. *Focus on the issue.* "This is a big issue, actually," he found himself saying. "And you're both right, in many ways. . . ." He thought frantically. This really wasn't his area of expertise. "There are two ways of looking at this," he continued, trying to look confident and self-assured. "You could argue, for instance, that if a condom firm ignores the millions of Africans dying of HIV, then soon they won't have a market for their products. If oil companies don't do their bit to encourage energy efficiency, they'll have themselves to blame when the world runs out of oil altogether and their profits run dry. Or you can argue that laudable aims like solving world hunger and teaching children in the developing world to read, are all very well, but if they don't make a profit, then a business has no reason to do them. But in today's environment, ethics is certainly becoming more of an issue. The globalization riots, for instance, and boycotts against companies that use sweatshops are really having an impact."

Jen found herself staring at Daniel again. Not only was he the most beautiful man she'd ever seen, but he was clever, too.

Lara elbowed Jen, who started slightly. "Ask him out," Lara whispered with a little smile. "You can call it homework."

Jen blushed and smiled back. "I think he prefers the guy at the front," she said with a little shrug as Daniel continued to talk, his eyes fixed directly on the front row for the rest of the lecture.

At lunchtime, Jen popped into Bill's office to look at his books.

"Hey, Jen!" He grinned. "What can I do you for? *Fundamentals of Management? Everything You Ever Wanted to Know About Business but Were Afraid to Ask?*"

Jen smiled at him uncertainly. "Do you have anything by Daniel Peterson?"

Bill looked nonplussed, and Jen quickly regretted asking. She might as well have said, "Do you know if Daniel Peterson has a girlfriend?" She wondered if he did have a girlfriend. Or wife.

"I don't think so," Bill said, frowning. "Daniel Peterson, you say? I don't know the name, I'm afraid."

"He, um, works here," Jen said before she could stop herself. "He lectures on internal analysis . . ."

Bill looked thoughtful, then grinned. "Dan? Dan's not an academic! He's what we call a practitioner. I believe he works in bookselling. Just guest lectures from time to time."

Jen nodded, trying to hide her excitement. A bookseller! He wasn't a Bell employee after all—he sold books. What a great job. She didn't usually think of booksellers as corporate strategists who would be lecturing at an MBA course, but that made him all the more appealing. He wasn't a corporate drone. And best of all, he didn't work for her father—at least, not entirely—he probably worked in some lovely little bookstore somewhere, lovingly displaying books about . . .

She frowned. What if it was a business bookshop? Someone who worked in a little independent bookstore was hardly going to end up giving lectures at Bell Consulting, even if he was just a guest lecturer. She wanted to ask Bill which bookseller he worked for, but stopped herself just in time. For all she knew, he might know Daniel really well and she didn't want Bill thinking she was a stalker.

"So," Bill continued. "Maybe something on information systems?"

Jen looked at him seriously and remembered Tim's warnings about Green Futures' finances.

"Have you got something on financial management?" she asked hesitantly. It wasn't a question she ever thought she'd ask anyone, and it didn't exactly trip off her tongue.

"Beginner or intermediate?" Bill asked with a big smile.

"Both," Jen said determinedly. "If that's okay?"

"Nothing wrong with a bit of ambition." Bill grinned. "And you take your time. Don't get much call for those ones, really."

"I can't think why . . ." Jen winked at him as she left, clutching the books to her chest and wondering whether they'd fit in her bag. There was no way she was taking the tube home without covering them up.

Daniel Peterson sat at his desk and gazed out of the window, deep in thought. There was bound to be some rule about dating students.

He frowned. Was she technically a student? And was he technically a lecturer? He wasn't, really—it was only a sideline. This was his second year of doing it. And he'd done it more as a favor than anything else. And his CV, of course.

But either way, it was a stupid idea. She wouldn't be interested in him anyway.

Daniel's brow furrowed. When she'd looked at him and gone pink . . . and all those "sorrys," she was just so adorable.

But it was ridiculous. Obviously. He was just looking for a diversion. He didn't even know her name, and "the girl from the men's room" was hardly a good moniker. No, this wasn't about her, he told himself firmly, it was about being bored in his job. He needed to tackle the root cause, not get strung out about some girl, however stunning she was.

He picked up the phone. "Jane, can you get me a meeting with Frank for this afternoon? Thanks."

That ought to do it. A meeting with the finance director should put all ideas of romance firmly out of his head.

∝ 6

Jen stared at the book in front of her and frowned. Had her life really come to this? She was sitting in the library, in Bell Consulting of all places, reading a book called *Financial Fundamentals,* which wasn't exactly what she'd had in mind when she'd taken on the challenge of a covert operation.

She turned the book upside down and pushed her chair back. Sure, she didn't want to rush into anything. Of course, she had to plan things properly and keep a low profile so that she didn't get caught before she found out anything of importance. But there was a fine line between lying low and doing sod all just in case you get caught. And right now she was definitely erring on the side of doing sod all. Anyone would think that she was scared of actually seeing her father or something. Scared of what she might find. Anyone would think that Angel was right about this whole thing. Either that or they'd think that Jen was considering a career as an accountant.

Jen closed the book and sighed. If she didn't do something soon she'd forget why she was here. She stood up and wandered over to the section of the library entitled Supply Chain, which was reassuringly empty, and walked slowly down the aisle, trying to work out a plan.

It was like Daniel said, she thought to herself. She needed to set out her mission and her objectives. Develop a strategy.

She walked back to her table and picked up her pad and pen, concentrating hard.

Mission: to end the corruption in Indonesia and bring the perpetrators to justice.

For a moment, she basked in the idea of having such a noble mission, but then she shook her head. That wasn't her mission, she thought, frowning. That was her strategy. The mission was to protect people whose houses had fallen down. Twice. People who trusted companies like Axiom to do what they promised. Her mission was to make sure that this time around, their houses were built properly, by firms that got the business because of their track record, not their ability to pay bribes. But how could she have any impact on something so big? She might as well have "world peace and an end to hunger" as her mission.

Now there was an idea.

She frowned, then decided to skip straight to the next line. Strategy: to uncover Bell's involvement in the corruption—specifically the involvement of one George Bell—and to alert the authorities.

Jen sat back, imagining herself handing her father over to the police in the manner of a *Scooby Doo* cartoon. He would look at her angrily and say that he would have gotten away with it, too, if it hadn't been for that meddling kid . . .

Except she wasn't about to uncover anything. She knew no more now than she'd known several weeks ago. And she wasn't a meddling kid anymore.

What would Gavin do, she wondered, trying to imagine her ex-boyfriend in her place. Much as she hated to admit it, he was pretty good at this stuff; he always seemed to know what to do, always marshalled everyone into helping. Maybe that was her problem—she was so used to following, to taking orders, that she didn't know where to start when there was no one to tell her what to do.

She frowned. She didn't want to be someone who took orders. Especially not from Gavin. She could do this. She just had to get started. Find a way in.

Jen looked at her list and realized how pathetic it looked. How pathetic she looked. Angel was right—this had been a stupid idea. Unless she was going to actually go up to her father's office and rummage around in his files, what was the point of her being here? Nothing, that's what. It was just another one of her mother's crazy ideas, and she'd been stupid enough to go along with it.

She put her pad back down and made her way out of the library. Maybe she should just quit, she thought despondently. Maybe she should do something else with her life, something that was actually going to achieve something. This had been a bad idea from the start, and to stay here was just adding insult to injury.

But what would she do instead? Go back to Green Futures?

She walked down the corridor slowly. It wouldn't be so bad, she told herself. At least she wouldn't have to finish her internal analysis assignment.

She headed for the lift and stood in front of it waiting, reviewing her reflection in its warped mirrored doors.

I'm just going to walk out, she told herself. *Go for a walk and clear my head. And if I decide to quit, then that's what I'll do. Mum will just have to live with it.*

She heard brisk footsteps coming down the corridor and looked up to see Jack, the consultant from the dinner and the lift, with a colleague she didn't recognize. She rolled her eyes. That's all she needed—another stuck-up consultant talking about student protesters.

But they didn't seem to notice her as they waited with her in front of the lift.

"He wants tickets to Indonesia?" one said conspiratorially.

"Yeah," the other one said. He was the one she'd argued with in the lift. "Fuck knows why. Wants them delivered personally."

Jen frowned, then looked away. She'd made up her mind to go, she told herself. She really wasn't interested.

"You on your way up now?"

"What does it look like?"

"D'you think this is to do with Axiom?"

The guy Jen had argued with looked at his colleague with contempt. "I'd never have thought of that," he said sarcastically, just as the lift arrived.

The doors pinged open.

"It's going down," said the argumentative one, who shot a look at Jen. "You want this one?"

Jen frowned.

"Actually, no," she said eventually, a nervous smile playing on her lips, "I think I'm going to go up."

The two consultants walked briskly out of the lift and didn't seem in the least interested in Jen, who walked out tentatively and tried to get her bearings. So this was the eighth floor. This was where her father worked, where board meetings were held. She'd been here before, many years ago, but right now it felt like a different lifetime. It looked different now, smaller, and she couldn't remember her way around.

She edged along the corridor, trying to look nonchalant, like she had every reason in the world to be there. If challenged, she would say she was lost, she decided. Was looking for the library. Or her tutor. Or . . .

"Hello, dear. Can I help you?"

A woman in her fifties was smiling at Jen. She smiled back. "I, um, was looking for the loo, actually," she said immediately.

"Just over there, dear. In the corner."

Jen looked over at the large LADIES sign and smiled awkwardly. She wandered over, but just before she walked in she took a sneaky look back and saw the two consultants walking into a large glass-fronted office on the opposite side of the floor. A room she recognized. She saw a man stand up to greet them. And the man, she realized with a start, was her father.

"We've got the tickets, Mr. Bell. So, who are they for?"

George stared at Jack in a way that told him this was a question that he shouldn't be asking. Jack looked away awkwardly.

"Peter was saying that Green Futures were out in force at the Tsunami dinner the other night," his colleague chipped in quickly. "Apparently your, um . . . Harriet . . . Ms. Keller . . . she was talking a lot about Axiom to people. Hinting that Bell might be implicated in the . . .

uh . . . corruption allegations. Just . . . thought you'd want to know."

George stared at him, then back at Jack, and they both shrank back.

"Thank you, both of you," he said gruffly. "And just for the record, the day Bell Consulting starts to worry about gossip is the day that hell freezes over. Do I make myself clear?"

"Absolutely, Mr. Bell."

The two consultants left, and George made his way back to his desk slowly. Was Harriet up to something? Should he be worried? He shrugged. She was always up to something. There was no point becoming alarmed. Harriet loved nothing more than gossip, a story. She knew nothing, and he was confident that it would stay that way.

He could never quite fathom how someone as intelligent as Harriet could be so utterly silly at the same time. He still remembered the day she'd walked into his office, a mere secretary, and had told him that the paper she was typing for him was all wrong and that she had a much better idea. He'd fallen for her right then and there, bowled over by her confidence, her insouciance, and, of course, her idea which, it turned out, was brilliant. But the very next day he'd heard her telling someone just as urgently about trees being more spiritual than human beings. She was scattered, George thought to himself. She'd never think about one thing long enough to work it out. She was hardly a threat.

It was amazing, George reflected, that she'd managed to run her own firm for so long. Amazing that her co-workers were able to work around her changing moods, her butterflylike attention span.

Well, at least he was out of it. At least he wasn't married anymore. What a marriage that had been, he thought ruefully. How exhausting.

And yet . . . he'd enjoyed some of it. The bits with Jen, mostly. Jennifer Bell, his daughter. He'd been so proud of her, had such high hopes.

He turned and stared out of the window. Life was full of compromises, he thought sadly. Full of tradeoffs and you-scratch-my-back deals. Did anyone really get what they wanted? Had he? He'd hardly seen Jen even when they were a family. He'd always been so busy, building his empire, building a future. And then she was gone, and he realized he barely even knew her.

Still, he told himself, turning back round to his desk. No point crying over spilled milk or wondering about what might have been. Much better to just get on with the job in hand.

George sighed. He sometimes wondered if he'd have been a better father if he'd had a son. Someone he could talk business with, play sports with. Women were so . . . complicated. Even now, even at his age, he found women hard to fathom. They wanted to talk all the time, started arguments from the least little thing. To George the world was a simple place of black and white. But all the women he'd known seemed hell-bent on turning it into a mass of uncertain, moving gray. He got up, walked to the door, and leaned out.

"Emily, why are women so complicated?" he asked his personal assistant.

She ignored him, as always. "Mr. Bell, sir, I've got Mr. Gates on the phone. He's wondering if you could pop over sometime this week."

"Okay. Put him through, will you? And, Emily, a coffee would be great. Get me a macchiato?"

"You mean a decaf macchiato," Emily said matter-of-factly, and ignored his grimace.

George marched back to his desk, picked up the phone, and put all thoughts of Jennifer out of his head.

From across the floor, Jen watched him beadily, then slowly made her way back down to the seventh floor.

Harriet Keller looked around her carefully. She needed somehow to capture the energy of the old days. Get Green Futures back on the map. And hopefully, this presentation would do the trick, would get everyone excited again.

"So you see," she said energetically to the fifty or so Green Futures employees congregated in the meeting room, "we have to use passion. Understanding. All around us, corporations are realizing that they can't ignore the community anymore, can't ignore global warming and poverty. We will continue to stand up for integrity, for love. And in doing so, we will change the world."

As she went to sit down, she nervously listened to the applause. Harriet needed applause, needed praise and validation, and she knew it. It wasn't something she was particularly proud of. She was well aware that it was a weakness, that she shouldn't care what people thought, but the fact was that she cared hugely. Nothing motivated her more than the adulation of others; nothing spurred her on more than the opportunity to prove herself—or, more often, to prove someone else wrong. She'd only started this firm to prove to her bloody ex-husband that she could, and what a triumph that had been. But now that particular motivation wasn't as compelling. And these days she didn't seem to be as interesting to the press, either. She sighed, then smiled as she saw Paul walking toward her.

"What did you think?" she asked immediately, trying to sound chirpy and confident.

He looked at her seriously. "Very, very good," he said. "I found it very . . . inspiring."

Harriet's eyes lit up and she smiled gratefully. "Oh, you're too kind, Paul, really. So you think it was okay?"

"It was much more than okay," he said immediately. "You should not doubt yourself so much."

"Oh, I know," Harriet said with a sigh. "But it is so very tough at the top. Really, it is. Everyone wants so much, and trying to balance my time—it leaves me exhausted. Particularly when Tim keeps telling me we should be spending less all the time. I can't run a business without spending money, Paul. I just can't."

"Everything will be fine," Paul said serenely. "You worry too much, Harriet. Have more confidence in your ability."

Harriet took Paul's hand. "Oh, Paul, I don't know what I'd do without you. You're the only one who really understands me, you know. The only person who understands what I'm trying to achieve, who can see the dimensions in which I work."

Paul smiled, looking a little embarrassed. "I do my best," he said simply.

"Next week," Harriet said suddenly, "we should have a party. Something to get people excited again. What do you think?"

Paul nodded seriously. "I think it is a great idea. I will,

unfortunately, be away, however. I have to see a client in Scotland."

Harriet looked crestfallen. "You have to go? But what will I do without you?"

"I will only be gone a few days. I think you will be okay. I know you will."

Harriet nodded stoically. "Yes, I will," she said with a little smile. "With your support, Paul, I know that I will."

She made her way back to her office, humming softly and planning in her head a party for Paul's return. She would invite all the journalists who'd interviewed her over the years. She'd make another little speech. Maybe allude to Bell and the corruption allegations. Show the world how important she and her firm were in upholding truth and justice and . . . Harriet's humming stopped abruptly when she saw that Tim the number cruncher was waiting for her.

"Harriet, I need you to go through the accounts with me," he said immediately.

Harriet waved him away. "Tim, I really don't have the time at the moment. I thought I employed you to look after the finances for me?"

Tim sighed. "I'm an accountant, not a magician, Harriet. The fact of the matter is that we're hemorrhaging cash at the moment and we need to make some cuts somewhere."

Harriet frowned, then remembered Paul's words. She needed more confidence in her ability. How right he was. If only Tim would see things in the same way.

"Tim, what is Green Futures' mission?" she asked, looking at him closely.

He frowned. "Holistic business, holistic growth," he muttered.

"Precisely. And growth takes funding, Tim, you know that. Perhaps there's more money going out than coming in right now, but I believe that we are doing the right thing. Do you believe that, Tim?"

Tim looked at her uncertainly. "Of course I believe in that, but if we lose much more money we . . ."

Harriet put her fingers to her lips, and Tim stopped talking. "We must invest to grow," she said softly, remembering the words that she'd used for her first *Financial Times* interview. "It is precisely because companies are so concerned with profits and the bottom line that corporate disasters continue to occur. Have faith, Tim."

Tim nodded and left her office, and Harriet sat down at her desk. He had sent her three e-mails, all tagged UR-GENT, and she deleted them one by one.

Focus, she reminded herself. *Tim can look after the figures—I need to focus on the bigger picture. And on organizing this party.* Pleased that she had a plan of action, she smiled and picked up the phone.

Tim walked wearily back to his office.

"Not a good meeting?" his assistant, Mick, asked in a deadpan voice.

"What do you think?" Tim said, his voice that of a defeated man.

"So she didn't think the one-and-a-half-million-pound black hole was a bit of a worry?"

"Didn't get a chance to tell her, did I?" Tim said. "She told me that focusing on the bottom line led to corporate greed."

Mick raised his eyebrows. "So we'll be going out for a nice expensive lunch on expenses, then?"

Tim sighed. "I don't see why not," he said, putting down his files. "If everyone else is going to spend money like it grows on trees, I don't see why we shouldn't either."

7

Jen pulled her coat around her more tightly and watched her breath become steam in the cold autumn air. *This had better be important,* she thought to herself irritably as she looked at her watch for the second time. Her mother had insisted that they had to talk and had then suggested this clandestine meeting in the park. Like they were working for MI5 or something.

She frowned. Maybe she was being unfair. Maybe her mother really had got hold of some important information and was being followed. Big corporations didn't like to be found out. They could both be in danger.

Jen laughed at herself. *Too much late-night television,* she thought, shaking her head and scolding herself for allowing her mother's hysteria to get to her. Harriet lived for excitement, for the appearance of danger and mystery. What she'd do if she ever faced any genuine danger, Jen didn't know.

She looked at her watch again. She had a lecture that afternoon with Daniel and she wanted a prime seat, toward the front. If she was late because her mother couldn't keep her own appointments, he would not be impressed.

"Darling, you're here!" Harriet was breathless, clutching coffee in her hands to warm them up.

"I'm surprised you're calling me 'darling.' Shouldn't we have code names or something?" Jen said with a little smile.

Harriet looked like she was considering the idea, then caught her daughter's expression and sighed.

"Really, darling, I don't know why you have to be so difficult. Now, isn't this nice?" She sat down on the bench next to Jen and looked around. "I do love the autumn in London, don't you?"

Jen looked at her curiously. "Are we here to talk about the weather?"

Harriet shook her head and turned to Jen, her eyes shining. "No. I've got some news."

Jen felt a little thrill jolt through her. "Me too. I was on the eighth floor the other day, and these guys were bringing Dad some tickets to Indonesia."

"He's going to Indonesia? When?"

"I don't know," Jen admitted. "But I'll try and find out. So what's your news?"

"I'm going to have a party!"

Jen frowned. "That's it? You get me on a park bench to tell me you're having a party?"

Harriet looked at her daughter despairingly. "A new-beginnings party. It's important, Jen. I was talking to Paul and it made me realize that I've allowed myself to get too caught up in the day-to-day stuff of running a business. I need to look beyond that, go back to my core mission. To be a beacon! I'm going to invite the press. I'm going to put Green Futures back on the map!"

"With a party?" Jen said flatly. *Why am I surprised*, she asked herself irritably.

Harriet's eyes narrowed. "Yes, Jen. With a party."

"Tim said you had some cash-flow issues. Can you afford a big party?"

"Tim should think before he opens his mouth. Look, Jen, I don't need advice on how to run my business from someone who thinks the world is run by spreadsheets. I thought you of all people would understand . . . Paul's going to Scotland next week and I thought you might like to help. . . ."

Jen looked at her mother in amazement. "You really didn't bring me all the way here to talk about a party, did you? Because your precious Paul has suddenly realized he's got other, more important things to do? Mum, will you look at yourself? This is crazy. I'm meant to be in lectures. I thought you had something important to tell me."

Harriet looked at Jen with wide eyes. "I see. So Green Futures isn't important to you? I suppose you're far too busy doing your *MBA.*"

"Which I wouldn't be doing if it wasn't for you and your big ideas."

"Well, if you're not interested in my big ideas, then I really don't know what I'm doing here," Harriet said in an injured voice. "I'm sorry if I disappoint you, Jennifer. I'm just doing my best, you know. Trying to hold everything together, as always. . . ."

She stood up and Jen sighed. That was Harriet's favorite card that she always used to win any argument—the "I'm a single parent and lone entrepreneur and am single-handedly trying to save the world" trump card that she could never beat.

"You're doing more than your best," Jen relented. It just wasn't worth arguing with Harriet, dealing with the long radio silence, the quivering lip, and the long, drawn-out making-up session in which her mother needed not just the last word, but all the ones before it, too. And anyway, it wasn't really Harriet's fault. Jen's irritation wasn't directed entirely at her.

"I'm just frustrated that I'm not doing better myself," she said with a shrug. "I'm not sure I'm the best spy ever . . ."

"We all do what we can, Jennifer, and no one can ask any more of us," Harriet said with a little smile, sounding much happier. "Now, I'd better go and start the planning for the party if I have to do it all on my own. It's going to be such a lot of work, but I know it's going to make a big difference. Let me know what you find out about your father's Indonesian trip, won't you?"

Jen nodded and sat still as Harriet kissed the top of her head and marched off across the park.

Poor Tim, Jen thought to herself as she watched her mother disappear. *Poor all of us.*

She sat for a minute, watching people walking through the park, enjoying the peace and quiet. Then she picked up her bag. It was time to get going.

Someone sat down next to her and Jen took it as a prompt to get up and go. But as she heaved the bag over her shoulder, the person spoke to her.

"So, is this where you do your own internal analysis?"

She looked up, startled, then felt her stomach somersault. It was Daniel.

"I . . . um . . . well, in a manner of speaking," she said carefully, glad that the cold air was preventing her face from going red this time. He was even better looking close up, with little curls around his hairline and the longest eyelashes she'd ever seen on a man.

"So . . . do you work near here?" she asked after a pause. "You work in bookselling, don't you? I'm Jen, by the way."

Daniel laughed. "Pleased to meet you, Jen. I'm Daniel."

Jen raised her eyebrows and he looked a bit embarrassed. "Yes, okay, I guess you knew that already."

He looked away quickly as if to regain some control over the situation. "Anyway, you were asking about my work? I suppose you'd call it bookselling," he said easily. "Although I rarely get to actually sell any books these days. Have you heard of Wyman's?"

Jen nodded. Wyman's was one of the bigger bookstore chains, and they were all over London.

"I was there just the other day!"

"Well then, you know who I work for."

Jen wondered what to say next. She didn't know much about bookselling—only book buying, which, she figured, probably wasn't the same thing at all.

"I was really interested in what you were talking about the other day," she said after another pause. "The choice between ethics and profit, I mean. It's something I've thought a lot about."

Daniel looked at her interestedly and Jen found herself staring into his eyes, which turned out to be a soft greeny brown, and was unable to look away.

"Who did you work for before this?" he asked, and Jen managed to tear her eyes away, only to look straight back into his again.

"Green Futures," she said. "The consultancy firm."

"I know what Green Futures is," Daniel said quickly.

"Harriet Keller, the storm trooper of ethical business. You work closely with her?" Jen nodded.

"Well, I can see why you're interested in ethics, then. To be honest, it's not really my speciality—you'll know a lot more than me if you worked for Harriet Keller. I just wanted to get the point across that you have to know what you want, otherwise you don't have a chance in hell of getting it. Now, we should probably be making our way to Bell Towers, shouldn't we? Aren't I meant to be lecturing you to death at three P.M.?"

Jen grinned and stood up. There were little droplets of ice forming on her coat and yet she felt incredibly warm as they walked back toward Bell.

She certainly knew what she wanted now. All she had to work out was how to get it. Maybe her mother's ideas weren't so bad after all, she thought to herself as she walked, sneaking little peeks at Daniel all the way back to the office. Maybe things were finally looking up.

That weekend, Jen found herself at her kitchen table, attempting to write her internal analysis assignment. Every time she wrote something, she read it with Daniel's eyes and immediately deleted it. Too naïve, too outlandish, too boring. She wanted to write an assignment that would make him look at her differently. An assignment that would bowl him over, make him want to talk to her about it, maybe over dinner . . .

She shook herself. *No one ever fell in love with an assignment,* she told herself firmly. And even if they had, she was pretty sure it wouldn't have been about internal analysis.

She looked at the question again. "Conduct an internal analysis of an organization or industry of your choice,

using the models and theories discussed in the course."
It was straightforward, at least. No trick question there.
But it was also about as inspiring as . . . well, as some-
thing very uninspiring. Jen sighed.

Unless . . . she frowned. If she were to do an internal
analysis of a bookseller, that would get his attention,
wouldn't it? If she could come up with things that
Daniel hadn't even thought of . . . Okay, maybe that
was unlikely bearing in mind that she'd been learning
about internal analysis for a few weeks and he was
teaching it. But still, he might find it interesting. He
might even be flattered.

Smiling, Jen got up and made herself a cup of tea, then
sat back down to work.

"I've ordered your usual."

Jen grinned at Angel. "Thanks."

"So you were working all last night? Like, actually
doing an assignment? I thought you were doing this
course under sufferance?" Angel's face was incredulous.

"I know, I surprised myself. But there's this guy who
lectures us. Daniel. I just . . . well, I wanted my assignment to be good."

Angel laughed. "You're actually going to get really into
this MBA, aren't you? You'll end up working as a Bell
consultant or something. It's so wonderfully ironic. . . ."

Jen grimaced. "I am not going to be a Bell consultant.
And I still think MBAs are hideous. But if I'm going to
do it, I may as well do it properly . . . Know your enemy
and all that."

"So this Daniel is the enemy?"

Jen blushed and Angel raised her eyebrows.

"Not exactly."

"I don't know anyone as complicated as you, Jen. Really, I don't know how you manage sometimes."

Jen looked at Angel curiously. "I'm not complicated at all. I'm perfectly straightforward."

Angel stirred her herbal tea. "Jen, you spend your life rebelling against things, then rebounding back again. Your father, your mother, Gavin. I lose track myself!"

"And you're so straightforward?" Jen challenged. "You say you don't want an arranged marriage or to be an Indian wife, but you never have a serious boyfriend. You won't drink coffee because of all the toxins, but I bet you were necking vodka shots last night as per usual . . ."

Angel's eyes twinkled and she put on her best demure face. "Vodka's very pure, you know. But okay, enough. I didn't say that complicated is bad, did I? It could have been a compliment."

"Was it?"

Angel laughed. "Yes and no. So, this Daniel person. Is he a good man? And has he got any money?"

Jen nodded as her muesli, yogurt, and bagel with jam arrived. For someone who said she hated her mother's attitude toward men and marriage, Angel managed to sound a lot like her sometimes. "You'd like him," she said with a smile. "He isn't like Gavin at all."

"Then I like him already. But he's your teacher, right? So nothing's going to happen?"

Jen shrugged and started eating. "He's probably married with five children. But it doesn't stop a girl dreaming, does it?"

❧ 8

"External analysis is perhaps the most interesting aspect of strategy." The lecturer at the front of the hall paused dramatically, and stared around the room ensuring that everyone's attention was focused directly on him.

Jen stared at him indignantly. *Where's Daniel,* she wanted to ask. *Why was internal analysis dealt with so quickly? It was just getting interesting . . .*

The past few weeks had been a blur of swotting up on internal strengths and weaknesses, drinking far too many cups of coffee with Lara and Alan, and skulking around in corridors not learning very much from the conversations she overheard, but taking copious notes anyway. She now knew about the love lives of what felt like half the consultants at Bell Consulting, as well as who was applying for new jobs and how little Bruce Gainsborough, whoever he was, was rated by his colleagues. But she knew next to nothing about her father or his trip to Indonesia.

Still, she'd finished her assignment for Daniel and done rather a good job on it, if she said so herself. She imagined him reading it, imagined him thinking about her as he read it, then shook herself.

"Internal analysis will only take you so far," the lecturer was saying. "As with people, looking inside your-self is not really going to help you decide your future. No, being self-aware may be a prerequisite, but then you need to start looking outside to the opportunities and threats on the horizon before you can work out your place in the world. And so it is for business. Consider the context of the business—who are its customers, what do they want, where do they live? Consider competitors—how strong are they and can you preempt their next move? What about your suppliers? Are they efficient? Cheap? What are the issues they're facing? And then think about the wider environment—what's happening in the world outside the business? Flood, famine, boom, bust, brain drain, immigration—they are all going to have implications for a business. It's your job to identify those implications, and to devise a strategy to make the most of the opportunities, and minimize any risks."

Make the most of opportunities and minimize risks, Jen thought to herself. That's what she needed to do at Bell. Her opportunities included bumping into Daniel accidentally on purpose, spying on her father, and listen-ing in on more conversations in the elevator. The risks included being accused of stalking Daniel, being found out by her father, and being asked why on earth she was in the elevator all day long.

"So, introduction over, let's look at some basic mod-els," the professor was saying. "The PEST is always useful—that's Political, Economic, Social, and Techno-logical influences. Would someone like to suggest a com-pany, and we can work through the PEST on it?"

A young man in the front row shot his hand up. "How about a condom company?" he asked with a slight smirk,

and everyone in the room agreed vigorously. Jen cringed—
she was never going to live this one down, obviously.

The lecturer looked disconcerted. "A condom company, you say?"

"We're comfortable with condoms," the young man
said as seriously as he could manage. "They're flexible
enough to really analyze effectively, and you can
really . . . capture the, uh, key issues."

A ripple of laughter spread around the room and the
lecturer sighed.

"Very well then. Political influences on a condom
company?"

There was silence.

Jen caught the eye of the lecturer and immediately
wished she hadn't.

"What about you," he said immediately. "Give me a
political influence on a condom company."

Jen thought frantically. "Um, how about the government's commitment to reduce the level of teenage preg-
nancy?" she ventured.

"Good!" said the lecturer with a smile. "That's one.
It's an influence that could work either way—either the
government could hand out free condoms, in which case
our condom company has to make sure that they hand
out its brand, or the government could preach absten-
tion, which could mean fewer sales. If its brand is important and is about fun, like Mates, it may actively
distance itself from government handouts because they're
seen as 'responsible.' So yes, lots of good stuff there.
Who can think of others?"

Jen felt a little smile creeping onto her face at the compliment.

"AIDS awareness," said someone else.

"Yes, but that's not political. A government's attitude to AIDS is what's political—do they acknowledge there's a problem and want to tackle it or are they ignoring it? Both will have implications for our company. Okay, economic influences?"

Lara stuck her hand up. "The cost of rubber," she said with a grin.

"Absolutely. Very big influence," the lecturer said to a great deal of giggling around the room.

He narrowed his eyes. "Social influences?"

"How much people are shagging," someone at the back shouted out, to more giggling.

The lecturer sighed. It didn't matter how old your students were; as soon as you had a group of people in a lecture theater they reverted to teenage humor.

"Someone turn that sentiment into a social influence," he said with a sigh. "What about you?"

He was looking at Jen, and she reddened again.

"Um, how about rates of marriage?" she tried. "And demographics—how many people are having children at what age, that sort of thing."

"Good. Why?"

"Because if there are lots of people married or in relationships who don't want to have children, condom use will go up."

"Excellent. Thank you. And finally, technological. Anyone?"

Alan put his hand up. "New developments like the male pill," he said seriously.

"Good. Anything else?"

"Vibrators," Lara said quickly.

"Explain?"

"Well if they're good enough, women may not need

sex with men anymore. . . ." She got a little round of applause from the few women in the room.

"Interesting idea," the lecturer said, "which we won't explore now—I'll leave that to you, shall I? Now, when you've done your PEST, you need to—" He was interrupted by the door opening. Jen looked up and froze. Her heart started pounding and she could feel the blood drain from her face.

"Mr. Bell!" the lecturer said, immediately straightening his posture and looking far more formal than he had five minutes before. "What a nice surprise. Would you . . . um . . . like to have a seat?"

George smiled broadly. "You just carry on, Julian," he said affably. "Thought I'd just take a quick look at this year's intake if it's all right with you."

"Oh, absolutely. Yes. We were just doing the PEST analysis," the lecturer said, obviously flustered. "On a . . . manufacturing company."

George nodded and started walking to the back of the lecture theater.

Jen looked around desperately, then dropped a pen on the floor and dived down after it. This was one risk she hadn't foreseen. And it could be the end of everything. Shooting a look at Lara, she hid under her desk and held her breath.

Lara looked at her curiously, evidently confused, and Jen tried to indicate that she was trying to hide, which she did with a series of hand gestures that frankly could have meant that she was hoping to travel to the moon one day. Still, Lara seemed to get the message and quickly deposited her coat over Jen.

"Mr. Bell?" she asked sweetly, turning round to face

him. "What's your take on the wacky world of condoms?"

Daniel grinned as he flicked through Jen's assignment. Bookselling. She'd done it on bookselling. Was she trying to tell him something?

It wasn't bad, either, he thought to himself. It was certainly more interesting than any of the other things he'd read that day. Management reports, financial statements, supply chain strategies . . . Why was it, he wondered, that the better you were at something, the less you got to do it? He'd been a great bookseller. And what had happened? He'd been promoted and promoted until he didn't do any bookselling anymore. Didn't get involved in promotions, in buying decisions, any of it. He just got to sit around talking to his chairman about cost efficiencies and to his finance director about whether to put a bookstore in Mall A or Mall B.

What should he write, he wondered. "A very interesting assignment with some good, original ideas"? No, that was way more complimentary than anything he'd written on any of the other assignments he'd marked so far. He needed to be consistent. But "Good. Interesting ideas" seemed somehow too curt.

She was bright, obviously. And her ideas *were* interesting. Maybe he'd wander down to Bell some time this week, bump into her, and give her verbal feedback. Over coffee or something . . .

He frowned. She'd probably be totally freaked out. Fuck it, maybe she was actually interested in bookselling. Maybe that's why she'd been so keen to talk to him, so keen to ask him about what he did. She wasn't interested in him at all.

He smiled to himself wryly. *Never mind, Daniel*, he told himself. *Nothing wrong with being an optimist.*

Then, carefully, he wrote "A–. Very good work."

Lara was staring at Jen with her eyebrows raised. Jen, meanwhile, was staring into her coffee, trying to think of a suitable explanation for her behavior in the lecture.

"So what, you're terrified of authority figures?" Lara tried, a little smile on her face. "Or are you a convicted criminal on the run?"

Jen cringed. She looked closely at Lara and took a deep breath. "Lara," she started nervously, "I've got something to tell you."

Lara's eyes narrowed. "Was it you who nicked my notes on the balanced scorecard?"

Jen shook her head crossly. "No, of course not. It's nothing like that."

"Okay, then, shoot."

Jen gulped, then put her hands together nervously. "You know this course. This consultancy firm."

Lara nodded like she was talking to a five-year-old. "Yes, Jen. That'll be Bell Consulting. I know it, you're right."

Jen punched her lightly in the arm. There was nothing for it—she was just going to have to come out with it.

"You have to promise—and I mean promise—not to tell anyone. At all. Ever."

Lara's eyes lit up. "Ooh, a secret. Okay, my mouth is sealed. What's the gossip?"

"I'm . . . well . . ." Jen began, her heart beating loudly.

"Yes?" Lara prompted impatiently.

"I'm George Bell's daughter. He doesn't know I'm here, doesn't know I'm doing the MBA, and he can't know."

"You're what? You're his daughter?" she said incredulously, spitting out coffee as she spoke. Jen wiped the coffee drops from her hand and nodded.

"And he doesn't know you're here?" Jen nodded again.

"But your name's Bellman." Jen raised an eyebrow at her.

"Oh, right, it isn't. Seriously, you're Jennifer Bell? You're his daughter?" Jen nodded glumly.

"I have one question for you."

"Okay," Jen said uncertainly.

"What the hell! Why don't you tell him? Jesus, you could be running this show in a couple of years. I don't understand."

"He's not really my father."

Lara looked at her strangely. "Look, if this is your idea of a joke, it's really not that funny."

"No, I don't mean . . . Look, he left us when I was thirteen. I haven't seen him since. And I don't particularly want to. See him, that is."

"So you're doing your MBA here because . . . ?"

"Because . . . okay, this is really, really secret."

Lara rolled her eyes. "Jesus, enough of the melodrama, okay?"

"Fine. I'm . . . I'm trying to find out if Bell Consulting is involved in corruption in Indonesia. You know the Tsunami aid money and the building program out there? Well, there are some dodgy deals being brokered. Dodgy houses being built."

"And why would you think Bell's involved?"

"Because one of the companies that just happened to get some of the prime contracts is Axiom, who are clients of Bell. Bell just happens to have offices in Indonesia, and its clients out there include several government departments. And" —she leaned over so she could whisper— "my dad's going out to Indonesia next week."

"Bloody hell," said Lara, a look of shock on her face. "So what are you going to do about it?"

Jen looked at her awkwardly. "I need to get into his office. Look at his papers."

Lara nearly fell off her chair. "You're going to break into George Bell's . . . sorry, your dad's office?"

Jen smiled nervously.

"Seriously?"

Jen nodded, and Lara looked thoughtful.

"I s'pose you're going to want my help, then?"

Jen shook her head, then hesitated. "Really?" she asked softly. "I mean, would you?"

"Hell, we're a team, aren't we?" she said matter-of-factly.

Jen grinned gratefully. "Does that mean we have to invite Alan along too?"

Lara laughed. "Oh that would be priceless," she said, her eyes twinkling. "Just asking him would be worth it to see the expression on his face!"

They both smiled and didn't say anything for several minutes.

"And when exactly were you thinking of breaking in?" Lara asked eventually.

Jen looked thoughtful. "I thought next week. When he's in Indonesia."

"Right," Lara said, doing her best to look totally unfazed. "Next week it is, then."

Bill was wearing a stripy jumper and army combats and his hair was tied back into a loose ponytail. Jen found herself about to ask how he got it to lie so flat and glossy, then kicked herself.

"So, Jennifer, how's it hanging?"

Jen smiled weakly. "Oh, you know," she said vaguely.

He motioned for her to sit down. "So, already on to your second module, huh? Are you finding the course work okay?"

Jen nodded. She knew she had to think of something to say, otherwise Bill was going to be forced to ask question after question and he'd feel bad and she'd feel awkward and he was meant to be her personal tutor; they were meant to be building a rapport.

The problem was that she couldn't think of anything to ask him about. Lara had been in to her see personal tutor that morning and they'd talked for two hours, covering (in no particular order), course work, whether it was a good idea to shag someone in your course—a theoretical question, Lara was keen to point out, since there was no one remotely shaggable around—rents in London, future career options, and whether or not her tutor's husband was cheating on her (in Lara's opinion the answer was yes, but she didn't say that). So how come, Jen wondered, I can't think of anything?

"We've just started on external analysis," she said eventually. "Environmental factors. Market positioning, that sort of thing."

Bill nodded interestedly. "Man, that's my favorite part," he said with a smile. "You can stop all that navel gazing and get out there, see what's happening in the real world. Am I right?"

Jen nodded uncertainly. All she could think about was breaking into her father's office, which filled her with equal amounts of excitement and dread.

"I suppose," she said noncommittally. "I mean, sort of. We're not actually going outside or anything." Now that Daniel wasn't teaching her anymore, Jen had lost her flurry of enthusiasm for her studies.

"Why don't you see some businesses for yourself, then?" Bill suggested gently. "Go visit some real-life managers somewhere? I'm sure they'd be interested in talking to you. You're going to have to pick an industry to write your assignment on anyway, so this could be part of your research."

Jen looked at him thoughtfully. "You mean just ring up a company and see if they'll let me come in and talk to them?"

Bill nodded. "Why not? Can't hurt to ask."

Jen thought for a moment, knowing exactly which company she'd pick if she had her way. She imagined herself at Wyman's, trailing after Daniel and talking to him about her assignment. Bookselling must have all sorts of external influences, and it was such a nice business, too. Very little pollution, no unethical practices—well, unless you counted those awful biographies of pop stars who were only nineteen and hardly had much of a life to write about, but then that was the publishing companies' fault, not the bookseller's. She snapped herself out of her reverie just in time to hear Bill ask about the rest of her life.

"You know, relationships, social life, that sort of thing?" he asked, his face suddenly changing into his life-coach "concerned" expression.

Jen looked away defensively. "Fine, fine," she said evasively, trying to convince herself as much as him.

"Pleased to hear it. And if you hit any problems, you

come to me—that's why you've got a personal tutor. To help you through stuff."

"Thanks, Bill. I appreciate it."

"You're welcome! Now you just keep those problems coming, and I'll just keep on helping. Deal?"

Jen grinned. She did actually feel better. "Okay, Bill," she said seriously. "It's a deal."

⁊ 9

Jen sat in front of her computer, took out her mobile, and dialed a number. Then she hit END and put her phone down again. For the fifth time.

Just do it, she told herself. *Just pick up the phone and call him. He liked your assignment. He gave you an A-minus. Now you just have to ask him if you can spend some time at his office, for research. It's an opportunity. Grab it!*

And the risks? she thought worriedly. *What if he laughs, says no, tells me he's too busy. He probably doesn't even remember me.*

She looked again at her assignment, with Daniel's writing on it and the official stamp at the bottom giving her the name and number of the marker. Daniel Peterson's direct line.

He'd be way too busy to see her. It was a stupid idea.

Although if she never even tried, she'd never know . . .

Closing her eyes and taking a deep breath, Jen pressed SEND on her phone and listened as it automatically re-dialed the number. After two rings, someone picked up.

"Hello?"

"Hi!" Jen said quickly. "I . . . I was hoping to talk to Daniel. Daniel Peterson."

"Well, that's lucky. You are."

Jen frowned. "I . . . Oh God, is that you?" she said suddenly. "I was expecting a PA or something . . ."

"She's having lunch," Daniel said amiably. "So, what can I do for you?"

Jen felt herself getting hot. "It's Jennifer here. We . . . we met at Bell Consulting and . . ."

"Jennifer from the men's room?"

Jen got hotter. "Yes. The thing is I . . ."

"And from the bench?"

"Yes." She could sense that Daniel was smiling, even over the phone, and it made her flustered. She looked at the piece of paper in front of her on which she'd written exactly what she wanted to say, but her eyes could barely focus on it.

"I was just wondering," she said hesitantly, "the thing is, we're doing external analysis at the moment and my personal tutor thought . . . I mean, I thought . . . I mean, well, we both thought actually that it would be good to get out into the real world, so to speak. Talk to someone about real business issues . . ."

"That sounds like a very good idea," Daniel said. "Which company did you have in mind?"

Jen went red. "Well, um, yours, actually." There was a pause and Jen held her breath.

"I see! Well, I'm sure something can be arranged," he said.

He's going to suggest I go and work in the bookshop, Jen thought to herself desperately. *He thinks I'm some weird stalker. He's going to hang up. He's going to . . .*

"I'll tell you what," Daniel said conspiratorially. "I've been thinking about getting out and doing a bit of research for ages but just haven't made the time to do it.

You could join me if you like—external analysis in action, so to speak."

Jen was taken aback. "Get out where?" she asked.

"Bookshops of course. To watch the great book-buying public make their purchases. I'm free on Sunday if you are. And I'll throw lunch in, too."

"Really?" Jen said incredulously. "I mean, really. No, that sounds very interesting. I'd love to. If that's okay . . ."

"Great. Meet you outside Book City on Oxford Street at one?"

"Okay," Jen said quickly, her heart suddenly floating on thin air. "One sounds great!"

"I liked your assignment, by the way."

Jen grinned. "I hoped you would." She frowned. Had she given too much away?

"So, one, then."

"One."

And feeling like a teenager, Jen hung up the phone.

Jen leaned over Lara, who was sitting in the library staring at a computer screen.

"Okay," she whispered. "Reconnaissance report is as follows: One P.M., his personal assistant goes to lunch. One-fifteen P.M. the two administrative assistants go to lunch. One-thirty P.M. his PA comes back with a sandwich and eats it at her desk reading the *Times*."

"And he's definitely in Indonesia?"

Jen looked at Lara shiftily. "I'm pretty sure he is," she said. "I've been up to the eighth floor three times this week and he hasn't been there, nor his coat or anything else. And one of his consultants definitely mentioned this week when he was by the water cooler the other day."

"Okay then, go on."

"Well, we've got to get in at one-fifteen P.M. exactly to avoid his PA. If you can be on lookout duty, I can find what I need in five or ten minutes, I'm sure. And I'll see if I can log on to his computer, too."

Lara turned round and rolled her eyes. "Are you really sure about this?" she asked eventually. "I mean, it sounded kind of exciting at first. And, you know, it still is. Kind of. But I was actually hoping to get an MBA here rather than being slung out for breaking and entering."

"You wouldn't be breaking and entering. The most they could get you for is aiding and abetting, and anyway, I told you, if anything goes wrong, just leave me there."

"So you can be slung out instead?"

"I'm not the one who actually wants an MBA. Seriously, just walk away and pretend you don't even know who I am."

Lara shrugged. "Okay, then. Let's hope it doesn't come to that, shall we?"

She smiled encouragingly at Jen, and Jen tried to smile back brightly, but her insides were churning.

"See you in the restaurant at one P.M.?" she asked Lara, who nodded silently.

Jen opened a book in front of her and waited for the seconds to tick by.

At one P.M. Jen and Lara were standing in front of the restroom, next to the lifts. Jen had a clear line of vision to Emily's desk and could see one of the administrative assistants. Lara was busily applying lipstick and talking about fictional relationship problems—at least Jen assumed they were fictional. They'd decided that if they were having a conversation about relationships and sex, no one would interrupt them or ask what they were doing.

"She's coming," hissed Jen as Emily stood up, put on her coat and started walking toward the lift. As she approached them, she paused briefly, looked as if she was going to stop and say something, then thought better of it, pressed the call button for the lift and, a few seconds later, disappeared behind the gray metallic doors.

Jen let out her breath and wiped away the small beads of sweat that were gathering on her forehead. This was all getting a bit too real, she decided.

"Why am I doing this?" she muttered under her breath, and Lara looked at her quizzically.

"Truth, justice, and world peace, wasn't it?" she said with a wry smile, and Jen grimaced.

Ten minutes passed, more slowly then Jen thought possible, and then, at last, she saw the visible administrative assistant stand up. A few seconds later, she too was walking toward the lift, followed by her colleague. It was now or never.

Quickly, Jen and Lara sprung into action. They walked as nonchalantly as they could toward George's office, then Jen quickly ducked in while Lara stood guard outside.

It felt very strange to be in her father's office, a room that she hadn't seen for sixteen, maybe seventeen years. It had the same smell—expensive leather, fresh flowers— and the same full bowl of fruit he insisted on getting delivered every morning and from which nothing was ever eaten.

On the walls were photographs—George with Bill

Gates, with Richard Branson; sailing, skiing, playing tennis. In each photograph his face drew you in—animated, strong, charismatic, powerful. And selfish, Jen thought to herself. *All this fun you were having—did you ever think about me? Ever wonder what I was doing?*

She shook herself. Now was not the time for recriminations, she decided. There would be time for that later.

She headed straight for her father's cabinet, a large wooden cupboard that, she discovered, housed not just his paperwork, but also his golf clubs and a dinner jacket. She frowned and scanned the shelves.

"Can I help you?"

Jen froze. She recognized that voice, although she couldn't quite place it. She turned around slowly just as she heard Lara answer.

"Oh, hi! I was hoping to catch Mr. Bell's secretary. I wanted to interview her for some research I'm conducting. Do you know where she is?"

Jen let out a breath silently and turned round again. She knew who it was now—it was one of the guys she'd followed into the men's room at the charity dinner. But thankfully he'd only seen Lara.

"I think she's at lunch, actually," Jen heard him say. "But she'll be back soon. She'll need to be—the big man's due back any minute."

Jen gulped. He couldn't mean her father. He was in Indonesia. Wasn't he?

"Even better!" Lara said, sounding for all the world as if she meant it. "I thought he was out of the country."

"Why would you think that?" His voice sounded vaguely suspicious, and Jen held her breath.

"Oh, something someone said. I must have got the wrong end of the stick . . ."

Jen scanned the cabinet for files. Alpha, AT&T, Barclays, Barton's, BOC Group, House of Fraser, the Ministry of Defense. Nothing on Axiom. Jen frowned. Where was the bloody file? There must be one somewhere, she thought desperately and carried on looking at the rows of files in case the Axiom one had been put back in the wrong place, but she got to Xerox and still came up with nothing.

She frowned and looked around quickly to see if there was anywhere else in the office that the file might be. There was a round table with six chairs around it, but there was nothing on it except for the obligatory fruit and a carafe of water. There were also two filing cabinets, but both were locked. Jen bit her lip—she couldn't believe she'd come all this way for nothing.

Then she noticed something on a low shelf. It was a pile of papers, on top of which was a handwritten note. She picked it up and felt her heart jump as she realized what it was.

George,
   Re our telephone conversation, thanks for helping out. Contracts will all be signed next week and I'll make sure you're copied in.

                                          Yours,
                                          Malcolm

Malcolm, as in Malcolm Bray? Jen thought to herself. Malcolm Bray was the chief executive of Axiom. But what did he mean by "helping out"?

Quickly, she folded the letter up and stuffed it in her

pocket. She heard the guy Lara had been talking to walk away and sighed with relief.

"Quick," Lara whispered, popping her head round the door. "Get out."

"I need a bit more time," Jen said quickly. "Just a few more minutes."

"There is no more time. Your father's not in Indonesia, is he? He's bloody well here!"

"Okay, so he'll be back soon—I only need a bit more time . . . ," Jen said dismissively.

Lara glared at her. "No, Jen, he's here, as in now," Lara hissed urgently. Jen looked at her in alarm and ran to the door. Across the floor, walking purposefully toward his office with two consultants in tow was her father. And in his hands was something that looked suspiciously like the Axiom file.

"Go!" she whispered to Lara, who shrugged helplessly and walked quickly back to Emily's desk, pretending to put something in her in-tray.

Jen looked around desperately. There was nowhere to run to. Nowhere to hide.

Unless . . . Quickly she opened the cabinet doors. There could just be enough room, she reasoned. If she could shift the golf clubs along a bit. Without pausing for breath, she dived in, closing the doors behind her just as her father walked through the door.

She squirmed around so that she could see through the crack between the two cabinet doors. Her father sat down at his meeting table, and two young men walked in. One of them was the guy Lara had been talking to.

"Right, so, Jack, tell me what this is all about."

"It's the Axiom problem. I think we need to make a

statement. Distance ourselves from the company. Tell them we can't work with them anymore."

There was a pause.

"You want Bell Consulting to cut one of our biggest clients adrift? To tell the press that we want nothing to do with Axiom?"

There was an uneasy silence in the room, then Jack started talking again. "This thing's getting too close. We're going to get dragged down."

George frowned. "You think we're going to get dragged down?"

"Yes, sir."

George looked serious for a minute, then he laughed. "Jack, you're a great consultant. I enjoy working with you. But I think you should stick to enterprise resource management, okay? Leave the press statements and side-taking to me. Do you understand?"

"But . . ."

"But nothing, Jack. I want you to leave this. Do I make myself clear?"

Jack and his colleague stood up. "Crystal clear. Thank you, Mr. Bell."

Jen watched as they left the room and shifted awkwardly. Her legs were killing her, pressed up against her chest, and she was terrified that she was going to make an involuntary movement before too long. *How much longer will he be in here,* she wondered. What if her father decided to work late? What if he didn't leave the office till eight P.M.?

"Emily, would you mind running out and getting me a sandwich?" Jen heard him say, and she prayed silently that he wasn't going to be in his office for the rest of the afternoon. "Something with cheese in it. Or meat."

She heard Emily come into the office. "And salad, Mr. Bell?"

There was a pause. "Tomato. I don't mind tomato."

"Very well."

Jen sat perfectly still as Emily left. She heard her father rummaging through some papers, then stand up.

"Well, I wonder what I'm going to do now," he said out loud to himself. "Maybe I'll go out for a bit."

Jen smiled with relief. He sounded a bit odd. But at least he was going out, which meant that she could escape. Her legs were killing her.

"Just one thing left to do," her father was saying, "and that is to find out exactly who it is that's hiding in my cupboard, and what the bloody hell you're doing there."

Before Jen could even register what he'd said, the cabinet doors swung open, and there in front of her, his face as surprised as hers, was her father.

∂ 10

"You!" George exclaimed. His face changed from anger to incredulousness to absolute shock. *He definitely recognizes me,* Jen thought to herself and was surprised how relieved she felt. If he hadn't realized who she was, she wasn't sure she'd have been able to forgive him.

Not that she was going to forgive him now.

"It can't be. Is it? You look so different. You've grown . . ."

His voice was fragile, so different from the confident, booming voice that Jen heard from inside the cupboard, and it unnerved her. He was an ogre, she reminded himself. A cheating, selfish, unethical ogre.

He held out his hands and Jen clambered awkwardly out of the cabinet, her legs giving way beneath her as she tried to work out exactly what she was going to say.

She leaned on his desk as he looked her up and down in amazement.

"It is you, isn't it?"

She nodded, and before she could say anything, he grabbed her in a hug. "Oh, my little Jen. Oh, my darling girl."

She struggled out of his grip. "I'm not your darling

girl," she said, trying to keep her voice steady. "I'm not your little Jen. Not anymore."

"You're right. Let me look at you. My God, you're a woman. What . . . What are you doing here? It's so wonderful to see you, but why now? And why . . . why in my cabinet? I thought I'd caught a thief in there."

She looked down at the ground, and George looked at her curiously.

"Jen?"

"Maybe you did catch a thief."

She bit her lip. Maybe Angel had been right: This was a dangerous game. If this wasn't her father, she'd be talking her way out of the situation, making a joke of it, doing her best to avert suspicion. But it was her father. And she wanted him to take notice of her.

"What do you mean?" George was looking confused. "Do you want money? I don't understand."

Jen looked up at him. "I want the truth. About Axiom in Indonesia. About the bribes that led to people dying last month . . ." Her voice was quavering.

George's eyes narrowed. "Axiom? What the hell has that got to do with you?"

This was more like it, Jen thought gratefully. It was much easier to be defiant and angry with a man who didn't look like he wanted to hug you.

"It's got everything to do with me. And the poor people in Indonesia who thought they were getting a proper home. And all those people around the world who donated money, thinking it would be spent properly . . ."

George paused and sat down at his meeting table. He offered a chair to Jen and she sat down tentatively. Adrenalin was still coursing through her veins.

"And you think that your father would be messed up

in that sort of thing, do you?" He looked sad and Jen forced herself to look away.

"I can't say I really know my father well enough to judge that," she said obtusely.

"No," George said with a sigh. "I don't suppose you do. But still, the suspicion came from somewhere."

Jen met his eyes briefly and again looked away. His face suddenly broke into a sort of smile. "Oh, of course. Your mother."

Jen went red. She'd felt kind of powerful until that moment. Now she felt like a sniveling teenager.

"Maybe."

"Harriet," he said carefully, "has a very vivid imagination, you know."

"You had tickets to Indonesia delivered to you last week. What were they for?"

Jen was getting hot now and was desperate to move the conversation away from her mother, away from anything personal.

George frowned. "How on earth did you know about those?" he asked, then shrugged. "They were for a colleague, actually. We have offices out there. I've just appointed a new head of professional services and he's going out next week to meet the team before he starts formally in January. But I'm sure you knew that, too. Right?"

Jen shifted uncomfortably in her chair.

"You never even came to see me," she suddenly blurted out, her voice soft but pained. "Not once."

Her lip was quivering, and it was all she could do to stop herself from bursting into tears. *Way to go, Jen,* she chastised herself bitterly. This is really going to show him you don't care.

"You made it perfectly clear that you wanted me out of your life," George said flatly. "It broke my heart to walk away, but what choice did I have?"

Jen stared at him, astounded. "You had every choice in the world. You could have seen me any time. You didn't even send me a good-luck card for my GCSEs. After all that work we did together."

"But you told me you never wanted to see me again."

Jen rolled her eyes. "No, I didn't. Don't you dare try blaming me for this. You slept with someone else. You walked out on us. I probably told you I hated you and I probably meant it, but that didn't mean you could just cut me out of your life."

"Cut you out? Jesus, Jennifer, it was me that was cut out. Your mother refused to let me talk to you, told me that you didn't want to see me. That it would upset you if I tried. And, just for the record, I didn't, as you put it, 'sleep with someone else.' I think your mother has rather rewritten history on that count."

Jen stared at him. This wasn't how this conversation was meant to go at all.

"What do you mean?"

"I mean that she was the one who did the sleeping. Not that it matters now. It's ancient history."

"She cheated on you?" Jen's voice was barely a whisper. "You're lying. She would never do that. She . . ."

"It wasn't entirely her fault," her father said softly. "We were having a rough patch. I wasn't home very much. She . . . I think she craved attention." George was looking awkward now, uncomfortable.

"But she had an affair? Are you serious?"

He nodded.

Jen pulled out a chair and sat down, her head spinning. This changed everything. Her mother had lied to her. Had kept her father from her. Harriet, her ethical and conscientious mother, was a cheat and a liar.

But did that mean that her father was the good guy? Somehow she doubted it.

"Jen, don't think ill of your mother," George said gruffly. "It was a long time ago, and I was far from the ideal husband. I'm just so sorry that . . . well, I'm sorry about what happened. Sorry I haven't seen you for so long. It's . . . it's unforgivable." He looked at her imploringly. "But I understand if you don't want me around. I've burned my bridges, I accept that. Just let me know if I can help you in any way—money, a job, you know. I'd like to be a father to you . . . somehow."

Jen looked at him, the father she'd missed for so long, the father she'd dreamed would come and find her and tell her how sorry he felt, was right here in front of her, wanting to be part of her life again, and she had no idea what to say. She felt her anger melt away, and she sighed. "Dad, the day you left I said a whole load of things I didn't mean. I was angry. I didn't want you to go."

It felt strange calling him Dad again after all this time. Using such an intimate, everyday term for the person whom until recently she'd thought she might remain estranged from forever. The man she'd been planning to betray.

"I thought I was doing the right thing. Keeping things simple for you. Oh, Jen, oh, I'm so sorry."

He stood up and came toward her uncertainly, the arrogant swagger replaced by something more humble.

"Is there still room in your life for a father?" he asked her tentatively.

Jen shook her head. Then she nodded. Then she shook her head again.

"Would you perhaps do me the honor of having dinner with me this evening?" he asked her, taking her hand and squeezing it.

Jen nodded. "And you swear you weren't involved in paying bribes?"

George smiled. "Jen, how much do you think Bell Consulting makes each year?"

Jen shrugged.

"Let me tell you. Our annual profit is in the region of twenty million pounds each year. It's been growing about five percent each year for the past ten years. That's an awful lot of money. Can you see us jeopardizing that kind of income to pay some bribes for a property deal on which all the world's eyes are focused?"

"But . . . but Axiom got the biggest contract and the houses weren't even built properly, and apparently there's been a cover-up, so no government officials can find out what really happened . . ."

"I'm not in the business of housing regulations, I'm afraid, or in the business of government, for that matter. But there are people who are, and I'm sure that they will be looking very closely at the houses Axiom built and at the paper trail around their contracts. But if you're interested in that, you should really be in Indonesia, not in my office."

Jen folded her arms. She felt awkward. Stupid. "Are they still your clients?" she asked eventually.

George frowned. "Have you heard the phrase 'innocent until proven guilty,' Jen?"

She nodded.

"Not a bad sentiment in my opinion. So yes, they are still our client. Any other questions?"

"The letter, thanking you for your advice. What was that about?"

George shook his head, smiling. "Tenacious little thing, aren't you? That was about our advice regarding the negotiations. Standard practice for us."

" 'Negotiations' as in bribes?" Jen persevered.

" 'Negotiations' as in negotiations."

Jen shrugged, deflated. "Why should I believe you?"

George looked her in the eye. "People only believe what they want to believe, and I dare say you won't be any different. All I can do is tell you the truth, and all you can do is judge whether you believe it. You believed your mother, remember."

Jen reddened. "I know."

"So will you have dinner with me?"

"I s'pose," she said quietly. Her head was spinning so fast she barely trusted herself to speak.

"Good," said George a little more cheerfully. "And then perhaps you can tell me how the hell you got past the Bell security and into my office."

"Seriously? He found you in his cabinet?"

Angel's eyes were wide. Jen nodded, a big smile plastered on her face, which had been there for two days solid now. Her father was a good man. Well, at least he wasn't a bad man. He had listened to her, told her about his life, been excited about her doing the MBA. He was her father, and she had him back again.

"And now everything's okay between you again? I mean, after just one dinner?"

"A dinner and lunch the following day," Jen pointed out.

"And you don't think you're rushing things a bit? This time last week he was enemy number one."

Jen looked at Angel, exasperated. "That was when I didn't know the truth. Mum lied to me. God, all this time I just took her word for it. I'm so angry."

"Have you spoken to her about it?"

Jen shook her head. "I don't know . . . Dad thinks I shouldn't. Thinks sleeping dogs should be left lying, or something. I don't think he wants the aggro, frankly."

"And you? What do you want?"

Jen shrugged helplessly. "I want to know why she lied. But I don't want her to get involved. I'm just getting to know Dad and it's . . . well, it feels precious. I'm afraid that if I tell Mum, if I challenge her, it might all go wrong again."

"So you're just going to leave it? Knowing she lied to you?"

Jen shook her head. "Of course not. I just want to leave it. For a bit, you know?"

"And in the meantime she still thinks you're spying on him?"

Jen managed half a smile and Angel looked at her exasperatedly. "And what about the MBA. It's over now, right? I mean, you're not spying anymore. So you're going to leave?"

Jen frowned. Why did Angel always have to ask the difficult questions, the ones that Jen allowed herself to pretend didn't exist?

"No," she said after a short pause. "I mean, well, Mum doesn't know, so I kind of have to keep doing it. And Dad was so excited that I was on the course . . .

I'll just do it for a bit longer. You know, until I decide what I really want to do . . ."

"Well, I take my hat off to you, Jen," Angel said, rolling her eyes. "Only you can take a complicated situation and make it a million times more complicated."

"So how's things with you?" Jen asked quickly.

"Well, I thought I had a lot going on in my life, but now it feels positively humdrum!" Angel said, grinning. "My brother's getting married, so I've got a big engagement party to go to. A sari to buy. Food to cook. Big commotion in my parents' house. And I have sixteen people in my yoga class now."

"Wow! That's fantastic!"

Angel smiled demurely. "It's not bad. So come on, then, tell me why we're meeting today instead of tomorrow? I thought our Sunday brunches were sacred!"

Jen blushed slightly. "I'm . . . meeting Daniel. It's a work thing . . . I mean, it's research. You know, for my MBA. But . . . well, anyway . . ."

Angel looked at her friend closely. "You're at a loss for words and as red as a tomato," she said. "You sure it's just work?"

Jen shrugged and grinned. "I guess it's complicated," she said, raising her eyebrows at her friend.

"Of course!" Angel said with a smile. "I should have known that, right?"

❧ 11

By twelve P.M. on Sunday, Jen was panicking. An hour before, she had been sitting at her kitchen table, dressed in her favorite jeans and with liquid eyeliner perfectly applied to make her eyes look double the size. She'd been ready for more than an hour and had been reading the newspaper, trying to stop herself from feeling nervous. She was just going to walk around some bookshops with Daniel. It was no big deal, she'd reasoned pragmatically. It wasn't even a date—it was work. Research.

And that's when the panic started. She was dressed for a date. She even had pretty blue knickers on and a matching bra. What was she thinking? This was her lecturer, a chief executive of a bookseller, and she was dressed like she was going out for a romantic liaison.

Quickly, she'd run to the bedroom and taken off her jeans. And her scoop-neck T-shirt that wasn't exactly revealing but was certainly more suggestive than a round-neck jumper. But what should she wear instead? What combination of clothes clearly said "I understand that this is a work-led excursion, but it is Sunday, and I am an attractive person that you might one day want to ask out. Not that I'm suggesting anything. Or about to throw myself at you . . ."

Jen cringed, picked up a pillow and pulled it to her face. This was a terrible idea, meeting Daniel. She'd deluded herself into thinking that he was actually interested in her when in reality he just wanted someone to walk round bookshops with him. He probably only suggested it to get her off his back.

Perhaps she should call Daniel and cancel. He'd probably be relieved—he'd probably invited her along before even thinking about it and was right now wondering how to get out of it.

Okay, breathe deeply. You can't call Daniel—you've only got his work number. Anyway, he does want to see you—why else would he have asked? And the jeans are fine.

Slowly, Jen had put her jeans back on, with a higher-neck T-shirt and a pale blue wrap cardigan. Then she'd gone back to the kitchen table and forced herself to slow her speeding heart rate with long, deep breaths and regular sips of water. *What can really go wrong*, she asked herself, then decided not to answer the question. This was a sort-of business meeting and sort-of date. Everything in the world could go wrong.

Jen stood up. Maybe she should do something to pass the time—it was a good twenty minutes before she needed to leave, and having time to think was always a bad idea before doing anything; she had long ago perfected the art of talking herself out of anything that could open her up to any risk whatsoever. The trouble was that Jen had always been nervous about doing anything outside her comfort zone—as a child she'd resisted everything from going to stay with her cousins without the reassuring presence of her mother, to performing in a school play, but somehow, since her parents had split up, it had become even worse. She justified this to herself regularly with the rationale that she was now the product of a broken marriage and it was natural that she should be more cautious. But it was a pretty crap excuse really, and Jen knew it.

I should read a book. Of course, she thought with the beginnings of a smile. *He's a bookseller. I need to be able to talk about books.*

Quickly Jen raced to the bookshelves in her sitting room and stared at them for several minutes in search of inspiration. Something impressive, she thought. James Joyce maybe. Or the biography of William Pitt that she'd seen in a bookshop window and bought on a day when she'd decided she didn't know enough about history, then never quite got round to reading. It had had very good reviews. And the more it sat there waiting to be read, the more it filled her with utter dread—page after page of factual detail with no sex, intrigue, or real plot of any sort. She felt like Alice in Wonderland wondering how anyone could read a book without pictures in it.

Still, Daniel was bound to be impressed if she could talk about a book on an eighteenth-century politician, wasn't he? Or was William Pitt seventeenth century?

Jen picked up the book and flicked to the introduction. Blah blah prime minister. Blah blah died young. Was a politician all his life.

You weren't meant to bring up politics, religion, or sex, were you? she thought suddenly. *Not on a first date.*

This isn't a date, Jen reminded herself. *It's research.*

She looked at her watch. Twelve-fifteen P.M. It was time to go.

* * *

Daniel was waiting for her outside the shop, wearing a beautiful well-worn gray cashmere coat and Jen felt an almost irresistible urge to reach out and touch it. Instead, she smiled as naturally as she could manage in the circumstances, said hello, and then stood there awkwardly for a second or two before Daniel held out his arm and said "Shall we?"

"So, do you go to bookshops much?" he asked once they were in the warm surroundings of Book City, turning round to look Jen right in the eye. "Or was your assignment research more desk-based?"

"Quite a lot . . ." Jen said tentatively. She was feeling incredibly nervous and was finding it hard to relax.

"When? When do you go and how long do you stay there and what makes you buy something?"

Daniel was still looking at her intently and Jen found herself getting hot. She took off her jacket, partly to cool herself down and partly to give herself an excuse to look away briefly. You could drown in eyes like that.

"Well," she said, taking a few minutes to try and remember not just when she went to bookshops, but what her name was, where she lived, and what day of the week it was. "I suppose I go a lot during my lunch hour—when I take one. And also on Saturdays—if I'm out shopping or something. Like the other day, I bought the latest biography of William Pitt."

"Which one?"

Jen reddened. "Which biography?" she asked.

"No, which Pitt? The younger or the elder?"

"There were *two* of them?" The incredulous comment left her mouth before she'd had time to think about it, to make an informed guess. But instead of looking at her as if she were utterly stupid, Daniel grinned.

"I'm sorry, that wasn't fair. So what made you buy it? We don't usually get many young women buying historical biographies. The typical demographic is men in their fifties and sixties."

Jen hesitated. "Actually, it was a self-improvement thing. I'd just decided I didn't know enough about British history."

"And do you now?"

Jen smiled weakly. "Actually I haven't read it. Yet."

Daniel grinned again, putting his hand through his hair, and leaving it there, twiddling some strands together between his fingers. Jen found herself staring at it and she shook herself quickly.

"So, back to the shop. What would make it better. What would draw more customers in? You're in the bookstore—what are you looking at?" Daniel asked her.

You, Jen thought, but didn't say it. Instead she looked around and her eyes fell on the tables in front of her. "The display tables."

"Only the display tables?"

Jen tried to concentrate—this was beginning to feel like an exam. "Well, unless I know exactly what I want," she said seriously. "Then I'll go and look by the name of the author or something."

Daniel nodded, his eyes bright. "And how often do you know exactly what you want?"

Jen thought for a moment. "Actually, not that often," she admitted. "I mean, I'll default to authors I know, but usually I just browse and wait for something to grab me."

This was great, she thought to herself—just the sort of thing she should be doing for her MBA course. She was really pleased. And if her smile seemed to have faded slightly, it was no big deal—it was like she'd thought all along; this was a work meeting. Daniel wanted her input to his strategy, not a cozy date looking at books together. It had been ridiculous of her to think anything else; his exact words had been . . . okay, she couldn't remember his exact words, but they had definitely included the words *research* and *external influences* and hadn't included anything like *date* or *kissing*.

She looked at Daniel and was alarmed to see that he was frowning.

"Is everything okay?" she ventured.

Daniel nodded quickly. "Yes, of course. I was just thinking how I miss all this. Miss being on the shop floor, talking to customers, watching them get excited by books. I started out selling books and now I rarely even get the time to buy one."

"So how did you get to where you are?" Jen asked interestedly. "I mean, from being a bookseller?"

Daniel smiled thoughtfully. "That's a very long story. But the shortened version is that I started my own bookshop, and when it did well I opened up another branch, and when I had a few of them dotted around the country, Wyman's offered to buy it and invest so that I could open up even more of them. I agreed, and I was made managing director."

"Wow! How long ago was that?"

"A year," Daniel said quietly.

"And are you enjoying it?"

He shrugged. "It's okay. The board are keen for more growth, maybe another takeover, possibly a move into international markets, that sort of thing. And they're right, of course. But I do miss . . . just, well, selling books. . . ."

Jen watched him carefully, noted the little crease above his eyebrow and the very slight sadness in his eyes. "Then that's what you should do," she said quickly. "Sod international markets, just do what you want to do."

"Is that what you're doing? What you want to do?"

Jen frowned. "Absolutely. I mean, you know, kind of. I mean . . ." she trailed off, realizing as she spoke that she barely even knew what she wanted to do, let alone how to go about doing it.

She smiled awkwardly. "Maybe it's easier said than done," she said with a little shrug.

Daniel stared at her, then grinned. "So, are you hungry?"

Jen smiled. "Shouldn't we be watching the movements of customers and the book displays?" she asked, her eyes twinkling.

Daniel smiled sheepishly. "Actually, I've got a whole load of market researchers doing that sort of thing. I was rather hoping instead that you might let me buy you lunch."

"You know," Jen said, two hours later, buoyed up by nearly a whole bottle of Châteauneuf-du-Pape that Daniel had ordered before mentioning that he was actually driving and so wouldn't be drinking more than a glass, "you're never going to get very far with your strategic planning like this. You haven't watched the movements of a single book-buying customer."

"I have!" Daniel said, looking mortally offended. "You're a customer, aren't you? And I think I've followed your movements pretty closely."

Jen looked down at her food, trying to hide her excitement. This hadn't been work at all. Daniel had whisked her off to his favorite restaurant, on a little road just off Oxford Street, and they'd been here for what seemed like hours, eating divine food and talking about everything from the price of taxis to the sad fact that as you get older you start sounding like your parents and think that all music in the charts is infinitely inferior to anything you listened to when growing up.

They hadn't talked about work once.

Except . . . suddenly Jen felt herself tighten. What if it was her driving the conversation? What if Daniel had wanted to talk about work and she'd been blathering on about there being no greater talent in the world than David Bowie?

"What about external influences," she said coyly. "We haven't talked about them at all."

Daniel looked at her curiously. "You really want to talk about external influences?" he asked.

Jen nodded, then shook her head, then nodded again. "I'm thinking about doing my next assignment on booksellers." She noticed Daniel raising his eyebrow at her. "After the first one went so well," she added.

"Booksellers the people or the companies?"

Jen grinned. "I haven't decided yet. You're my first bookseller." She caught his eye and blushed. Maybe she'd had a glass of wine too many, she thought to herself. But then again, she didn't really care.

Daniel raised his eyebrows at her. "You're planning to meet more?"

Jen shook her head and he smiled.

"Okay, then. For what it's worth, I think you're rather a welcome positive influence," he said gently, moving his hand to rest on hers. "And I'm sorry if I was firing questions at you earlier. It's what I do when I'm nervous."

Jen looked at him incredulously. "You were nervous?"

Daniel shrugged. "Maybe," he said with a little smile. "I thought you might want me to talk shop all afternoon—no pun intended. I didn't know if . . . well, you know."

"If?" she prompted gently, wondering whether it would be very forward to link her fingers through his.

"If you'd like coffee," he said matter-of-factly, and Jen frowned slightly as Daniel motioned upward. She followed his eyes and saw the waiter hovering over them.

"Ah," she said quickly. "I see what you mean."

After coffee, Daniel got the bill and insisted on driving her back home. They walked round the corner to where his car (a beautiful vintage Alfa Romeo Spider, Jen noted) was parked and he insisted on opening the door for her—although it was probably because the door required a good kick before it would open rather than because of any kind of gallantry.

As the car pulled away and made its way onto Oxford Street, Jen sat back and assessed the day. Daniel was perfect, she decided. Intelligent, funny, didn't take himself too seriously, and those eyes . . .

And he was even taking her home. He was a gentleman. He was kind. He was . . . oh God. What happened when they got back to her flat? Would he expect her to invite him in? Why else would he have insisted on going home via her flat?

But she couldn't just invite him in—it was so clichéd, and suggested things that Jen wasn't quite ready to suggest. At least she didn't want him thinking that she was ready to suggest them, even if right now she kind of wanted to . . .

No, she wasn't the sort of person to invite someone in so soon, even if it was just for a cup of tea.

Although, at the same time, she wasn't quite ready for the afternoon to end . . .

Jen frowned, wished she hadn't drunk quite so much wine, and did a quick mental pros and cons list. Pros, she'd have him for a few more hours; she wanted him to kiss her; it was the polite thing to do; God, she wanted to rip his clothes off. Cons, she might never see him again, her flat was a mess . . .

"Everything all right?" Daniel asked.

"Great, thanks!" Jen said brightly.

The car purred down through Green Park and Chelsea until they arrived at her road in Fulham, and Daniel drew the car to a standstill.

"Thank you so much," Jen said quickly. "It was really kind of you to give me a lift. And the lunch, too . . . I had a really lovely time."

"Me too," said Daniel, turning off the ignition and turning to look at Jen properly. It was the kind of look that usually signalled that there might be kissing in the very near future. Jen undid her seat belt.

"So, which one's your flat?" Daniel asked, looking up at the building ahead of them.

"Oh, it's not in this building—it's the one across the road."

Daniel turned to look. "That one, with the tramp standing outside?" he asked.

Jen turned to see what he was looking at. "Yes," she said. "The one with the . . ." She peered more closely, then let out a little yelp. "Oh, God. That's not a tramp. That's Gavin, my ex-boyfriend."

Daniel raised his eyebrows and quickly sat up a bit straighter. "Oh, right. I, er, better let you go, then."

"No, don't. I mean, I don't know what he's doing here. There's no reason why you should go . . ."

Gavin had turned around and was staring at Daniel, who was doing his best not to stare back.

"No, really, it looks like he wants to talk to you. I . . . I've got to get back anyway . . ." he said, his voice suddenly less intimate.

"I'm so sorry," Jen said despondently. "I . . ."

"Look, it's really no problem," Daniel said quickly with a sudden and false-looking smile on his face. "You go and . . . well, you go."

As she got out of the car, Jen leaned down to look at him one last time.

"See you," she said, with a slight question mark at the end.

"Yeah. It was fun," Daniel said with a wink, and turned the engine back on.

Jen watched him drive off, then turned round to face Gavin.

"And what the hell do you want?" she asked crossly.

❧ 12

"What are you doing here?" Jen asked again.

She looked irritably at Gavin's mousy hair, which looked like it hadn't had a wash in several weeks, and his lopsided grin.

"I came to see you, gorgeous. Didn't realize I'd be interrupting anything. He a friend of yours, is he?"

Jen ignored him, taking out her key and opening her front door.

"You're looking . . . good," Gavin said in a voice that suggested he thought the opposite. "Smart, I mean. Shiny hair."

"You're looking like shit," Jen replied cautiously. "What's with the clothes?"

Gavin grinned. "And I thought you liked a bit of rough. Well, next time I'll know to bring my sports car."

Jen raised her eyebrow at him and he shrugged. "Just been helping organize a rally against a supermarket," he said, lolloping into the kitchen and helping himself to a large glass of milk. "Ended up meeting some really cool travelers so I've been kicking around with them for a while."

Jen nodded. "So that would explain the hair," she said curtly.

Gavin grinned sheepishly. "I think it suits me, actually. Mind you, I could kill for a bath. If we're friends, that is?"

He looked at Jen hopefully and she tutted like an irritated mother. "You can't just keep coming round here," she said brusquely. "I'm not your girlfriend anymore. I've got my own life now."

Gavin looked hurt. "But you're my friend," he said. "I can go, if you want. Steve said I could sleep on his floor . . ."

He picked up the large, musty-looking bag he'd been carrying and moved slowly toward the door. Jen let him get halfway there, then relented. "One bath. That's it."

"And some food?" His eyes were twinkling now. "You do the best food, Jen. Just one meal, and tomorrow I'll be off, I promise."

"Tomorrow?"

Gavin grinned and leaned over to kiss her on the cheek. "You wouldn't kick me out, would you? Not now I'm here. Not when you haven't seen me for so long?"

Jen folded her arms and looked at him. Gavin was unlike anyone else she'd ever known. Energetic, charming, hopeless at practical things but better than anyone else at what he did best—drawing people in, getting support, and winning people over. Everyone wanted to look after him, everyone wanted to be close to him. But he was like a stray cat—affectionate and loving when he needed something, then off like the wind once his appetite was satisfied. As his girlfriend, Jen had been envied and pitied in equal measure by those around them. But, she'd discovered, not being his girlfriend anymore didn't seem to offer the protection from him that she'd expected.

"You're going to have to find someone else to spring

your little visits on, Gavin," she said eventually. "You can stay tonight, but that's it. Seriously. Don't you have another girlfriend?"

She asked the question partly to test herself. To check for her response if he said yes. She was pretty sure she was past caring.

"Not like you."

"You are so transparent, Gavin. Stop with the flattery, okay? I've already said you can stay."

"You're the best, Jen. You really are."

She rolled her eyes and opened the fridge, watching Gavin walk to the bathroom and start to run his bath.

"So, you still working for your mum?" Gavin asked, simultaneously talking and wolfing down a plate of Jen's signature green Thai curry.

Jen frowned. "Kind of."

"Kind of?"

"It's . . . complicated."

Gavin grinned. "I love a bit of complication. So go on, then."

Jen shrugged. "Okay, but it's a secret."

"Cross my heart and hope to die. Actually, I don't hope to die. Why the fuck would I hope to die? But I won't tell anyone."

"I'm doing a bit of corporate espionage."

As Jen spoke she could feel elements of her mother rise up within her, wanting to show off, to impress Gavin with her dramatic tales of spying, and she squirmed slightly.

"Cool."

Jen frowned. It was just "cool"? No questions? No looking at her with newfound respect and wonderment?

"Yes," she continued. "It's related to this whole corruption scandal in Asia. The Tsunami money? I'm . . . well, I'm leading the team trying to find out who's involved from the UK." Was she really this shallow, she wondered, as she spoke. Was she still desperate to impress Gavin? She was making it sound like she was working for the government, single-handedly running an investigation, when all she'd done was follow her father around and then discover that it wasn't even him in the first place.

"That's really cool. So who is it?"

Jen picked up her empty plate and took it over to the sink. "Oh, we're following a few leads," she said vaguely.

"What leads? Come on, this is interesting."

He was sitting up now, looking at her expectantly. Jen sighed. This was her fault for wanting to sound good. She thought for a moment, then sat down again.

"Well, we thought it might be Bell Consulting. You know—they've got offices over there, government clients, and Axiom—the construction firm—well, they're a client too. But it isn't them, so I'm kind of back to square one."

"Bell Consulting? That's your dad's firm, isn't it?"

Jen nodded, feeling herself getting a bit warm. It was probably the curry, she told herself.

"And how do you know it wasn't him?"

"I just . . . know."

"What, because he told you?" Gavin laughed and Jen shot him a look.

"Maybe."

He looked at her in mock amazement. "You're serious, aren't you! He told you he wasn't involved and you believe him. Oh, Jen. Oh, little sweet Jen."

"I am not little or sweet," she said hotly, suddenly remembering why she'd been so keen to show Gavin just how much she was achieving on her own. She'd spent two years running around after him and he'd returned the favor by constantly making out that she was the one that needed looking after, that she was too naïve and trusting. *Mind you*, she thought to herself, *I went out with you for long enough. Maybe you had a point.*

"Look, he didn't just tell me. There was more to it than that," she said matter-of-factly, taking Gavin's plate to the sink and washing it up. She felt self-conscious, defensive.

"Whatever you say." Gavin was smiling to himself and Jen took a deep breath. She would not rise to the bait. She would not let him get to her.

"So this guy in the car today. He your boyfriend?"

Jen put the plates down. "Maybe."

"What, he hasn't made up his mind yet?"

She turned around, her eyes flashing now. "Maybe, if you hadn't pitched up today. Maybe, if you weren't waiting outside my flat, *he'd* be here now."

Gavin grinned. "Oops. Did I get in the way? Hey, it's not a bad thing to let him know he's got competition, you know. It'll keep him on his toes."

"You're not competition," Jen said crossly. "And if you don't mind, I'm going to make it an early night. Are you going to be all right on the sofa?"

"Do I have a choice?" His eyes were twinkling again and Jen sighed.

"No, you bloody don't."

As she moved toward the door, Gavin stood up,

blocking her path. "So I guess it's my fault you're not shagging that bloke tonight, is it?"

She narrowed her eyes. "Shut up, Gavin."

"Only, I feel like I owe you. You know . . ." He put his arms around her and leaned in to kiss her, an action that was so familiar to Jen and yet felt entirely and utterly wrong.

"Fuck, I've missed you, Jen," he moaned as she pulled away forcefully. "What?" he demanded. "What's the matter?"

Jen looked at Gavin and shook her head. "I'm not interested anymore, Gavin. You're on the sofa, and I want you out tomorrow."

He shrugged. "Shame," he said with a little smile. "You're pretty sexy, you know, Jen."

As Jen made her way to bed, she wondered if Daniel shared that sentiment.

๑ 13

The next morning, sitting in his office, Daniel felt his mind wandering and forced himself to focus as his chairman droned on about the advantages of selling and then leasing their property portfolio. He found it about as interesting as watching paint dry.

"Why don't you leave this with me?" he eventually suggested, desperate to get Robert Brown out of his office. He was feeling agitated, like a caged lion.

Robert nodded and got up to go. "How's the growth strategy going?" he asked as he headed for the door.

Daniel paused for a second, trying to push the image of Jen out of his head—the elusive, beautiful Jen who made words like *strategy* and *stakeholder* sound sexy and exciting.

"Oh, you know, coming along," he lied. The truth was that he was finding everything about his job arsewipingly boring at the moment. It was all growth charts and balanced scorecards and mergers and acquisitions, and nothing to do with books or marketing or customers. The stuff that he was actually good at.

"Well, let me know if you need any help." Robert gave Daniel a little nod as he spoke, then left. Daniel got up and started pacing about his office. He had been in this job, what, ten months? Eleven maybe? And what had he actually achieved in that time? Nothing. Absolutely bloody nothing. But what could he achieve when everything he used to do was now out of his hands? He had a team who dealt with publishers, another who dealt with publicity. There was a director of marketing, a whole division that dealt with customer experience, and as far as Daniel could see, there was nothing left for him to do except stare out of the window and wonder how the hell he ended up here.

He leaned over his meeting table and read a few headlines on the *Financial Times*, which was spread out on top of it. An investigation was being launched into the finances of an oil company. The share price of a manufacturing firm had dropped following a slow quarter.

Dull, dull, dull. He hadn't gone into business to manage. He'd gone into business to invent, to find new ways of doing things, to innovate. And somehow he'd ended up here, at the top and bored out of his skull.

Damn it, he thought to himself, and picked up the phone.

"Anita Bellinger's office."

"It's Daniel Peterson, from Wyman's. Is Anita around?"

"One moment, please." Daniel drummed his fingers on the table as he waited.

"Daniel? What a nice surprise! I didn't think you had time for us publishers anymore. What can I do for you?" Anita sounded thrilled to hear from him.

"I wanted to talk through your list, if that's okay. I thought maybe we could have lunch sometime."

"Is there a problem, Daniel? I went through our list with your buyers last month and they seemed very happy."

Daniel frowned. Of course she had. Yet another thing that he didn't get to do anymore. "Anita, I just want to talk about books. Is that okay? I'm paralyzed here, staring at spreadsheets and listening to people talk about business process reengineering, and I want to remind myself what the hell I'm doing this all for."

"I understand completely, Daniel. No problem at all," Anita said quickly, hearing the frustration in his voice. "Look, I'm going away for Christmas, but we'll set something up as soon as I'm back, okay? And Daniel, everything is all right, isn't it?"

Daniel smiled gratefully. He knew he could depend on Anita. She'd known him when he was just starting out, had done him huge favors and taught him everything he needed to know about bookselling, from deals with publishers to getting displays right. If anyone could get him excited about his job again, it was her.

"It's fine, really. Look, thanks, Anita. I'd say I owe you, but you already know that, right?"

"Have a good Christmas, Daniel. Get some rest. And have some cash ready for all the books I'm going to tell you about."

Daniel grinned and hung up, then turned back to his spreadsheet.

"And you're absolutely sure that you're following the diet I gave you?"

George stared petulantly at his doctor and huffed loudly. "You calling me a liar?" he challenged.

"No, George. I'm asking a question, that's all. It's your health that's at stake here—if you don't want to take it seriously, then I'm not going to force you."

George lowered his eyes to the floor. Blasted diet. Buggering exercise program. It was inhumane—he was expected to survive on a diet of vegetables and walk ten thousand steps a day. Ten thousand! He'd carried the ridiculous pedometer the doctor had given him for one whole day and had made a grand total of 2,500 steps. And that had been a particularly exhausting day, too—he'd had no driver and a meeting in town, which meant walking out onto the street to hail a taxi. His doctor was becoming worse than Harriet—she'd always been trying to get him to eat carrots and vile things called chickpeas, but he'd had absolutely nothing to do with any of it. And didn't intend to start now.

"I thought I paid you good money to look after my health for me," he said sulking. George had no time for weakness—in others or himself—and the idea that he might be anything other than invincible was too much to bear. "Anyway, you chaps always over-egg the pudding, don't you? Always very cautious. I'm more of a risk-taker. Live fast and—"

"Die young?" Dr. Richards interjected. "George, take it from me: You don't want to die young. And you certainly don't want to find yourself bedridden or incapacitated, do you?" George looked at his feet.

"No, I didn't think so. So no more cigars. No more red meat. Get some exercise. And stay off the claret, okay?"

George shrugged. "I'm not happy about this," he said crossly. "Not happy at all. I might still get myself a second opinion."

Dr. Richards stood up and shook George's hand warmly. "I would be disappointed if you didn't," he said with a smile.

* * *

George left Dr. Richards's surgery in Harley Street and decided to walk back to his office and notch up some steps on that Woods pedometer. It wasn't often he got time to himself during the day, and it was rather nice and bright. Bloody cold, but the English were built to withstand low temperatures, he thought to himself. It was the sun that got them into trouble.

He wondered what Jen was doing now. She'd be in Bell Towers, listening to a lecture or maybe working in the library. God, how incredible it all was. A week ago he had a daughter only in name. Today, he was a proper father again, and she was a little chip off the old block, too.

He wished he was allowed to brag about her. Tell Emily, tell his colleagues—particularly the ones who spoke endlessly about their offsprings' achievements. But she'd made him promise not to, and anyway, he could wait. The last thing he wanted was for Harriet to get involved, after all. He had enjoyed some precious time with his daughter and he didn't want anything to get in the way.

And of course he had to remember the circumstances. She was his daughter, but she'd been hiding in his office for God's sake. He was pretty sure she believed him, but he had to be careful.

Maybe he'd call her. See if she was free for lunch. He quickly took out his mobile phone and dialed Jen's number. It went through to voicemail.

"Jen? Just your father here, wondering if you're free for lunch? If not, don't worry. I'll . . . well, I'll talk to you soon, I hope. Work hard now! Cheerio."

Did he sound ridiculous, he wondered? He probably seemed like an old man to her. It was easy to ignore the passing of time, to let years go by and assume that they hadn't touched you, he thought to himself. That you were still the young, dynamic man you always were. But children had a way of bringing you crashing down to earth. Jen was, what, twenty-eight? He was fifteen years older than he'd been when she last saw him. His hair was graying, his stomach protruding, his face sagging. What must she think? Had it been a shock to her?

He frowned. *Come on, George,* he told himself gruffly. *Snap out of it. You've got things to do.* Still holding his mobile phone, he dialed another number.

"Hello, Paul Song speaking."

"Ah, Paul. Just checking in to see how the trip to Acech went. Shall we meet at the usual place tonight? Say seven P.M.? Good, good. Look forward to it."

Thrusting his phone back in his pocket, George upped his pace and strode back toward St. James.

❧ 14

The next day, sitting in one of his favorite restaurants, George eyed the juicy steak in front of him greedily. It was beautifully rare, just as he liked it. This was the food humans had been eating for years, not beans and bits of leaves. He was confident that the medical establishment would figure out pretty soon that all the advice they'd been handing out was just plain wrong.

"So," he said with a smile, "got much planned over Christmas?"

His old friend Malcolm shook his head. "Nothing too eventful. Usual family gathering back in Surrey—son's coming down with his two children, you know the sort of thing. Too much food and drink, and then back to work with an almighty hangover!"

George smiled and nodded, trying to feel happy that his own Christmas would be a rather more solitary affair. *Peace and quiet,* he said to himself—*nothing like it.*

"I imagine it'll be nice to get away from the horror headlines for a while," George said, washing his mouthful down with a gulp of Margeaux.

Malcolm raised his eyebrows. "Too right," he agreed. "Bloody journalists stirring everything up. Ought to be a law against it."

George nodded sagely. "So you're bidding for the re-building work, I take it?"

Malcolm poured George another glass of wine. "Oh, I should think so," he said with the hint of a smile. "Now, have you seen the pudding menu? I think we're going to be in for a treat."

Jen sighed and looked at Lara nervously. It was all very well, being all friendly with her father and arranging nice cozy lunches like the one they'd had yesterday, but that wasn't going to help her now. "I know my pen's going to run out," she said, shaking her head. "Lara, lend me a pen, will you?"

Lara handed Jen a biro. "It's not the pens I'm worried about—it's whether my brain's going to run out," she said dramatically. "I bloody hate exams. Don't see why we have to do them. Particularly not the week before Christmas. I mean, that's just sadistic."

Jen shrugged. They had about ten minutes until their first semester exam, and nerves were running high. She told herself she didn't care if she passed or failed, but she knew deep down inside that she did. She'd never failed anything, and she wasn't about to start now.

"Hi, Jen, hi, Lara." They looked up to see Alan hovering above their table.

"Hi, Alan," Jen said brightly. "Looking forward to the exam?"

He looked thoughtful. "It is always good to have an opportunity to consolidate your learning," he said seriously. "But I wouldn't say I'm looking forward to it. More of a necessary evil. I have a question, though—would you say that stakeholder analysis should be part of the internal or external analysis? I mean, they're a business's stakeholders, so they're internal, but they're not in it, so they're external. Right?"

"Oh, shut up, you bloody brainbox," Lara said irritably. "I have no bloody idea, and if you only had a proper life, you wouldn't either."

Alan looked down at her with a confused look on his face. "I just wondered . . . ," he said defensively, then sat down.

"Well, it's time to go in, I reckon," said Jen, gathering up her things.

"Go in where?"

Jen turned round quickly. She recognized that voice. But it couldn't be Daniel, could it? He'd be at work, surely?

It *was* Daniel. Looking utterly gorgeous in rolled-up shirtsleeves and dark-blue wool trousers. He grinned at Jen sheepishly and as he put his hand through his hair she felt her stomach flip over several times. She stood up quickly, nearly knocking the table over.

"Daniel! Hi!" she said in a voice that was slightly too high pitched. "It's our exam. Starts in five minutes. So, are you . . . are you teaching here today?"

Daniel grinned. "No, just picking some of the consultants' brains," he said lightly. "I also wanted to say good-bye—I'm off to Northumberland to spend Christmas with the folks tonight."

Jen felt a sudden stab of disappointment, but forced herself to smile. "Oh. Right. Well, um . . ." She wanted to kiss him. Wanted to wrap her arms round him. But she could feel Lara's and Alan's eyes burning into her, and anyway, it wasn't like he was her boyfriend or anything. Once again, she cursed Gavin for having turned up unannounced. If he hadn't been there on Sunday, she'd probably be kissing Daniel right now.

"See you when I get back?" he asked quietly, forcing her to lean in toward him, so close she could smell his skin.

"God I hope so," she breathed, then pulled a slight face. "I mean, well, that would be nice . . ."

"I rather thought so, too. Good luck with the exam!"

As he walked away, Jen sank back onto her chair.

"Well, Alan," Lara said in a deadpan voice. "Would your stakeholder analysis of that little interaction consider Daniel Peterson an internal or external influence?"

Alan stood up. "Since I don't have a proper life, as you so kindly put it, I couldn't possibly say."

Lara shrugged. "Ready, Jen?"

Jen was still smiling inanely. "What? Oh. Yes. Yes, absolutely." And, walking on air, she followed Lara and Alan into the exam room.

"I forgot all about Ansoff."

Jen frowned as Alan put his head in his hands and leaned down onto the table in front of him. She quickly moved an ashtray out of the way.

"Come on, Alan, it's over. There's no point going over it now." She smiled halfheartedly as she spoke, knowing that she hadn't just forgotten Ansoff's matrix, but had also forgotten all the other models and theories she was meant to have used in the exam—her head had been too full of Daniel to focus on an exam question about a vineyard in California that was losing money.

"Isn't there?" Alan asked, slowly pulling himself up straight. "I thought that was the point of going to the pub—going over the exam and working out where we went wrong. Prepare ourselves for failure. Mind you, I'm already prepared. Been preparing all my life."

Jen rolled her eyes. "Alan, don't be ridiculous. You got a first in your degree, for God's sake—I wouldn't call that failure. You're just suffering from post-exam stress disorder. Lara will be here with the drinks soon and you'll be fine."

Alan regarded her dolefully. "I won't be fine. Lara was right about me—I don't have a life. All I've got is passing exams and if I do badly, well, there'll be nothing left."

"Alan, don't be stupid—there's loads more to your life than exams."

"Like what?"

Jen frowned, searching her mind for something positive to say. She liked Alan, she really did, but they'd only ever really spoken about the course.

"Like your personality, Alan. You're a nice bloke."

He shook his head balefully. "I'm a boring bloke. That's why I haven't got a girlfriend."

Jen grinned. So that's what this was all about. "You want a girlfriend? Is that the problem? Alan, there are probably girls tripping over themselves to go out with someone like you."

"I don't exactly see them queuing up."

"Well, they wouldn't, would they? I mean, you do have to talk to people a bit before they'll declare their undying love for you." Jen looked over to the bar to see what was holding Lara up and saw her emerging from the Ladies. Oh God, she realized, she hadn't even gone to get the drinks yet.

Alan shook his head. "I can't do that whole talking thing. I don't know how."

" 'Course you do. You talk to me and Lara, don't you?"

Alan looked at her shiftily. "Only about work stuff. When you two start talking about shoes or the weather or holidays I just switch off."

Jen frowned. He was right—she'd had plenty of conversations with him about the balanced scorecard, and plenty more arguments with him about the nature of business, but she'd never talked to him about anything else.

"Okay, so try it now. Tell me about your family. Are you seeing them for Christmas?"

Alan shrugged. "Yes."

"That isn't exactly telling me about it."

Alan sighed. "Yes, I am. I have a normal family. They live in a house. And we'll be having turkey for dinner. That's it."

"Where do they live?"

"Chester."

"Is it nice?"

Alan looked at Jen, then scratched the back of his neck. "Not really. Look, I'm sorry, I've just had a bad morning, that's all. Just forget all that crap I've been spouting."

Jen smiled, slightly relieved. Then she frowned and leaned over. "Alan, when was the last time you went out on a date?"

He looked uncomfortable. "I dunno. A while back, probably."

"Be more specific."

Alan looked around and started to go red. "I dunno," he said, more defensively. Then he shrugged. "Never, okay? I've never been on a date. I had a girlfriend from school, went out with her for ten years, and then she dumped me a year ago for some bloke she met at work. End of story. And it doesn't matter anyway . . ."

Jen nodded, trying not to look as shocked as she felt, watching Alan struggle to maintain his composure. She thought for a moment.

"Would you like me to help you?" she asked eventually. "Alan, you're a great guy. You should be going on dates. You just need to . . . relax a bit. Learn the art of conversation."

"Fat chance," he said quickly, but he looked as if his ears had pricked up a bit.

"Come on," Jen urged. "Just give it a go. What have you got to lose?"

Alan pushed his glasses back up his nose. "You'd really help?" he asked, his voice suddenly smaller somehow.

"Help at what?" Lara had returned from the bar and was depositing drinks on the table.

"Ansoff," Jen said quickly, winking at Alan who smiled gratefully. "I'm going to help Alan to understand Ansoff's matrix better."

Lara rolled her eyes. "You'd better help me too, then," she said. "I can't even remember who Ansoff is."

"So, your exam yesterday. I hope you did well?"

Jen looked at her father nervously, but was relieved to see that his eyes were twinkling. He'd been obsessed with exam results when she was growing up, and she'd half expected him to berate her for not working hard enough. Although, since she was having lunch with him every other day, she figured it was partly his fault if she didn't do well. "I think that anyone who thinks that exams this close to Christmas are a good thing is deranged," she said matter-of-factly, sitting down carefully as a waiter fluttered over her, placing a napkin on her lap and pouring her some water.

"But doesn't it feel more like Christmas now that the exam is over?"

"I suppose," Jen conceded. "But that's like saying that you should starve yourself before a meal just so that you enjoy it more."

George laughed. "You always were argumentative. Just like your mother."

Jen raised her eyebrows.

"Okay, and a bit like me," George said immediately. "So, tell me, how are you?"

Jen grinned. "Well, not much has changed since I saw you on Monday. And since we spoke on the phone yesterday."

George nodded. "Tease me if you like," he said, pouring Jen a glass of wine, "but it won't dampen my enthusiasm. It's just so good to have you back. To be . . . part of your life."

Jen noticed a little tentative look on George's face as he spoke, which almost immediately disappeared, replaced by his usual, confident smile.

"So," he continued quickly, "what are you going to have? I thought I might go for turkey."

Jen shook her head and looked at the menu. "Turkey? You must be joking. Aren't you going to be having enough of that on Christmas Day?"

George flinched slightly, then he smiled broadly. "Can't ever have enough turkey in my book," he said. "But if you're too much of a wimp to take it, I suggest the steak. It's really rather wonderful."

Jen frowned. "Dad, what are you doing for Christmas? You do have plans, don't you?"

George looked at her incredulously. "Plans? Of course I've got plans. Too many invitations, truth be told. Can't decide which ones to turn down."

Jen smiled, relieved. If he'd said he was going to be on his own, she'd have had to spend Christmas with him. Which would be fine as far as she was concerned, but breaking the news to Harriet . . . well, it didn't bear thinking about.

"You're going to your mother's, I presume?" George continued as if reading her mind. She nodded.

"You could appear more enthusiastic. She is your mother, you know."

Jen looked at her father curiously. Harriet was never this charitable about him.

"I am looking forward to it," she said cautiously. "But you know what Christmas is like. Lots of people, lots of drinking, the inevitable arguments . . ."

George shook his head. "Nonsense. Christmas is a wonderful thing. Didn't you used to enjoy our Christmases? I remember every one."

He looked at her wistfully, and Jen suddenly felt a huge urge to hug him, to sit on his knee like she did when she was five and feel utterly and completely protected and contented. Mothers were wonderful, she thought to herself, but they just didn't have broad enough shoulders sometimes.

"Me too," she said quietly. "Especially the one when you got me a bike." They'd spent the whole day together that Christmas, George encouraging her to ride without her training wheels, and her screaming with delight when she finally mastered riding solo.

George laughed. "Well, I'm afraid I don't have a bike for you this year, but I hope you'll like it all the same."

He pulled out an envelope and passed it to Jen. She opened it and found a Christmas card—"with all my love, from your father," and a certificate with her name on it and a picture of a funny-looking planet. She wrinkled her nose, trying to remember if she'd ever told her father she was interested in outer space, and drew a blank.

"It's a star," George said softly. "I always promised you the moon, and I failed abysmally, but you've got a star now, in your name. I . . . I hope you like it."

Jen stared at him and felt little tears start to prick at her eyes. "It's beautiful," she said, digging her nails into her palms to try and maintain a bit of composure—she was in a smart restaurant, after all. "Thank you, Dad. I . . . I didn't get you anything."

George frowned. "You're here, Jen. Believe me, for an old fool like me, that's Christmas present enough."

Jen nodded silently as the waiter came over to take their order. He was right, she thought to herself as she ordered. Being here with her father was the best Christmas present she could have wished for.

❦ 15

"We wish you a merry Christmas, we wish you a merry Christmas, we wish you a merry Christmas and a Happy New Year!"

Jen smiled tentatively as her mother handed her a glass of sherry and sang along to Geoffrey's terrible piano accompaniment. Harriet hated to be alone at Christmas and regularly invited virtual strangers to spend the festivities with them rather than face an empty dining table, and Jen had always enjoyed it before. But now all these people just seemed like barriers between her and her mother, preventing Jen from speaking her mind. Stopping her from asking Harriet whether it was true she had an affair, and why she'd lied for so many years about George not wanting to see her. She sighed— maybe it was a good thing all these people were here. Right now she was so confused about everything it was probably best to keep quiet.

Jen bit her tongue and looked around the room to see who she'd be spending the day with. Geoffrey was a Green Futures's stalwart—he'd been at the company nearly as long as her mother and was also a regular at Christmas. Then there was Hannah, who'd joined the firm around the same time as Jen and who always eyed

Jen with a certain level of suspicion, and Mick, who worked for Tim in the accounts department. She didn't know him very well at all. Finally in the corner, nursing a drink that looked suspiciously like whiskey neat, was Paul Song.

He did a little mini bow when he saw her, and she wandered over unenthusiastically. "Good trip?" she asked conversationally. "Mum said you were away."

He nodded. "Yes. I was in Ireland. A very beautiful place. Very enjoyable."

Jen frowned. "I thought Mum said Scotland," she said. Paul blanched.

"Of course, sorry. I get confused. Yes, it was Scotland. Definitely Scotland."

"Come on, darling, sing along. Good tidings we bring to you and your kin . . ." Her mother motioned for Jen to join them. Jen eyed Paul suspiciously and moved over to where the others were standing.

"We wish you a merry Christmas and a Happy New Year," she chipped in halfheartedly and helped herself to a handful of peanuts.

"Very good for your skin, peanuts," Hannah observed. "Cashew nuts, too. Actually, all nuts."

"To eat or rub in?" Jen asked.

Hannah looked at her oddly. "How would you rub a peanut into your skin?"

"Rub a peanut into your skin?" Harriet said, wandering over. "I've never heard anything so ridiculous in my life. Who wants you to rub peanuts into your skin, Hannah?"

"Jen does," Hannah said, eyeing her cautiously.

Jen smiled weakly and sat down on the sofa. She considered telling Hannah that she'd meant the oil—peanut oil—but decided it would probably be best to let the whole matter rest.

"If you were going to rub them in, I suppose they might be a good exfoliator," Hannah continued thoughtfully. "Although you'd probably have to break them up a bit first."

"Nuts have a very low glycemic index," said Mick in a deadpan voice. "My ex, Shirley, used to eat them all the time. Said they had good oils in them."

"See?" said Hannah triumphantly. "Good for your skin. Like I said."

"Personally, I thought that oil was fattening, but that just shows how much I know about diets," Mick continued. "Like potatoes. One minute they're low fat, the next they're forbidden. I can't keep up. I just used to say you eat what you want. 'Course, then she said I was trying to keep her fat. When I said I wasn't, she said that proved that I thought she was fat. Or something like that. She always found something to criticize, did Shirley."

Jen stared at Mick, mesmerized by his monotone voice. "Why did you split up?" she enquired.

Mick looked up in surprise, as if he hadn't expected anyone to actually be listening to him.

"Don't know, really," he said dolefully. "Said I didn't really understand her. She had a point, too. I didn't know what she was going on about half the time."

Jen nodded sympathetically as her mother wandered back into the kitchen, followed swiftly by Hannah.

"You got a boyfriend?" he asked interestedly.

"Kind of. Yes." Jen felt a little warm feeling rush over her and took a few seconds to enjoy it. Daniel. The very thought of him made her feel so much better, even if strictly speaking they weren't exactly boyfriend and girlfriend yet.

"Oh," said Mick. "Oh well. I suppose there are other fish in the sea. Now that's something my mother used to say a lot, and I don't know why. What's anything got to do with fish?"

Jen raised her eyebrows as if to sympathize with the sentiment, but she wasn't really listening to Mick anymore. She was thinking about Daniel. Wondering what he was doing. Northumberland suddenly seemed an awfully long way away.

"You all right?" Mick asked.

She realized that she'd been staring into space for a couple of minutes. And that she'd been left alone on the sofa with Mick. Everyone had gone into the kitchen apart from Paul, who was staring into his drink. Jen picked up her glass.

"I think I need a refill," she said quickly, swigging down nearly an entire glass of sherry in one go. It filled her stomach with a welcome warmth and sent a rather nice rush to her head. "Can I get you one?"

Mick shook his head. "Alcohol. That's fattening, too," he was saying as he followed her into the kitchen.

Harriet, as usual, was holding court, standing at the head of the kitchen table with everyone else sitting round in silence, listening to her.

"And that's when I had the brainwave," she was saying, as everyone listened attentively. "A poster campaign in all their shops with pictures of the children they were helping from the local neighborhood. It was a triumph. . . ."

Jen sat down and listened appreciatively as her mother regaled the room with stories about Green Futures, its clients, its early wins, her various television appearances. She could hold a room like no other, and Jen had always loved her stories, loved the fact that she was Harriet's daughter. She'd felt so proud.

But now Jen realized that she'd heard all these stories a hundred times before. And she didn't know if she could believe a single one.

"So come on then, little miss MBA," Geoffrey said when Harriet had finished a story with a flourish. "Are you going to tell us what it's like at Big Bad Bell?"

Jen looked at him uncertainly, then looked at Harriet. *No one was meant to know,* she said with her eyes.

Harriet smiled nervously. "Darling, I couldn't keep it a secret forever. And I've only told everyone here. They're practically family."

Jen looked at her incredulously. "Mum . . . ," she started to say, then shrugged. What did it matter if everyone knew, if Harriet had been unable to resist the urge to tell an exciting story, even if it resulted in her breaking a promise to her own daughter?

"I thought about doing an MBA once," Mick said behind her. "But I did an accountancy qualification instead. Wanted to work in finance so I thought it would be best. Difficult to know, though, isn't it?"

"Yeah, thanks for that, Mick," Geoffrey said with a little smile. "Come on, Jen, spill the beans. Tell us about the bastards at Bell Consulting. I have to say, better you than me."

"I'd rather not talk about it if it's okay," she said stiffly. "Do you need any help with the food, Mum?" she asked quickly. Questions were bubbling up inside her, and she didn't know how long she could last playing the role of happy daughter.

"Food?" Harriet asked vaguely. "Oh, you mean Christmas dinner? Well, actually, there's been a bit of a change of plan on that front, too. I was thinking, since we are fortunate enough to have Paul here, that he could cook us a traditional Tibetan Christmas meal. And he very kindly agreed, didn't you, Paul?"

Paul nodded and smiled, and Jen looked at him uncertainly. "I didn't think they celebrated Christmas in Tibet."

"Oh, well, sometimes they do," he said quickly. "Really, this is more of a generic celebratory meal, though."

Jen nodded, trying to hide her disappointment. "So, no turkey and mince pies, then?" she asked, attempting to sound jovial and failing miserably.

"No, darling," Harriet said firmly. "Now, let's put on some music, and we can open our presents!"

Jen bit her lip and went to find the myriad presents she'd wrapped. She never knew in advance who would be at her mother's for Christmas, so she tended to overbuy, bringing a sackload of generic presents that would suit anyone, just in case.

"Right, here you are," her mother said brightly, depositing a beautifully wrapped parcel in her lap.

Slowly, she unwrapped it. She peeled off the thick cream paper, and then started to unravel the tissue paper that lay beneath, and finally found herself holding a lacquered, white box. Carefully, she opened the box and found herself staring at a wooden block.

"It's a musical instrument," her mother said excitedly. "Paul brought it at my request, all the way from China!"

Jen held it up and looked at it more closely. "Wow!" she said brightly. "So, what does it do?"

"Well, you bang it, of course. Look on the side—there's a little stick attached."

Jen looked, and sure enough, there was a little baton with a circular blob on the end. She banged the piece of wood and it sounded like . . . a piece of wood. "Thanks, Mum," Jen said quietly. "Really, it's great."

She handed over her mother's present, and Harriet opened it with great gusto. Inside was a first edition of *Winnie the Pooh*. It had been Harriet's favorite book when she was little, and she would read it to Jen night after night.

Harriet looked at it quickly. "Oh, a book. How sweet. How lovely. Right, now, Paul, why don't you open your present?" She deposited a large parcel in front of Paul, who frowned as he pulled away the wrapping. Jen forced herself to smile, trying not to get worked up about her mother's dismissal of the present she'd spent so long tracking down.

"*Zen and the Art of Motorcycle Maintenance!*" Harriet announced, clapping, before Paul could speak. "Isn't it perfect!"

He smiled, looking at the book curiously.

"I'm sure you've already read it," she continued excitedly, "but I just looked at it and thought of you."

Paul nodded seriously. "Of course," he said, putting the book down.

Jen eyed him suspiciously. "Of course, what?" she wanted to ask, but Harriet was already handing out gifts to everyone else and telling them how perfect the presents were before they had time to react themselves. *Has she always been this annoying,* Jen wondered, *or is it a new thing?*

By four o'clock, Jen was exhausted. The Tibetan hot pot had been surprisingly delicious, but there was no doubt that it had left a huge gaping hole in her stomach where Christmas pudding and mince pies should have been, and she'd spent about as much time as she could bear listening to Harriet tell everyone the story of how she'd set up Green Futures from scratch, the story of how she'd singlehandedly saved a large stretch of woodland in southeast England, and the story of her trip around the world to spread the message of corporate social responsibility and how grateful everyone had been.

Eventually, when Harriet stopped to draw breath, Jen stood up and walked over to her. She couldn't stay silent, she'd realized. She just didn't work that way. She needed to talk to her mother, needed to know the truth, and she needed to do it now. "Can I have a word?" she asked.

Harriet smiled beatifically. "Of course. Everyone, Jen's got something to say."

Jen cringed. "No, I meant in private."

Harriet looked confused, then smiled. "Of course, darling. Let's go to the kitchen. So," Harriet said as soon as they were out of earshot, "do you have some news on your father? You've gone rather quiet lately."

Jen sat down and Harriet joined her, looking at her expectantly. "I spoke to him."

"Spoke to whom, darling?"

"Dad. I spoke to Dad."

Harriet frowned. "You spoke to George? I don't think I understand. Did he know it was you?"

Jen nodded.

"Oh God," Harriet gasped. "So the secret's out? How did he react? Was he very angry?"

"You had the affair."

Harriet started, her eyes wide. "I'm sorry?" she asked angrily. "What did you say?"

"Dad told me that you had the affair, not him."

Harriet looked at her daughter indignantly. "And you believe your father rather than me? Trust the man who betrayed me, who left you without a second glance . . ."

"Did he really? Or did you leave him?"

Harriet frowned. "Darling, it was all such a long time ago. Does it really matter now? The point is that you and I . . . we're a team. We're . . ."

"So you *did* have an affair?" Jen's voice was monotone. She told herself it was because she was beyond caring, but in reality it was her way of keeping a check on herself, to stop her voice turning into a hurt, angry squeak.

Harriet looked closely at her daughter, then slumped back against her chair. Hesitating, she tried to take Jen's hand, and when Jen quickly moved it away, she nodded, a look of resignation on her face.

"Jen, darling, I did what I thought I had to do. George may not have had an actual affair, but he might as well have done. He was never there, never left that bloody office. And when he said he was leaving, I just couldn't bear the idea of him taking you, too. Darling, I wanted to protect you. . . ."

"You lied to me." There were tears pricking at Jen's eyes and she wiped them away angrily.

"I didn't think you'd understand. I knew George would be too busy to see you, that he would only disappoint you as he had done already, time after time, missing your birthdays, your concerts. I thought . . . I thought it would be easier. . . ."

Jen looked at her mother and could see the insecurity

in Harriet's face, but it only made Jen more angry, more resentful. "He's my father," she said quietly.

Harriet nodded. "You're angry," she said. "And I understand . . ."

"You understand?" Jen asked incredulously. "You understand? Is that it?"

"Paul said that you'd react like this, and I just thought . . ."

"Paul knew?" Jen spat. "Paul knew about this and I didn't?"

"He helps me, darling. I talk to him. I . . ."

"And how much do you pay him to listen, Mum? How much money do you pay him to tell you that you've done the right thing, that it's okay to lie to your daughter? That it's perfectly okay to convince me that not only does my own father not care about me, but that he's also tied up in some corruption scandal. And it's all utter bollocks!"

Harriet's eyes widened. "That's unfair, Jennifer," she said, her voice faltering. "This has got nothing to do with Paul. And I think I know a little bit more about your father than you do. He's a selfish, self-serving man, and I hoped I could show you that. . . ."

"Selfish and self-serving? What, unlike you?"

"I've only ever done my best," Harriet said quietly. "You don't know what it's like to be lonely, Jennifer. Don't know what it's like to have to start from scratch."

"Lonely? Mum, you took my father away. I think I've got a pretty good idea."

"I wanted what was best for you, that's all."

"What was best for *you*, you mean," Jen said angrily. "You just can't help it, can you? You have to control everything, have to run the show. Well I've had enough of you trying to run my life."

Harriet looked at her with surprise on her face. "Run your life? I barely get a look in. I never know what you're doing, where you're going, anything."

"That's just not true!" Jen said exasperatedly. "And I've had enough. I'm not going to be your pawn anymore."

"I sense tension." Jen looked up, shocked to see Paul emerge through the door. How long had he been there? Had he heard everything, she wondered? "Perhaps some herbal tea would be a good idea? This kitchen has a difficult space—it encourages conflict."

Harriet took his hand. "Oh, Paul, that's a wonderful idea. Jen, why don't we have some herbal tea?"

She looked at Jen hopefully and Jen stared at her. "Herbal tea? Are you serious?"

"It's very calming," Harriet said, her voice quavering. "Please, Jen . . ."

Paul put his hand on Harriet's shoulder. "Jennifer is upset, and that is okay," he said quietly. "She is finding her place in the world, and it's a difficult time for her."

Jen frowned, then felt an enormous rush of energy cascade through her. It was all suddenly very simple. She looked her mother straight in the eye, then pushed her chair back and stood up.

"Actually, it's not as difficult as I thought it would be," she said calmly. "Paul's right that I'm finding my place in the world—and one thing I'm sure of is that it isn't here. So if it's all right with you, I'm going home." Slowly, she made her way into the sitting room, pulled on her coat, picked up her bag, and headed for the door.

"Darling, don't go," Harriet said weakly, getting up

and following Jen toward the front door. "It's Christmas. . . ."

"Right now I don't really care," Jen said tightly, not noticing that everyone had wandered out into the hall to stare at her. She couldn't stay here another minute. Opening the door, she took one last look at her mother and walked out, closing the door behind her and finding herself outside on the deserted winter street.

It was one of those cold, bitter nights where every little bit of exposed skin burns against the wind. *This has to go down as the worst Christmas ever,* she thought to herself sadly. She suddenly remembered a bar of chocolate she had in her pocket and opened it, wolfing it down hungrily. She sat down on her mother's stoop and contemplated her position. Christmas Day, on her own, freezing cold, and a good half an hour's walk from home.

Still, she knew where she was now. The truth was out.

She walked over to her mother's bin to deposit her chocolate wrapper and frowned slightly when she opened the lid. There, hidden under a Marks and Spencer's bag, were several takeaway boxes with THE TIBETAN KITCHEN written on them. *Surely Paul hadn't cheated,* she wondered with a smile. Perhaps he wasn't all he'd made himself out to be either.

She shrugged—in that case, they truly deserved each other. Still, that didn't mean he had to get away with it completely. Smiling to herself, she took out one of the boxes and carefully placed it just outside her mother's front door.

Then she turned, buried her hands deep inside her coat pockets, and started the long walk home. Her mobile phone was in one of her pockets and, pulling her collar up against the wind, she took it out to transfer it to her bag. As she did so, she saw that she had a text message. Moving under a lamppost, she hit VIEW.

HPPY XMS. FNCY A DRNK SMTM WHN I GT BCK? DANIEL X

She stared at the message. Daniel "x"? He was kissing her by text? He wanted to know if she fancied a drink sometime?

Jen looked around. Suddenly she wasn't a total saddo who was on her own at Christmas—she was a romantic heroine walking through a winter wonderland. Nothing seemed quite so bad anymore.

Do I fancy a drink sometime? she thought to herself happily. *Ooh, I think I could be persuaded.*

❧ 16

"Dum, dum, dum, dum, gonna use my style, gonna use my sidestep, gonna use my, my, my imagination, yeah . . ."

Jen hummed along to Chrissie Hynde blaring out of her stereo as she lay in the hot, steaming bath, watching her skin gradually go wrinkled and pink. *It's just a drink,* she told herself. *Just a drink with Daniel. Nothing worth getting steamed up about.*

But even as she thought the words she knew she didn't believe them. As far as she was concerned, this was their first proper date. The first date that definitely had nothing to do with work, MBAs, or anything else. No one would be waiting outside her flat at the end of this date, and there would be no walking around bookshops. No, this was absolutely worth getting steamed up about.

Jen lifted one of her legs out of the water and started to shave it. She'd have had them waxed but getting an appointment at short notice had proved to be completely impossible—all the salons were either closed over Christmas or booked up. Of course, shaving would mean that next time she had them waxed her beautician would tut at Jen and give her that reproachful look that made her feel like she'd admitted to running a small slave-trade operation rather than simply whipping out her razor in an emergency. But that was nothing that couldn't be sorted out with an extra-large tip.

When she finished, she reluctantly heaved herself out of the water and immediately felt a cold draft hit her. That was the problem with "character" apartments like hers. They looked lovely, but the windows were always centuries old and you could never get properly warm. Like country houses—Jen had learned many years ago that if you ever got invited to someone's country house (or rather, someone's parents' country house), you had to bring not just jumpers, but blankets, thick socks, thermal underwear, and woolly hats *and* you'd still be cold. *Maybe that's why the English have stiff upper lips,* she thought to herself as she dried herself quickly and slathered on body lotion. *Maybe they were frozen that way.*

Quickly, Jen wrapped her old, battered, but much-loved terry towling bathrobe around herself and stuck her feet in her trusty Ugg boots. It wasn't a look that screamed "sex goddess," but it was warm, and right now, that was what really mattered.

Did she even know how to scream "sex goddess" anymore, she wondered, taking out some tweezers to pluck her eyebrows. It had been, what . . . she counted on her fingers . . . quite a few months since she'd last had sex. And the last time had been a not particularly fulfilling post-Gavin fling with Jim, a friend of a friend, who had been very drunk (as had Jen), and which had led to an excruciating morning after, in which both she and Jim had been keen to get him out of her flat as quickly as was humanly possible.

Not that she'd necessarily be having sex tonight or anything. Not definitely.

She peered at her reflection in the mirror, trying to ascertain what makeup to wear. Her skin was pale, with red blotchy bits around the nose and chin—the result of Christmas drinks and the bitterly cold weather. So, foundation then. Lots of concealer.

She wandered over to her stereo and put on Style Council at full volume. There was nothing like the prospect of a love affair to make everything seem a bit more shiny and new. It was the same feeling (although, you know, a lot better) that she used to get in September when she was starting a new year at junior school with a neatly pressed uniform that hadn't yet been covered with ink or bits of lunch; her pencil case would be full of bright new pens; and her new classroom would signal loud and clear that she'd moved up in the world. There was so much expectation, so much hope that this time things would be better—that she'd suddenly be in with the in-crowd and know all the pop songs her schoolmates sang in the playground, and wouldn't get a single red mark in her exercise book or, worse, the ominous "Please see me."

Of course, it usually only lasted a week or so before she realized that a new desk and clean uniform didn't make her any different. Her mother still refused to let her listen to pop music on the radio or even to watch *Top of the Pops,* which led to a significant disadvantage in the playground; she still daydreamed too much, mobilizing her teacher's red pen every time she sat down to write something. And it was usually the same with love affairs—all too quickly the sheeny, shiny, new love interest turned out to be a man like any other, "forgetting" to call, refusing to plan more than a week ahead, insisting on going to a pub that was showing "the game," whether it was football, rugby, or cricket.

She sighed, then shook herself. Now was not the time to think about such matters. She was getting ready for a date, and who knows, maybe this time *would* be different.

"You look . . . gorgeous."

Daniel was smiling, and Jen felt herself go a bit wobbly inside. "Th . . . thank you," she said, shivering. A cold December night was not the time to wear a skirt and high heels, she knew, but practicality wasn't everything. Earlier that evening Jen had peered outside at the snow gathering on her windowsill and had spent a few minutes trying to convince herself that sheepskin boots were, in fact, pretty attractive and would demonstrate just how relaxed she felt in Daniel's company. Particularly when she'd opened her front door to an icy cold gust of wind. But she knew that legs did not look their best in flat, chunky boots, so eventually she had compromised with a fairly substantial yet still quite delicate pair of highish black pumps. And she was absolutely bloody freezing.

"Shall we get you inside?" Daniel suggested, and held open the door. They were at Ketners, a bar in Cambridge Circus, just down from Oxford Street and a stone's throw from Soho.

Jen nodded gratefully and found herself walking into a small, cozy room with waiters in black suits and groups of people sitting around tables drinking champagne.

"I guess people are in a celebratory mood," she said to Daniel, and he grinned.

"Actually it's a champagne bar," he whispered. "I heard that girls like champagne. Sorry, women. Um . . ."

He looked perplexed and Jen smiled. "*Girl* is fine," she said. "It's usually only when you're a teenager that you want to be called a woman. Once you're the wrong side of twenty-five, *girl* is always welcome. Although not if you say it in a patronizing tone. Oh, and never say *lady*. That's the worst."

Daniel nodded seriously as they were shown to a small table in the corner of the room. "I'll try and remember that," he said. "But in the meantime, what shall we order?"

Jen frowned. "We have a choice?"

"Absolutely. Straight champagne, champagne cocktail, vintage champagne, new champagne, pink, white . . ."

"Okay, okay, I get the picture. Just straight champagne for me."

Daniel nodded and a waiter appeared out of nowhere. "A bottle of champagne," he said. "And some nibbles. Olives, bread, that sort of thing."

The waiter disappeared, and the two of them were left alone. Jen found her stomach doing flip-flops.

"So, good Christmas?" Daniel asked.

Jen rolled her eyes. "I wouldn't call it good, exactly. Interesting, maybe."

Daniel grinned. "Don't tell me you come from a dysfunctional family, too?"

Jen nodded. "There's no way yours can be as bad as mine," she said with a little smile.

Daniel's eyes glinted slightly. "Oh, so we're competing, are we? Well, okay, mine aren't exactly dysfunctional, but they do live in the middle of nowhere and they like trifle on Christmas Day, not Christmas pudding. And they take the Queen's speech very seriously indeed. Why do you think I was texting you on Christmas Day? I was desperate!"

Jen pretended to look hurt. "Oh, so it was just because you were desperate, was it?"

"No, no, God no, I didn't mean . . ." Daniel realized too late that Jen was joking and went red. "Oh piss off," he said jovially. "So go on then, what makes your family the crown bearers of dysfunctionality?"

Jen shrugged uncomfortably. She was still raw after the argument with her mother.

"That bad?" Daniel asked sympathetically and Jen found herself softening.

"Oh, nothing too serious. I've just got parents who lie, cheat, and hate each other, that's all," she said. And as she spoke, it suddenly didn't seem quite so terrible anymore. It was actually kind of funny. Well, nearly. The thing was, she felt so natural with Daniel, like she could say anything to him, tease him, open up to him. Was this what people meant when they talked about love at first sight?

"You must have had a very interesting childhood!" Daniel grinned. "So do they get on well? In spite of the lying and cheating, I mean . . ."

"They're divorced, actually."

"Ah. Sorry." Daniel looked slightly uncomfortable.

"It's okay. It happened years ago."

He nodded. "Maybe they were just too similar."

Jen frowned. "Similar? They are in some ways. And at the same time they're nothing like each other. Mum's into crystals and healers and ridiculous spiritual gurus who are nothing of the sort, and Dad . . . well, Dad is a workaholic. He's . . ." She trailed off, not knowing what to say, not wanting to admit that she didn't really know her father. She knew what she thought he was like, and she knew what he'd been like recently, but the two were so different that now she realized that she had no real idea what he was like at all, apart from her childhood memories when her parents argued most of the time and he always seemed to be at the office.

"He's competitive," she concluded. "And actually, you probably know him. He's . . . well, he's George Bell."

Jen watched closely as Daniel's eyes widened. "Crikey. Okay, you win. So, seriously, you're George Bell's daughter?"

Jen nodded. "No one at Bell knows," she said seriously. "It's kind of . . . complicated." She thought of Angel as she spoke and smiled to herself slightly.

"So you're actually Jennifer Bell, not Jennifer Bellman?"

Jen cringed slightly. "Yeah. I . . . well, I kind of ran out of inspiration on that one. And I was terrified I'd forget what I was supposed to be called."

"I prefer Bell. It suits you. So do you take after him? Or are you more like your mother? Only I think I should be warned, don't you?"

He was grinning and looking right into her eyes, and Jen felt herself sinking, losing the ability to think straight, to think about anything except him, how close he was, how wonderful it felt.

"Neither of them," she said softly as Daniel reached forward and kissed her. "Both of them. Some of them. The . . . just the good bits . . ."

Five hours later, Jen was in the back of a taxi with Daniel, her head spinning with excitement. She was sitting, head nestled on Daniel's shoulder, with his arm wrapped around her. She was holding his hand, and he was stroking her hair with his other hand. She'd be ready to die and go to heaven right now if she wasn't so excited about what was to come.

Jen closed her eyes briefly, trying to commit the entire evening to memory, every last detail. There had been the kiss, of course. That had really been the start, the moment that she'd stopped feeling nervous. With that one kiss—or, actually, quite a few if anyone was counting—Jen had felt something stir inside her, something that made her feel like laughing and crying at the same time.

Which, she recognized, was a little over the top as reactions go, and at first she blamed the champagne. But then, at dinner, they'd talked like they'd known each other for ages. She talked and talked about her parents, telling Daniel things that she hadn't even admitted to herself. And every so often he would squeeze her hand or lean over and kiss her—and when she was done, which was about the time pudding arrived, he took over the talking. He talked gently about himself, his childhood in Scotland then Northumberland, his decision to go to university—which crossed the family tradition of working in farming—his early successes, and his current existentialist angst about what the point of everything was.

And when they'd finally finished, neither of them had wanted to go home, so he'd taken her to Ronnie Scott's, spirited her upstairs to a little dance floor where they played salsa music and the two of them danced together, alone, cheek to cheek, and Jen truly thought that if they carried on dancing, the night would never have to end.

Finally, when Jen found herself with her head on Daniel's shoulder with her eyes closed, he whispered

that perhaps it was time to go home now, and she nodded sleepily, knowing that tonight wherever Daniel
went, she would go, too.

"Come on sleepyhead, we're nearly home," Daniel
said, ruffling Jen's hair and waking her from her little
dream.

"Whose home?" she asked sleepily.

"Yours, of course." Daniel grinned. "I thought it might
be a little presumptuous to take you back to mine."

Jen shot Daniel a sideways look. "My flat's a mess," she
said sheepishly. "You'll have to keep your eyes shut."

"What if I promise not to remember anything I see?"

"No," said Jen. "I don't want you forgetting tonight,
if it's okay with you."

As they pulled up outside her building, Daniel peered
at the front door. "Just checking," he explained as Jen
hit him playfully. "You're not expecting any other ex-
boyfriends, are you?"

Jen got out of the cab and made her way to the front
door, suddenly terrified that maybe Gavin was there,
that in some hideous twist of fate he'd found himself
stranded in London for a second time. But to her relief,
her doorstep was empty. As she turned the key, Daniel
came up behind her and started to kiss her neck. She
turned to kiss him and they fell against the door, pushing it open. Then, silently, they made their way to her
first-floor flat, where she unlocked the door and held it
open for him.

"Nice high ceilings," he said appraisingly. "It's lovely."
Daniel walked over to her and put his arms around her,
and as he leaned down to kiss her, Jen wrapped her arms
tightly round his neck.

Daniel slowly took off her coat, and she unbuttoned

his jacket, and then he was kissing her neck, pulling off her sweater.

Brrrrrrrrrrrrrrrrrrr. Brrrrrrrrrrrrrrrrrrrrrr.

Jen started.

"Is that your phone?" Daniel murmured. "Why don't you turn it off?"

Jen nodded as Daniel released her, and she picked her mobile out of her coat pocket. Then she frowned.

"It's Dad," she said, intrigued. "Why would he be calling at this time?"

She hesitated. It was strange—she'd only plugged his number into her phone the other day and it felt odd and exciting to see DAD flashing on her phone's display. But she was here with Daniel. She'd had enough of family in the past few days. This was her time and she wasn't going to let him intrude.

Purposefully, she pressed END on her phone, then switched it off.

"Everything okay?" Daniel asked gently, and she nodded, letting him scoop her up in his arms and half carry her into the bedroom. Then she let him undress her completely, and she helped him out of his clothes, too. And minutes later they were writhing on the bed, Jen pressing herself into him and trying to remember the last time she felt so exhilarated.

"I want to make love to you," Daniel whispered, and Jen nodded, maneuvering him on top of her and allowing him to take complete control. As he entered her, she gasped, and as they rocked back and forth she felt her world drop away. Nothing mattered more than the here and now. Daniel inside her. On top of her. All around her. She felt herself rising, falling, spinning, and then at last she gasped, pulling Daniel into her, squeezing him with a strength she didn't know she had, then, afterward, she didn't know how long afterward, loosening her grip, lying back in wonderment.

"Fuck me." Daniel sighed, and rested his head on the pillow next to hers.

"I think I just did," Jen said dreamily, her limbs entangled with Daniel's, as she floated off to sleep, flushed, exhausted, and deliriously happy.

Jen awoke to someone stroking her hair, and immediately opened her eyes to see that there was a cup of tea being thrust in her direction.

"I didn't know if you took sugar," Daniel said apologetically. "So I put one in—I thought after last night you might need the energy."

Jen allowed herself a little giggle, then pulled herself up to a sitting position. "You've made toast!" she exclaimed and Daniel shrugged.

"There wasn't much bread left. And you've got absolutely bugger-all in your fridge. But yes, I managed some toast if you're hungry. And I bought a newspaper as well."

Jen reached up and kissed him. "You are perfect," she said happily. "This, all this, is just completely perfect."

Daniel got back into bed and Jen greedily wolfed down a slice of toast dripping with honey, opening up the newspaper and scanning it for interesting stories. Snow was expected in London that week. There had been widespread criticism of transport problems on New Year's Eve. And Bell Consulting was implicated in the Tsunami corruption scandal according to sources . . .

Jen stared at the page. Bell implicated? How? Why?

She read quickly. A source close to Bell Consulting

had uncovered a letter that the newspaper had seen, which suggested that Bell played a role in securing valuable contracts for its client Axiom Construction. A letter thanking George for his help!

She frowned. They couldn't be referring to the letter she found, could they? Impossible. She still had it. And no one else had "uncovered" it. No one else had seen it.

No one except Gavin.

"Now, I don't know if you've got plans today," Daniel was saying, "but . . ." He paused. "Is everything okay?"

"Um, no, no, not really," Jen said, her heart pounding. "I . . . oh, fuck." Her brain was going into overdrive. It had to be Gavin. That stupid prick had gone and leaked it to a journalist! It was exactly the sort of thing he'd do. Why on earth had she even mentioned it to him? Oh, God, how could she be so stupid? Was that why her father had called last night? Had the journalist called him? Her heart was thudding in her chest. She'd only just got her father back and now she'd betrayed him, all because she hadn't been able to stop herself wanting to impress Gavin, to let him know just how important she was. Would he ever forgive her?

Her landline phone started ringing, and Jen thought about ignoring it, then changed her mind. If it was going to be her father again, disowning her, then she may as well get it over and done with. With any luck it would be Gavin instead and she could tell him exactly what she thought of him.

She looked at Daniel apologetically and scrambled for the phone, getting there just in time.

"Hello?" she asked tentatively.

"Is this Jennifer?"

Jen frowned. She didn't recognize the voice. "Yes. Who's this?"

"Oh, good. Jennifer, this is Emily, your father's personal assistant. I'm afraid I've got some bad news."

Jen realized guiltily that she was speaking to the woman whose every move she had tracked in order to sneak into her father's office. "Right," she said resignedly and braced herself. She was being booted off the course, she thought to herself. Her father never wanted to see her again.

Daniel watched curiously from the bed as Jen's face went from a guilty red to absolute white in the space of a few seconds.

"Right. Okay, then. Yes, immediately," he heard her say, and frowned.

"Everything all right?" he asked, getting out of bed and sitting on the side as she walked back toward him as if in a dream.

She looked at him vaguely and pulled a sheet around herself as if suddenly noticing her nakedness. "Um, no. Not really," she said, turning slowly to meet his eyes. "Emily, my dad's personal assistant, is coming to pick me up in about five minutes. He's . . . he's had a heart attack."

17

Jen stared at the body of her father, limp and still, connected to tubes and machines that beeped and flashed protectively around him, and felt inadequate. Her mind was full of ifs, unable to focus on one before another pushed its way into her consciousness. If only she hadn't spoken to Gavin about Bell Consulting. If only she hadn't screamed at her father that she hated him and never wanted to see him again when her mother had told her he was leaving. If only she'd found out the truth earlier. If only she'd answered the phone when he'd called. If only she was a better person, a better daughter. If only she wasn't so utterly selfish that even now she was picturing Daniel in her bed and wishing that she was there with him and that none of this had happened . . .

It was all her fault, she knew that. And yet all she wanted to do was blame someone else. Gavin, mainly, for talking to the newspapers. It had to be him, she reasoned; it had his name all over it, he was the only person she'd told about the letter. Plus he was the biggest opportunist she knew—doubtless this little leak would earn him brownie points with the journalist and get him coverage of his latest escapade. But did he even stop to think about the impact? Did he ever worry just a teensy bit what might happen to her? Of course not. Bastard.

Well, now he could add giving George Bell a heart attack to his list of achievements. No doubt her father had heard the story was going to run, and it sent him over the edge. She wondered whether it was the story itself or the fact that he thought he'd been betrayed by his own daughter that had caused the attack.

No matter. The point was that Gavin was going to get it. He was going to be so sore by the time she'd finished with him that he'd spend the rest of his life apologizing and it still wouldn't be enough.

Who else, she wondered, now in her stride. Who else could take some of the blame? Well, there was always her mother—she'd been responsible for sowing the seeds of suspicion in the first place, after all. She'd forced Jen into spying on her own flesh and blood. The man who wanted to be a father to her and whom Harriet had lied about all along. Yes, it was all her fault. Well, hers and Gavin's.

And then there was Daniel. If he hadn't asked her out, if he hadn't *been* there, it might have been different. She'd have picked up the phone, she'd have been there when her father called . . .

Jen felt a little tear trickle down her face and she wiped it away. She was seriously losing the plot here if she was attempting to somehow finger Daniel in the culpability stakes. Him of all people. The loveliest person in the world. She seriously needed to get a grip on herself. It was entirely her fault anyway—she'd been showing off to Gavin, and she'd allowed her mother to talk her into doing the MBA because she was bored, because she wanted something else to do, and spying on her father seemed as good an idea as anything else.

Didn't mean Gavin wasn't going to pay for going behind her back, though. Jen had already left one shitty message for him on his mobile phone, and she was planning to leave another one every day until he called her back and apologized. She wanted to know how he'd managed to take a copy of the letter, too. She'd checked, and the letter was still where she'd hidden it, so how would the newspaper have seen it? Not that it mattered now.

Slowly, she moved toward her father's bed and sat down in the chair next to it. She stared at him, trying to memorize his face, trying to make it fit with the face she used to know so well. The doctor had only said that he would probably pull through; there was no guarantee that he actually would. And even if her father did get better, if he was as angry as she expected him to be, this might be the last chance she got to look at him close up.

As she looked at him, she made a little promise to herself. If he pulled through, she was going to be the best daughter ever. She was going to spend time with her father, make him proud of her. It would be like one of those slow-motion film sequences where they'd run down the beach together, build sandcastles, and have long chats about life and the universe. Maybe not the running bit—he had just had a heart attack, after all. But definitely the talking bit. She looked at her watch. Eleven-thirty A.M. Right, from now on, she was going to look after him. From now on, things would be different.

"How long have you been here?"

Jen was startled to hear her father's voice, and opened

her eyes quickly. She stole a quick look at the clock on the other side of the wall and realized that she must have been asleep for a couple of hours. Okay, so the good-daughter routine started from one thirty P.M.

"A while," she said tentatively. "Dad, I'm so sorry. I'm so . . ." Without meaning to, she started to cry, all her frustrations and guilt pouring out of her in warm, saltwater tears that clung to her eyes and nose.

"Come on, now," George said quickly. "There's no need . . . I'll be right as rain soon enough. Come on, Jen. Come on, sweetheart."

"I thought . . . I thought I might lose you. Again," Jen blubbed, sniffing loudly and taking a tissue from her father's bedside table. "And I'm meant to be strong for you too, and look at me. I'm hopeless. I'm a terrible daughter."

"No one's losing anyone," George said, his voice weak and breathless.

Jen nodded seriously. "You're right. Of course, you're right. So, what happened?" she asked, wiping away her tears and frowning to make herself concentrate on the present situation instead of contemplating her many failings as a human being. She was going to be strong, take whatever her dad had to say to her on the chin.

"Bloody nuisance, that's what happened," George said, attempting a wry smile. "Sooner I get out of here the better, wouldn't you say?"

Jen nodded silently, wondering whether he was talking about the article or his heart attack. "But what . . . what prompted it? The heart attack, I mean," she asked tentatively.

You, she imagined him saying. *You were responsible*

for that article, weren't you? The one that's going to ruin my business? You prompted my heart attack . . .

But instead, George shrugged. "I expect it's my fault for not eating rabbit food and running mindlessly in the gym for hours on end. Bloody waste of time. Can't abide the places. So, Jen . . ."

She looked at him nervously. "Yes?"

"How was your Christmas? Have you been doing lots of work on your MBA studies? I meant to call, but you know how it is . . ."

He doesn't know, Jen realized. *He hasn't seen the papers yet.* The thought filled her with relief for a second—the heart attack wasn't her fault! But then she realized that it wasn't the great news she'd thought it was. He was bound to find out anyway—the word *yet* was a bit of a killer. And when he did find out, he'd probably have a relapse.

She smiled hesitantly, remembering that she was meant to be having a normal conversation. "Oh, you know what Christmas is like," she said, trying to sound as cheerful as she could. "Too much time spent with family for my liking . . ." She blushed, realizing too late what she'd said. For so long she'd only thought of her mother as family. "I didn't mean . . . I mean . . . ," she stammered and George grinned.

"Couldn't agree more. So, your studies?"

Jen shrugged and smiled slightly. "It's my holidays, Dad. I don't want to work."

The words echoed the conversation they'd had the Christmas before he left. Perhaps *argument* would be a better word for it. She'd slammed a door, he'd threatened to dock her pocket money, and all because he wanted her to study more for her GCSEs.

George smiled in recognition. "How did your GCSEs go, by the way?" he asked softly.

"Straight As," Jen said, choking slightly. "Thought you'd never ask."

Her words hung in the air for a moment or two, then George smiled cheerfully. "Good thing I made you work through the school holidays, then, isn't it?"

"You're late."

Jen looked at her friend guiltily and gave her a quick kiss. "Angel, I'm sorry. I've been at the hospital. I'm only ten minutes late, though."

They were at Shepherd's Bush tube, an outpost of West London that housed the BBC, a small amount of gun crime, increasing numbers of London families who couldn't afford to live in Notting Hill or Holland Park, and Shepherd's Bush Market, where you could buy everything from sweet potatoes and plantain to bootlegged DVDs and outfits with more bling than anything in R Kelly's wardrobe.

Jen had promised Angel two weeks before that she'd be there, and after five reminder phone calls and two text messages, she hadn't had the heart to cancel, even though going shopping for wedding outfits didn't quite chime with her new "perfect daughter" routine, especially as she'd only been doing it for two days. Still, she supposed that being a good friend was probably pretty important, too. And anyway, her father had spent most of the day before sleeping, so with any luck he wouldn't notice that she wasn't there.

"Fifteen. You're fifteen minutes late, I have eleven outfits to buy and we only have one afternoon, so fifteen minutes matters, you know?"

Jen nodded seriously. "You really need eleven outfits? I thought you 'viewed arranged marriages with suspicion and disagreed with the cultural paradigm behind them,' " she said, quoting directly from Angel's own tirade a few months before. "How come you're so keen to conform now?"

Angel narrowed her eyes. "I am not conforming; I'm supporting my brother in his choice. Life is not black and white, Jen, as you well know—there's a lot of gray, and the trick is to navigate it without losing too much integrity along the way. I do not want an arranged marriage or to spend my life cooking curry for five children. If my brother's happy to live that life, then it's fine by me."

Jen lowered her head. "I'm sorry, I didn't mean . . ."

"I know," Angel said briskly. "So anyway, to answer your question, yes, I do need eleven outfits, and that's quite an achievement seeing that I've got it down from sixteen. Honestly, Jen, you have no idea. The pre-engagement party, the engagement party, the welcoming her family into our family party, the welcoming our family into hers party, her formal hen party, her real hen party, the pre-wedding dinner . . . and so it goes on. Believe me, eleven outfits isn't bad for an Indian wedding." She stopped talking suddenly and looked at Jen. "I'm sorry. I didn't even ask—how is he?"

Jen smiled. "He's okay, actually. I mean, the doctors say he'll be absolutely fine. Another week or so in hospital, a strict diet of lentils and vegetables, and he'll be back to normal."

"You've been to see him a lot." Angel asked the question without inflection, almost as a statement. But Jen knew what she was getting at. "A lot" was an understatement, actually—she'd been there for two days straight, telling him all about her life, refusing to buy him chocolate muffins and bringing him bananas and apples instead. It felt almost like it used to when she was younger. Just a bit more self-conscious.

"I guess," she said noncommittally. "So, where are we doing all this shopping?"

"Follow me."

Angel led her down through the market to Goldhawk Road and into a shop with silky-looking fabrics adorning the window. Angel grinned at Jen. "This is where we buy the official stuff."

She raised her eyebrow at the assistant who came wandering over to them. "I need to order five saris," she said firmly, putting on her mother's strong Indian accent. "None of your rubbish fabrics, I want pure silk only. And I don't have much time. Okay? Well, go on then!"

As the assistant ran off obediently, Angel winked at Jen. "I'd make a great Indian matriarch, no?"

Two hours later, they finally left Shepherd's Bush and made their way down toward Kensington High Street.

"And now," Angel said, "we go to Karen Millen."

Karen Millen's windows were glitz city. It was the January sale and the end of the Christmas party season, and the displays were full of skirts with glittery patterns, bejeweled corset tops, and jackets covered in sequins. Angel's eyes lit up and Jen rolled her eyes. She could never understand Angel's fascination with gold and shiny things. She was a vegetarian yoga teacher, which in Jen's book meant that she should be wandering around in the sort of things that Christie Turlington wore—long

lean lines, flowing and natural looking, and not looking
like she'd raided J-Lo's wardrobe.

She trailed after Angel, watching wide-eyed as her
friend descended on rack after rack of clothes, taking
one of nearly everything and handing it to a rather bemused sales assistant.

Finally, Angel reached the end of the shop and sighed.
"Well, that will have to do for now," she said with a little sigh, and disappeared into the changing rooms, leaving Jen sitting on the chairs usually reserved for bored
boyfriends and husbands. She was beginning to understand why men weren't so keen on shopping—it wasn't
anywhere near as fun when you weren't buying anything yourself.

She found her eyes wandering to a rack positioned
near the changing rooms, on which navy pin-stripe suits
were hanging alongside sparkly hot pink vests and silk
leopard-print tops. Jen could almost see them on a magazine page explaining how to dress work clothes up for
an evening do with a deft change of top and the use of
accessories, something she'd never exactly seen the point
of since she'd never really distinguished between day-
and nighttime dressing. Sure, she'd put on high heels if
she was going out, maybe a bit of lipstick, but she found
that jeans had a wonderful way of moving seamlessly
from work to play. They could be worn to an evening
out, but were equally at home slobbing out in front of
the television. A perfect combination, she felt.

She looked away again and Angel came out of the
changing room in Outfit Number One: the official hen
night. Top: not too low, but glitzy enough to say "I'm
making an effort." Skirt: just below the knee in a silk
bias cut with enough sequins to look worth the £85 price

tag, reduced from £150. Shoes: ridiculously high, but then Angel didn't seem to have a problem with heels. She was only five-foot-three and had spent her teenage years practicing walking in her mother's shoes until her feet were almost shaped diagonally. Maybe that's why she was such a yoga fiend, Jen thought to herself. It was a chance to straighten everything out again.

"So?" Angel demanded. "Does this say 'I'm obviously doing okay for myself and reflect well on my family, I know how to dress well but am definitely not in the husband market yet?' "

Jen thought for a moment. "That's exactly what it says," she said seriously. "At least it covers the chic and fabulously wealthy part. Just explain how that look says 'not in the husband market' for me?"

Angel shuddered. "That was just wishful thinking. My brother's fiancée has a brother, and I just know the family is already hatching a plan for me. Okay, so, time for outfit number two. This one has to say 'good-time party girl who still reflects well on her family but also knows how to enjoy herself.' Okay?"

Jen nodded, slightly bemused as Angel disappeared back inside the changing room. After a while her eyes wandered back to the clothing rack.

She'd never actually worn a suit and had always been suspicious of those who did. Suits were about conformity, a demonstration of power—in other words, everything she hated. And they weren't particularly practical either. Protestors didn't tend to wear one of Calvin Klein's finest when conducting a sit-in on a field up for development, and at Green Futures the look was more "geography teacher" than "smart city consultant." Some of the guys there wore sandals with socks, for God's sake. Tim was the only one to wear a suit, and he was an accountant. It would look weird if he didn't.

Bell was a different story, of course. Everyone wore suits. Even people in the MBA program wore them sometimes—when they were giving presentations, that sort of thing. And her father . . . well, he looked strange out of a suit, like female physical education teachers when they turned up at staff meetings wearing skirts instead of their usual tracksuits. It was just . . . wrong, somehow. On weekends, George used to mooch around in cords or slacks and a jumper over a shirt that didn't have a stiff collar—none of which went together particularly well and all of which made him look faintly ridiculous. In a suit he was George Bell of Bell Consulting. Out of one, he was just like anyone else.

Well, she didn't have that problem. She didn't need to wear a suit to be someone. She was fine as she was.

She caught a glimpse of herself in the mirror and recognized that perhaps she wasn't *that* fine. Passable, maybe, but she wasn't going to set the world on fire looking like this—an old baggy T-shirt and old jeans. And that suit hadn't exactly been a 1980s-style power suit, after all. It had low-waisted trousers. The jacket looked kind of cool, really. She could actually ignore the fact that it was a suit altogether and just wear them as separates . . .

Slowly she stood up and made her way over to the rack, picking up one of the suits and holding it up against herself. She wondered what she'd look like in one. Wondered what it would feel like, striding around in a pinstripe number like this with her father watching her proudly from the sidelines. *"Hello, I'm Jennifer Bell. Yes, George's daughter. Oh, you know him? Yes, we are*

*close, actually. You think I look like him? Well, you
know, you could be right about that—perhaps I do. So
anyway, I believe you need some help with leveraging
your core strengths to drive up your business performance? Let me see what I can do . . ."*

She frowned. What was wrong with her? She hated
suits. She wouldn't be seen dead in one, full stop, end of
story. Quickly she put the suit back.

"Do you want to try it on?"

Jen turned to see a sales assistant looking at her and
blushed. "Oh, no," she said quickly. "I was just looking.
I mean, I'm not really a suit kind of person . . ."

"It's more of a going-out suit than a work one," the
sales assistant said. "That's why it's hanging with the
sparkly tops."

The sales assistant pointed at the tops, and Jen felt the
need to look at them with interest as though she hadn't
seen them before.

"Oh, I see," she said, smiling at the sales assistant to
emphasize that she did indeed see.

"So, do you want to try it on?"

Angel stuck her head out of her cubicle. "These
trousers are all wrong. I need another size. And some
different shoes . . ."

The sales assistant nodded and walked over to Angel,
turning back to Jen as she reached the cubicle. "You can
go in there," she said, pointing at the cubicle next to
Angel's.

Jen hesitated, then, holding the suit several inches away
from her as if it were a wet dog, she strode quickly into
the cubicle. *I'm just going to try it on,* she told herself
firmly. *There's nothing wrong with that.*

*   *   *

"Wow!" Angel said appreciatively five minutes later as they both came out to take a little look at themselves, self-consciously standing in front of the large mirror and checking their behinds for unattractive creasing. "I've never seen you in a suit before. It looks great!"

Jen shook her head bashfully, but she knew she wasn't convincing anyone. She did look great. Much better than she looked in her jeans, which had become so comfortable that they no longer held any shape, draping over her legs as if hungover and unable to think what else to do.

"It feels odd," she said, unable to take in the authoritative-looking woman staring back at her from the mirror. "It isn't me."

"What's 'you'?" Angel asked with a shrug. "We're not simple creatures, are we? You're doing an MBA—you were bound to get more business-ey."

Jen looked at Angel indignantly. "I'm not doing an MBA. I mean, I am, but I'm not . . . you know . . . doing one. Not properly . . ."

"You're doing a pretty good job of it though, aren't you. Studying for that exam before Christmas, getting yourself a new boyfriend who actually has a proper job and doesn't spend his time sleeping on other people's floors. And your father . . ."

"You think I'm selling out?" Jen asked hotly.

Angel shook her head. "You're the one who thinks that. I think you're moving on. And it suits you. But look, we're not here to deal with your identity crisis—we've got mine to worry about. So tell me the truth, do I look too slutty? I do, don't I? I can just hear my mother's voice—'Anuragini, do you wish to bring my house into disrepute? Have you no respect for your family? Oh, why do I have such a daughter? Why do you never listen to me?' "

She mimicked her mother's accent perfectly and Jen giggled. "I think you look fab. And this is the *unofficial* hen-night outfit, right? So will your mum even see you?"

Angel groaned. "You really have no idea, do you? Of course she'll see me. Not in person, but through my cousins' descriptions, which will get more and more exaggerated as people pass on the story until my mother hears that I was wearing nothing but a thong."

"So it probably doesn't matter what you wear then, if you're going to get aggro anyway," Jen suggested.

Angel smiled. "I knew I brought you along for a reason. Perfect logic. I like that. Okay, so, now I need a 'demure, respectable sister who doesn't put the bride's family off her brother' outfit. Are you going to get that suit?"

Jen shook her head. "God, no. No, absolutely not. I mean, it's just not . . . Well, just no. No, I'm not."

"So, yes, then?"

Angel grinned and Jen looked at her hopelessly. "What's happening to me, Angel?"

"You're playing a new role," she said simply. "Get used to it."

❧ 18

Jen got home with an hour to spare before she had to leave again to meet Alan for her promised coaching session. This was meant to be her Christmas holiday, she thought to herself, but she'd never been so busy. She took her new suit out of its smart paper bag and hung it up in her wardrobe, then ran herself a bath. Was Angel right? Was she just moving on? Could you do that so easily—just put on a new skin, turn into a new person with different ideals, different thoughts, and different loyalties? It felt so . . . weird. And so easy. Surely you had to agonize over stuff like this. Go into hibernation for several months. Face some sort of ritual at the end of it, a test of some sort.

She smiled to herself as she poured scented oil into her bath. Maybe the MBA was the hibernation and the final exam the ritual. She imagined everyone on the MBA doing a tribal dance and being pronounced fully fledged members of the business community. Then the smile disappeared off her face. Jesus, was that what she was doing here? She'd been thinking so much about impressing her father, she'd forgotten that in the process she was becoming everything she'd ever hated.

Jen frowned as she undressed. Everything was topsy-turvy—her mother was now the liar; her father the person she wanted to protect. Business wasn't so evil anymore, whereas Gavin the eco-activist had betrayed her. She'd just bought a suit, and now she was about to spend her Saturday night out with Alan, the MBA geek, teaching him how to chat up women. Well, only *part* of Saturday night; she'd promised Daniel that she'd be at his place by ten P.M. at the latest. Daniel, her new boyfriend with his own flat, his own business, his own everything. She shook her head and got into the bath. If fate had some grand plan for her, some explanation that made sense of the strange new world she seemed to be inhabiting, she wished she could have a little peek at it.

An hour and a half later, Jen made her way into a dark and dingy pub on the corner of Tottenham Court Road for her assignation with Alan, a pub he'd chosen and which in retrospect Jen wished she'd known was at the top end of the street, because she could have got off at a different tube stop and avoided a twenty-minute walk.

She found Alan at a table in the corner, and he looked up at her nervously.

"What a nightmare journey!" she said, sitting down in a heap. "Alan, why did you have to choose somewhere so far away?"

Alan took off his glasses and wiped them clean with his handkerchief. "Look, I've been thinking about this and I'm really not sure this is such a good idea," he started nervously. "I don't even want a girlfriend. Don't need one, at any rate. I've got my MBA work to do and . . ."

Jen sighed and looked at him firmly. If she was prepared to accept change in her life, then Alan was damn well going to do it, too. "Alan, you *do* want a girlfriend, and this *is* a good idea. Look at you—you're a quivering wreck, and it's only me sitting here! Tell you what, I'll get some drinks and you can think through ways to start conversations with girls. Then you can try them out on me. Okay?"

Alan looked utterly unconvinced, but Jen headed up to the bar regardless. Change was scary, she reminded herself. She would have to help Alan through it gradually. And she was definitely the one to sort him out, she thought to herself purposefully as she ordered a pint of bitter for him and a gin and tonic for herself. The doubt and uncertainty that had been dogging her since she'd bought that suit a few hours before were gradually subsiding, leaving in their place the conviction that moving on was an incredibly positive experience. And that she was now the expert in it.

"So," she said with a smile five minutes later, plonking the drinks on the table. "Hit me!"

Alan looked perplexed. "Hit you?" he said nervously. "What, like a high five?"

She sighed and sat down. "I meant *tell me*. Your chat-up lines."

"Oh, right. Do people really say *hit me*?"

Jen shrugged. "I don't know. But that isn't really the point. So come on."

Alan went red. "I don't really have any chat-up lines," he said awkwardly.

"Okay, put it this way. You're in a pub, right here, and I'm a strange woman who has just sat down at your table because there's nowhere else to sit. And when I say strange, I mean you don't know me, not that I'm actually *strange*. I'm . . . I dunno, a pretty, intelligent-looking woman. Nice shoes, that sort of thing. So I'm sitting here and I'm obviously not with anyone, and you like the look of me. What would you say to me to start a conversation?"

Alan looked at Jen strangely. "I wouldn't. I'd probably take out a book so that I didn't have to talk to you."

"Right," Jen said uncertainly. "Well, that's an interesting approach. Okay, what about at a party. One where you've seen someone you like?"

"I don't go to parties. I hate them. You have to talk to strangers."

Jen thought for a moment. This was turning out to be a lot more difficult that she'd hoped. "Okay, Alan. Look, the thing is, if you want to get a girlfriend, you're going to have to talk to strangers. You did okay when you met me and Lara, didn't you?"

"That was different. I could talk about work with you straight away. You didn't expect me to talk about films I've never seen or foreign places I've never been. I can't do small talk."

Jen took a slug of her gin and tonic and sighed. Who was she kidding—she hated small talk, too. Hated going to parties full of strange people.

"Okay," she said eventually, "let's forget parties and pubs. Let's think work situations. Maybe if you liked the look of someone on the MBA course. That's got to be easier, right?"

Alan looked at her worriedly. "I don't fancy anyone on the MBA course," he said quickly. "I don't know what people have been saying, but it isn't true. I'm not . . ."

"I said *if*," Jen said quickly, emphasizing the word for effect. "I'm using the MBA course as an example. A theoretical one. You know—*if* you did fancy someone, how might you go about talking to them?"

Alan was looking hot and uncomfortable. "I don't, though," he said gruffly. "I knew this was a bad idea."

Jen put her drink down. This was going to require all her ingenuity and patience. "Alan," she said slowly, "think about it. Lots of people meet people at work. It's the perfect place—lots of like-minded folk all in the same office. If you can't ask someone out at work, where you spend half your life with the same people, then you're going to find it a lot harder anywhere else."

"I told you," Alan said defiantly, "I don't fancy anyone in the course. And even if I did, and I asked them out, they'd only say no, and then I'd have to enroll in a new MBA program. No, it's a terrible idea."

Jen took a deep breath. "They won't necessarily say no," she said quickly. "Not if you plan it carefully enough. What you've got to do is figure out little ways to find out if they might be interested. To give them subtle signs that you might be. So that if and when you do ask them out it isn't a total shock. You see? That way you don't set yourself up too much."

"You mean risk management?" Alan asked seriously.

Jen looked at him, exasperated. The man really could not talk about anything other than business strategy. It was a hopeless case, and if she had any sense she would bail right now and go to Daniel's flat. He'd have food waiting for her, wine, those arms . . .

Then she had a thought.

"Risk management, you say?" she said carefully. "Well, actually, yes. That's exactly what it is." She picked up her glass again and took another sip. "In fact, why don't you think of this whole exercise as stakeholder management?" she said, watching as Alan's face turned from suspicion into interest. "Your prospective girlfriend is a potential stakeholder. You've got to work out how interested in you she is, analyze her preferences and interests, and then develop your strategy. It's just like an MBA assignment, only not on paper. A *practical* assignment."

"You mean, find out if she's interested in films before inviting her to the cinema?"

Jen glowed. "Alan, that's exactly it. But you wouldn't suggest that a business cold-call a customer, would you? Not unless they're selling double glazing and don't mind being hung up on a million times. No, you'd suggest building up to it first, right? Make sure that the customer has heard of the company, knows its products."

Alan nodded.

"Right," Jen continued. "So maybe you wouldn't just invite this girl to the cinema straight off—first you might mention a film you've seen. Ask her if she's seen it, whether she enjoyed it. Ask her what she liked or disliked about it. Market intelligence, you know? Suddenly you're having a conversation, and if it goes well, the next time you talk about films it could be a natural thing to ask her to the cinema to see a film."

Alan nodded seriously and started to make notes on a pad of paper.

"Like Amazon," he said as he wrote. "Knowing what you bought last time and then making recommendations the next time you visit the site. Customer relationship management?"

Jen took a deep breath. "Exactly," she said.

"And this stuff actually works?" he asked.

Jen smiled as she remembered her own early conversations with Daniel about MBAs, books, ethical business, family squabbles.

"There are a lot of couples out there," she said firmly. "They all had to start somewhere."

"Hello, gorgeous."

Jen grinned and reached up to kiss Daniel, who wrapped his arms around her, picked her up and swung her round, depositing her in his hallway.

"What took you so long?" he asked, ushering her into his flat. "I didn't know whether or not to cook."

Jen's eyes traveled around the hallway, taking in the photographs of Daniel in diving gear; on a mountain; smiling, with his arm around a woman . . . Her eyes narrowed as she frowned involuntarily.

"My sister," Daniel said with a twinkle in his eye. "She lives in the States. So?"

"So, what?" Jen asked, slightly embarrassed at having been caught out.

"So where have you been?"

"Oh, right. I was with a friend from the course. Alan."

Now it was Daniel's turn to frown. "Right," he said, walking toward the sitting room. "Well, I hope you had a good time."

Jen smiled to herself as she followed him. "We did, actually," she teased Daniel. "We were talking about relationships, mostly."

Daniel turned round and stared at her. "Relationships?"

"And how he can get himself one," Jen said, grinning. "He's a bit of a geek, actually. I was . . . kind of teaching him. How to get a girlfriend."

"I see," Daniel said. "Well, just so long as he isn't eyeing you up. . . ."

Jen raised her eyebrows at him. "I really doubt it," she said quickly. "So, what did you decide?"

Daniel looked at her curiously. "Decide about what?"

"About whether to cook. You said you didn't know whether to cook or not."

"Ah. Well, I decided not to. I figured that if you were hungry we could get takeout, if that suits you."

Jen nodded. "Sounds perfect. So, what have you been up to since I saw you last?"

Daniel rummaged around in a drawer, pulled out some menus, and handed them to Jen. "Italian, Chinese or Thai—take your pick. What have I been up to? Oh, not much. Working, sleeping, waiting around for my gorgeous girlfriend to turn up . . . and trying to figure out some winning ideas for a presentation I'm doing in a couple of weeks."

"I fancy a black bean curry with chicken," Jen said, handing the menus back. "So what's the presentation?"

Daniel rolled his eyes. "It's to the board. Which would be fine, but I just don't seem to be able to see eye to eye with my chairman these days. I need some big ideas that will blow them away, but he keeps talking about cost cutting like that's the answer to all our problems."

Jen frowned. "Problems? I didn't think Wyman's had any problems."

Daniel shrugged. "Everyone's got problems. All of our competitors are problems, as are the costs of real estate in London and the demise of the high street. They're not insurmountable problems, but they keep us busy. So, black bean curry? Sounds good—I think I'll join you."

He picked up the phone and made the order, then joined Jen where she was sitting on the sofa.

"And what have you been doing lately," he asked tenderly. "Missing me, I hope?"

Jen looked at him playfully. "Why should I have missed you, when all you've been thinking about is the cost of London real estate?"

Daniel nodded seriously. "Harsh, but fair," he said solemnly. "Did I also mention that I've missed you desperately and have been unable to sleep because of it?"

Jen looked at him archly. "You can do better than that," she said with a little smile.

He put his hand through his hair. "Okay, so sleeplessness isn't enough. How about self-flagellation? Would that impress you?"

Jen giggled. "Did it hurt very much?"

Daniel nodded. "Yup. Quite a lot, actually. I was hoping you might kiss it better."

"I see," Jen said thoughtfully. "And where did this self-flagellation . . . manifest itself?"

"Um, well, I guess here," he said, pointing to his cheek. Jen reached over and gave it a little kiss.

"Anywhere else?" she asked, her eyes glinting.

Daniel frowned, then unbuttoned his shirt slightly to reveal his broad chest. "Here," he said, pointing to the area just below his neck. Jen reached over and kissed it.

"And here," he said softly, pointing to the top of his back.

"You know, you might need to take off your shirt," Jen said thoughtfully.

Daniel nodded seriously. "If you think it might help," he said, unbuttoning further. "Do you think it would be a good idea if you took yours off too?"

Jen found herself smiling involuntarily. "You're the one who should've been coaching Alan this evening, you know," she said as she allowed Daniel to unbutton her shirt and kiss her neck. "I just told him that he should ask lots of questions."

"Questions?" Daniel asked, taking off her shirt and putting it to one side.

"Yes," Jen said, trying to concentrate as Daniel's lips started to explore her body. "I said he should find out what girls like, and then he'll have something to talk to them about."

"Do you like this?" Daniel asked, taking off her bra and moving his lips onto her breast.

Jen nodded. "Mmm hmmm."

"And this?" He was taking off her trousers now.

"Oh, yes."

"And how about this?" he asked as he quickly got undressed.

Jen sighed. "I think I like that most of all."

Twenty minutes later, the doorbell rang, and Daniel reluctantly disentangled himself from Jen, ran to the bedroom, and pulled on a robe.

Jen slowly sat up and wandered over to the mantelpiece, over which was hanging a smart walnut mirror. She peered at herself—flushed cheeks, hair all over the place, and a loopy grin on her face—and mooched back to the sofa. Her brain seemed unable to think about anything other than the here and now—the day's events seemed a lifetime ago; Bell Consulting and her mother seemed like distant memories. Was there any better stress reliever than sex? she wondered idly to herself. Was there any better sex than sex with Daniel?

He walked back in carrying two plates, handed one to Jen and placed the other on the floor. Then he left the room and returned a few seconds later with a bottle of wine and two glasses. "We can eat at the table, if you want—or here. Up to you."

Jen had her plate firmly in her lap. "Here's good," she said, secretly pleased that she wasn't going to have to move. She'd put her shirt back on, but other than that she was naked and quite comfortable curled up on the sofa.

"So what are you going to do about Wyman's problems?" she asked vaguely as she started to eat. Either she was very hungry or this was the best black bean curry she'd ever had. Daniel was sitting right next to her and the feeling of his knee brushing against hers every time he moved his fork toward his mouth sent little frissons of excitement through her. He was so perfect. This was so perfect.

Daniel rolled his eyes. "Fuck knows, and right now I really don't care. I'm more interested in looking at your legs."

Jen blushed slightly. "Well, I quite like looking at your legs, too, but that doesn't stop me from being interested in your work," she said, smiling slightly.

Daniel looked at her and shrugged. "Oh, I don't know. I'll come up with something. Hey, you're the MBA student—I should be coming to you for ideas."

Jen grinned. "Yes, you should," she said with a twinkle in her eyes. "And while my advice doesn't come cheap, I did learn from the master, Daniel Peterson himself, so it's well worth the money."

Daniel smiled. "Okay, then. So, I've provided you with curry—that must buy me one or two ideas, surely?"

Jen nodded seriously. "And it's very good curry, so yes, I think at least two ideas. So . . ." She thought for a moment. Her head felt like cotton wool; endorphins had blocked out all coherent thought, and she could barely remember a thing from her course.

"How about your supply chain?" she said eventually. She'd written an essay about the supply chain in her exam and felt it had a suitably serious-enough sound about it to impress Daniel.

He raised his eyebrows. "Supply chain, you say. Go on . . ."

Jen frowned. He wanted more? She thought for another minute. "Oh, I don't know. Buy up a publisher. Or do a deal that ties them in to producing just for you. And you can't start eating my chicken just because you've finished yours!" She looked indignantly at Daniel, whose fork had just landed in her plate. He grinned mischievously, and she scooped some of her curry onto his empty plate.

"Actually, that's not a bad idea," he said thoughtfully.

"What, you're going to buy a publisher?"

He shook his head. "Tying them in. I wonder if there's any mileage in a joint branding deal."

Jen, finding herself full, put her plate down and picked up wine, then leaned her head on Daniel's shoulder.

"You need to tie in your customers too," she pointed out. "Make them want to shop at Wyman's rather than anywhere else. Have loyalty schemes and stuff."

Daniel put his arm around her. "So, loyalty schemes would tie you in?"

"They might."

"Would regular black bean curries do the trick?"

"Curries would be a start," Jen said with a little smile.

"A start," Daniel said thoughtfully. "Well, I suppose a start is something."

He pulled her toward him, and as her lips met his, she felt goose bumps on the back of her neck.

"This helps too," she said with a contented sigh, as Daniel's lips traveled down to her neck. "This, combined with the curries, is pretty compelling, actually."

❧ 19

"Welcome back, folks, hope you all had a great holiday." Jen looked around the lecture hall, smiling as she caught people's eyes. She remembered how alienated she'd felt the first time she'd sat here, how desperate she was to get out as quickly as she could. Now look at her. She was one of them. And she wasn't even embarrassed about it.

"As you know," Jay continued, "in the next few weeks we'll be looking at another stage of strategic analysis—namely the SWOT analysis. That's Strengths, Weaknesses, Opportunities, and Threats to those who don't know or who did know but drank enough booze during the holidays to forget. So, to walk you through the finer points, please welcome Dr. Mary Franks, who is joining us from the London Business School this term."

Jen took out her new pad and paper and prepared to start taking notes, but her mind was still dreamily absorbed in thoughts of Daniel. Kissing her. Smiling at her. Talking till two in the morning because neither of them wanted the evening to end.

"Good morning, ladies and gentlemen, and thank you, Jay. So, the SWOT analysis. Well, many of you will know of the SWOT. But few of you will be using it properly, and even fewer will really be getting the most from it.

"Essentially, the SWOT analysis helps you make sense of your internal and external analyses. It's your opportunity to put the two together and to look at the whole—what the company's strengths and weaknesses are, as identified in the internal analysis, and how the strengths can be maximized and the weaknesses reduced. But you add to that the opportunities and strengths as identified in your external analysis—and then you can see how the company is positioned, what it needs to do, whether or not it's really fit for purpose."

Fit for purpose, Jen wrote carefully. God, if anyone was fit for purpose, it was Daniel.

"Let's take an example, shall we? Someone give me a company to work with. One that has relatively straightforward strengths and weaknesses—that we can get to grips with the internal workings of."

There was silence for a few moments, during which a guy at the back started to suggest Duracell, but he was quickly shouted down.

"A condom company," said Lara seriously. "We've analyzed them before, and I think we're all familiar with their internal workings."

"And some of us are all too familiar with their weaknesses," chipped in a woman at the back who was proudly sporting a large, pregnant belly. A ripple of laughter filled the room and Jen started to giggle.

Mary looked uncertain. "Condoms, you say? Well, okay, then . . ."

"Which is why it is crucial that we leverage our strengths to maximize our output and reduce our overheads . . ."

Daniel nodded vaguely and hid his BlackBerry under the table as Robert, Wyman's chairman, twittered on about growth and efficiencies.

Fancy a drink tonight you sexy beast? Am in deadly meeting. Call me! D x

He sent the e-mail and tried to look nonchalant when the familiar *ping* was heard by the entire board.

"Just some routine business that needed an answer," he apologized. "Sorry, chaps. So, we're leveraging our strengths . . ."

"Yes, Daniel," said Robert seriously. "I was rather hoping that you might have something to say on that."

"So, for our market-leader multinational condom company, we have strengths: brand awareness, high quality, size—no, don't laugh, I'm talking about the company—and market leadership. Weaknesses: reliance on one product, we think—although I will look into James's comment on sex toys—reliance on suppliers, size—because being big can be a weakness as well as a strength—and lack of innovation."

Poor woman, Jen thought to herself as around the room everyone was collapsing in giggles while Mary did her best to keep a straight face and plow on.

"Opportunities would be James's sex toys or other sex-related products, increasing market share, sourcing new materials or buying a latex manufacturer, and tackling new markets. Threats would be new entrants to the market, other types of contraception such as the male pill, and suppliers raising their costs.

"Can you see that by putting these together, you are starting to arrive at options: You are starting to see how it all fits together and how ready the company is for the future it faces. If you can do a good SWOT, then the next stage of your analysis will be very much easier."

Jen nodded seriously as her mind shifted away from Daniel and on to more pressing matters. She knew all about threats and weaknesses—her father still didn't know about the article about Bell, and it was only a matter of time before he found out. The nurses had so far been very obliging, keeping all newspapers and television from him in the interests of his relaxation, but that would only work while she was the only person visiting him. Now that everyone was back from their holidays, he could find out at any minute, and she still hadn't worked out quite what she was going to do about it other than cross her fingers and hope a lot.

She looked down as her phone started buzzing, and as she read a text from Daniel, she found her worries dissolving. Everything would be fine, she told herself, a goofy smile plastered on her face. How could it not be fine?

"So, for tomorrow, I'd like you to read pages thirty-three to ninety-four of your textbook and undertake the exercises recommended," concluded the professor. "Thank you, everyone, and see you tomorrow."

๑ 20

"So, how's the patient?" Jen asked tentatively. Her father had been in the hospital for four days now and even though she'd convinced the nurses that allowing him a newspaper of any description would be a bad idea, she was still convinced every time she came in to see him that this would be the day he turned on her; this would be the day he'd produce a gnarled old copy of the *Times* and point an accusing finger at her. He'd start off looking wounded and upset; then he'd get really angry and start throwing things around; and he'd conclude by telling her that as far as he was concerned he didn't have a daughter anymore, like Blake Carrington told Sammy Jo in *Dynasty* when she helped to kidnap Crystal—or was Sammy Jo his niece? Jen couldn't remember, but she didn't suppose it really made a huge amount of difference.

"Better, now you're here," George said gruffly. "I told the nurses today that I've had enough and I'm going home. I've got to get out of this dump."

"I wouldn't exactly call it dump," Jen said cautiously. *He doesn't know yet. I'm safe for another day.* "I mean, you do have a private room, a button that gets the nurses scurrying in after you, nice food, lots of books, fresh flowers . . ."

"Nevertheless, I'm getting out of here today."

"No!" Jen said, alarmed. "If you leave now, you'll get ill again. You need to rest." As she spoke she told herself that she had his best interests at heart—and actually she really did; if he left the hospital he'd find out about the article and it would be bound to make his heart worse. Plus the longer he stayed here, the longer she had to prove to him that she was a good person who just happened to make mistakes every so often, as opposed to a total bitch from hell who would sell her own father up the river. That had to be good for his mental health, right?

"I need to get back to work," George said firmly. "I have important things to do."

"Other people can do them," Jen said quickly. "Come on, Dad, haven't you heard of delegation?"

He looked at her and raised his eyebrows. "I delegate lots of things," he said dismissively. "But some things can't be delegated. And I need to get back to them."

"What things?" Jen pursued. "You're ill, you can't work. Tell me what they are and I'll help you."

George rolled his eyes. "Just things, that's all. I need my phone, my laptop."

"If you had those things, would you stay here a bit longer?" Jen asked thoughtfully. "I mean, if I got them for you, would you stay here until the doctors say you can go? Look, it's Friday now anyway, so there's no point leaving now. Give it till after the weekend at least."

George looked unconvinced. "They won't even let me have a television in here."

Jen reddened guiltily. "Tell me what you need and I'll

get it for you. But promise me you'll stay here a few more days."

George grimaced. "My keys are over there. You know the address? My laptop is in the sitting room. And my phone . . . I think it's in a coat pocket in the hallway. Can't believe I left it behind."

"No problem. I'll get them for you. I'll bring them over tomorrow."

George looked at her and there was the slightest trace of a smile on his face. "I'm so proud of you, you know," he said quietly. "So pleased you're back in my life, even if it was under rather strange circumstances."

Jen glowed and smiled slightly. "Me too," she said quietly.

"There are so few people in the world that you can trust," he continued. "But family . . . well, I think you can trust family. Wouldn't you say, Jen?"

Jen nodded silently.

"Done any more work on your MBA?"

"You want me to visit you *and* work?" Jen said with a little smile.

"That's exactly what I want."

"Okay. I'll see what I can do."

"Thanks, Jen. You're a good girl."

Jen smiled back, wishing she could feel so sure.

"Daniel, you're looking thin. Are you eating properly?"

Anita's voice was concerned, but her eyes were twinkling, and Daniel reached over to kiss her once on each cheek. She was sitting at a table in the window, her pale features and blond hair shining in the sun, and she left a light lipstick trace on Daniel's face.

"You're very kind to be worried about me." He grinned.

"I'm worried about my authors, Daniel, that's all. I need to make sure you're fit and well enough to make sure that people buy their books, and if that means I need to feed you first, well then, so be it."

"You know, it's been too long, Anita."

Anita raised her eyebrows at him. "And we both know whose fault that is," she said caustically. "Now, are you ready to order?"

Daniel quickly looked at the menu and nodded.

"Don't tell me. You're having pasta." Anita smiled, picking up her glass of water and taking a small sip. "I'd guess ravioli."

"Actually, no," Daniel said with a little grin. "I think it's time to break a few habits, don't you? I thought I might have steak."

"My, my. You really are changing, aren't you."

Daniel shrugged. "Maybe I am. But bear in mind that it used to be me buying you lunch, and I was broke, so no wonder I always ate pasta."

Anita smiled. "And look at you now," she said, raising her eyebrows. "Managing director. You're quite the success story, you know."

Daniel shook his head. "Hardly," he said.

"You don't think?" Anita asked quizzically.

"I think I'm hungry," Daniel replied evasively, turning to his menu.

They ordered and Anita shook back her hair. "So come on, tell me what this is all about, Daniel."

Daniel looked at Anita's intelligent, expectant face and sat back in his chair.

"Do you ever look at your life and wonder how the hell you ended up where you are?"

Anita frowned. "Tell me you're not having a mid-life crisis, Daniel. I'm not sure I can cope with that at lunchtime; I'd need a drink, for one thing."

"No, no, nothing like that. It's just . . . I worry I may have taken a wrong turn. At some point. You know, I spend my life in meetings and I can't be arsed contributing to them. I'm meant to be running a company and I just don't think my heart's in it anymore."

Anita smiled. "Management is exceedingly dull, Daniel. That's why you get paid so much to do it."

"You think I'm stupid to be complaining?"

"I think complaining is the wrong way to go. Doing something about it is more my style."

"My chairman wants growth and cost-cutting at the expense of everything else. Big bookshops, loads of them everywhere, pile 'em up and sell 'em quickly. That's not what I started the business for. I feel like I'm betraying something."

Anita sighed. "That's the way of the world, Daniel, but there's still room for niche players. Wyman's used to offer the best advice on books. What happened to that review magazine you used to publish? That was great."

"Considered too expensive and dropped," Daniel said despondently. "By my own marketing department, after thorough research that I could hardly disagree with."

"But you're the managing director. Of course you can disagree."

"Not really. It's too operational. Anita, that's just the problem," said Daniel, playing with his fork. "I have nothing to do with books anymore. I just look at spreadsheets."

"I suppose it isn't your job to focus on the books anymore."

"I know . . ."

Daniel sighed and Anita took his hand. "Come on, Daniel, you're just having a rough patch, that's all—you'll work your way out of it. But let's not get too depressed, shall we? Tell me what else is going on. Are you still breaking hearts all across London?" She smiled, hoping to break Daniel out of his despondency, and was relieved to see his eyes twinkling.

"Actually, no," he said, his face suddenly becoming lively with color. "I've . . . well, I've met someone."

Anita clapped her hands. "Daniel, I can't believe you've been sitting here talking about work when you've got such incredible news! You mean to say that the eternal bachelor has finally been tamed?"

"Maybe," Daniel said with a little smile. "Tell you what, you let me bore you stupid with every little detail about Jen, and I'll listen to everything you've got to say about the books and authors on your list. Who knows, you may manage to remind me why the hell I went into this business in the first place. . . ."

The next day was Saturday. Jen got up early and, after a quick breakfast, took the tube to her father's house. It felt strange going there, seeing the place he'd lived his life without her, without her mother; the house where he'd lived for the past fifteen years, going about his life like any other person, like she'd never even happened.

Still, it was also a chance to nose about a bit, check out the photographs, rummage around for a little glimpse of the private life of her father. Not his *very* private life—that would be weird, and also pretty revolting, really—no one wanted to think about their parents having a private life even with each other and she certainly didn't want to find pictures of women about the place. Or, worse, items of clothing . . . Jen shuddered as she opened the front door. Maybe she'd forget the rummaging. Maybe she'd just find the laptop and phone and get out of there.

It was a big house, one of those smart white St. John's Wood houses with railings outside and big gates with locks on that make it look like the inhabitants are desperate to keep the world out of their home. And no wonder, she thought, her eyes widening as she took in the paintings all over the walls, the sculptures, the expensive furniture. There were no squishy sofas, no dog-eared books scattered around; just dark wood, velvet, and leather.

She walked around, her footsteps echoing off the walls and making her feel self-conscious. It felt strange to see this vast array of things, all belonging to him, none of which she'd ever seen before. Somehow she'd always imagined him in some parallel universe, living in the same house they'd lived in together, but without her or Harriet. Either that, or living in a really depressing bed-sit, like Arthur from *Eastenders* moved into when he left Pauline.

She walked into the kitchen and saw a half-drunk glass of port on the kitchen table, and a newspaper from December twenty-eighth, the day he had gone into the hospital. She blanched. Somehow the heart attack seemed more real now that she was actually in his house—now she could imagine him sitting here; using the phone over there.

Quickly she put the plate and glass in the dishwasher and made her way to the sitting room, an opulent room with two large ornate gold mirrors hanging above the two fireplaces. There, on the coffee table by one of them was her father's laptop. She picked it up, unplugged it, and carefully wrapped the cord around it, looking for its case.

She couldn't see it anywhere, so she went into her father's study, where she found it leaning against the desk.

Just as she was about to pick it up, she was startled by the phone ringing, its harsh trilling piercing the silence. She stared at it for a few moments, unsure whether or not to answer it. Finally, she decided she would—it might be important, she reasoned, and the caller should at least be told that her father was away at the moment.

She picked up and before she could say anything, a voice started to speak urgently.

"Hello, George? It's me. Where've you been? I need to talk to you."

Jen frowned. She knew that voice, but it felt strange hearing it here. "Paul?" she asked. "Is that you? It's Jen here."

There was a little click. "Hello? Paul?"

But it was too late—the connection went dead. Jen stood still for a few moments, trying to think of a reasonable explanation for why Paul would be calling her father, needing to talk to him. But she was at a loss.

Unless it was another of her mother's ploys, she wondered. Was Harriet using Paul to spy on her father now that she and Jen weren't speaking? It was possible, she supposed, but Paul hadn't even said his name. It was like he knew her father really well. And why would he hang up when he heard her voice?

She suddenly realized that Paul would no doubt tell her mother that she'd been at her father's house and had picked up the phone, which meant that she'd be getting an irate phone call herself before too long. Still, she could face Harriet's inevitable tantrum later. Right now, she wanted to know just what was going on.

Slowly, Jen put the phone down, put the laptop in the computer case, and walked back into the hallway, where she found her father's mobile in his coat pocket as he'd promised.

And then she stopped again. On the hallway mantelpiece, next to a large carriage clock, she saw something that looked familiar. It was a wooden block, just like the one her mother had given her for Christmas. She thought of Harriet giving it to her excitedly. *Paul bought it at my request, all the way from China!*

Jen made her way slowly toward it and picked it up. It felt and looked the same. She turned it over. His had a little label on the bottom: MADE IN INDONESIA. She put it back uneasily. It couldn't be the same one, could it? Hers was from China, not Indonesia. Unless they were made in Indonesia and shipped to China. Or maybe hers wasn't from China at all.

What is going on? she wondered uncomfortably. Why was her stomach tying itself up in knots? And why was she so keen to find easy explanations, to pretend to herself that everything was just fine?

She leaned against the door and took a deep breath. What had her father said? *It was so hard to find people you could trust.* Well, he could trust her. She'd had enough of scheming and sneaking around. She'd come here to pick up her father's laptop and phone, and she'd done that now. So she was just going to open the door and go home.

And hope against hope that this didn't all blow up in her face.

❦ 21

George sat staring ahead grumpily. It was eight o'clock on Saturday morning, and he was wide awake and bored. What was the point, he asked himself, of being the chief executive of one of the best known management consultancy firms if you still ended up like this, tubes in every orifice and subject to the whims of nurses and doctors over whom you had no bloody control whatsoever? What was the point of being fabulously wealthy if you couldn't buy your health? To buy your way out of bloody hospitals before the buggers got you with one of those hospital bugs or nicked one of your kidneys when you weren't looking?

He looked around his private room, taking in the institutional bed that he'd been in for nearly a week now, the drip and machines beeping at him from beside his bedside cabinet, the cheery wallpaper that made him want to jump off a cliff, and the gaping hole where a television should be. No news, nothing that might agitate him.

It was insufferable. It was outrageous. He had a private doctor. He took pills. He *shouldn't be here*.

And the pain. The pain was worse than he'd expected. Not that he'd expected a heart attack—that sort of thing happened to other buggers, not George Bell. But still, he'd never realized it would hurt so much. It had started as a bad case of heartburn. Too much cheese, he'd thought to himself. And port, perhaps.

But his usual antacids hadn't done anything, and when he'd turned to the hard stuff, the tablets his doctor had prescribed for emergencies, they hadn't done a bloody thing either. George had decided to call his doctor, to tell him in no uncertain terms that next time he was prescribed something for "emergencies," and something that cost not an inconsiderable amount of money, too, he'd expect it to work. But there'd been no answer. Then the pain had spread outward, stopping him in his tracks. His left arm had started to tingle, and then the pain had spread along it, causing him to shout out. He'd made it to the sofa and tried Emily, but she wasn't answering either. Bloody Christmas had meant that everyone was out, away, somewhere else. And so George had sat there for twenty minutes, breathing slowly, wondering whom to call, what to do. And then he remembered his daughter.

Somewhere deep inside, George had actually been rather pleased to have such a dramatic reason to call Jen. No "can I buy you lunch" or "I wondered if you wanted to pop over for a coffee" for him and his estranged daughter. No, on balance, he thought that "Jen, I'm having a heart attack, and I need your help" was far more interesting.

But, naturally, she'd been out, too.

So eventually, having even considered calling Harriet in a moment of madness and swiftly rejected the idea, he'd dialed 999, reasoning that after decades of being screwed by the tax man, he should take advantage of an ambulance at least once. Get a bit of value out of the state. He'd described his symptoms, and twenty minutes later two young men had turned up, put him into a wheelchair, and taken him to John and Lizzie's Hospital where he'd been trussed up like a chicken, connected to some awful beeping machines, and prodded every so often by a doctor who looked like he'd barely left school.

And now look at him. On his own. Weak and away from the office. It was too much to bear.

He sniffed despondently. Of course, he was supposed to be convalescing. Bloody joke that was. His private room was about as private as a public convenience—people wandering in and out at all hours, never knocking, never asking permission. Given rabbit food to eat and encouraged to drink lots of water. Most vile drink around in George's opinion. Tasteless. Absolutely bloody tasteless.

On top of all that, no one would let him see a single newspaper. *No work,* he'd been told by the nurses. *Nothing that might upset you.* What they didn't realize, George kept trying to point out, was that not having access to newspapers was far more upsetting than reading the rubbish printed in them.

George's thoughts were interrupted by the phone. He'd had to fight for the luxury of having a phone, too—they'd tried convincing him that having a phone might also create more stress. Idiots. If he didn't get a phone, he'd patiently explained, he would not be the only person round here with a heart problem. Of course, Emily was guarding the number as if it were the Holy Grail, which meant that next to no one actually called him. But it was there for emergencies. He just hoped that this wasn't going to be one of them.

"George here," he answered gruffly, hoping for some

news. Hoping for some information that would ease his mind if not his heart.

"George! Good to hear you, old chap. It's Malcolm."

George frowned and pulled himself up to a better sitting position. He paused before answering, gathering his thoughts. He didn't like to talk to Malcolm Bray, Axiom's chief executive, without having his wits about him.

"Malcolm! How good of you to call."

"Well, I just heard the news. Sorry to call so early, George, but, well, it was a bit of a shock. You know I would have come down to see you if I hadn't been tied up. So how is the old ticker?"

George groaned. "Bloody awful. And being in hospital is not helping. It's a dreadful place, you know. Sooner I see the back of this room the better. There's nothing to do here but read out-of-date magazines."

"My sympathies are with you. I felt the same when I had my knee done. Nowhere is as bad for your health as hospital, eh?"

George agreed heartily.

"Well, I look forward to seeing you when you're fit and well," said Malcolm cheerfully.

"Absolutely. Must have a drink one of these days."

"I'll get my secretary to fix something up. Oh, just one thing before you go . . ."

"Yes?"

There was a pause. "I gather you haven't read the newspapers."

George clicked his tongue. "My medical notes on the Internet, are they?" he quipped sarcastically. "No, I bloody well haven't read the newspapers and if I don't get one soon, someone somewhere is going to lose their job."

"Oh, well, not to worry," Malcolm said quickly. "There's just been some more rubbish printed on this Indonesian thing, that's all. Nothing to worry about. You just concentrate on getting better."

"Not to worry?" George asked concernedly. "That means that something's gone wrong, doesn't it?"

"Oh, no, everything's fine. Really."

"Right," said George, sounding unconvinced.

"Good. Good to hear it. Thanks, George. And we'll catch up very soon."

As George put the phone down, he felt an uncertain feeling rise up within him. He needed his mobile phone and his laptop, and he needed them now. Where the hell was Jennifer?

"Good afternoon, Mr. Bell!"

Oh sod. It was the older nurse. The cheerful one. George preferred the young, sullen one—she looked as if she enjoyed her job about as much as George was enjoying his stay in hospital. They didn't talk to each other and George could be as grumpy as he liked. But this one—she was interminable.

"Lovely day, isn't it! Deary me, these curtains haven't been opened! Let's bring some sunshine in, shall we?"

"It's January," said George. "I hardly think we're going to get much sunshine."

"Nonsense! Winter sun is lovely and warm. Now then, isn't that better? And how is the patient eating? Oh dear, not good. Did you not feel like breakfast today?"

"I did feel like breakfast, actually. I just didn't feel like eating that drivel. Chap needs bacon and eggs. Hot but-

tered toast. Not that . . . that . . . mush." George was
talking on autopilot; his mind was elsewhere, worrying.

"Now, now, we want to get your heart better, don't
we? That means healthy eating, Mr. Bell. Good, nour-
ishing food. Lots of fiber and fruit and none of those
awful fry-ups!"

George focused on the nurse for a minute, taking in
her own curves, and was tempted to ask whether she'd
managed to kick the fry-up habit herself, but decided
against it. Those bedpans could be very uncomfortable.

"I want to have a cigarette." His fingers were drum-
ming now and he could feel himself becoming agitated.

"Of course you do. But you're not going to, are you,
Mr. Bell? We're not going to give in to Mr. Temptation,
are we? We're going to be strong and ignore our crav-
ings. You've got your nicotine patches, haven't you?"

George stared miserably at the box on his bedside
cabinet. "I don't want a patch, I want a cigarette. Better
still, a cigar. And I want you to stop being so bloody
cheerful."

"Oh, you've got to stay cheerful, Mr. Bell. Otherwise
where would we be? There's enough reason to be sad,
what with children dying in Africa, even on the ward
upstairs. Heartbreaking, isn't it? Then there's those poor
people in Indonesia with no homes, no money, and
there's that big hole in the aid money and no one knows
where it's gone. It's a terrible state of affairs, Mr. Bell.
And what I say is, be grateful for what you have and be
cheerful while you can."

"The aid money's disappeared? Disappeared where?"

"If I knew that, then it wouldn't have disappeared,
would it?" the nurse said hurriedly, suddenly remembering that she wasn't meant to be discussing the news with

this particular patient. "Now you get some rest and don't worry yourself."

"Fat chance," George said under his breath as she left the room. Sheepishly, he picked up a tissue and blew his nose. One of the little-known side effects of a heart attack, he'd discovered, was the propensity to cry at any given moment and for absolutely no reason whatsoever. He'd developed various strategies for dealing with it—including sending people from the room on errands, blowing his nose and surreptitiously wiping his eyes at the same time, and talking loudly about being allergic to hospitals. But what he hadn't mastered was stopping them from coming in the first place. Bloody nurse just had to stroke his head and he felt little tears pricking at his eyes, felt an irresistible urge to press his head to her chest and to blub like a baby. *Bloody disgraceful*, he thought to himself, and probably due to the drugs. Quicker he could get out of here the better.

"I'm not going to cry," he heard himself say, and immediately placed a pillow in front of his face to smother his shame. "I'm George sodding Bell and I am not going to cry."

"George, what on earth are you doing?"

George started. That didn't sound like the nurse. Slowly he removed the pillow from his face.

"You?" he said, surprised. "What are you doing here?"

Jen drummed her fingers nervously on her kitchen worktop as she waited for the kettle to boil and poured herself a cup of tea. She was doing her best to put Paul Song and that phone call out of her mind, but it was like trying to keep water out of a leaking boat—every time she managed to think of something else, Paul Song kept trickling back into her head, leaving her exasperated and confused. There had to be an explanation, she kept telling herself. She just had to trust her father and *not get involved*. After all, look what had happened last time—hiding in cabinets and leaks to the press. It wasn't exactly a record to be proud of.

Moving back to the kitchen table, she pulled out her papers. Maybe if she lost herself in her studies she'd forget all about it.

Assignment 3: Conduct a SWOT analysis of a business or industry, using models and theories covered in the course.

She frowned and started to make notes. *Chosen industry: bookselling. Chosen business: Wyman's. Internal strengths: Daniel . . .*

She crossed that bit out and found a little respite from her Paul Song quandary. Daniel, who was always a welcome intrusion into her thoughts. *Is a sexy managing director a strength that could be leveraged?* she wondered idly. She sighed. If she was really going to do some work, she needed to do some proper research. Find out about industry margins, profit levels, that sort of thing. She should go to the library and go online.

Or, she suddenly thought, she could spend the morning organizing broadband for her apartment. Sure, it could be considered a diversion tactic, but it would save so much time in the longer term. No more having to wait in turn at the Bell library, or, worse, her local municipal library, where there were only two computers. No more sitting in Web cafés on a Sunday where they charged by the hour. Not that she'd ever done that; she hadn't taken the MBA seriously enough before. But now things were different. Now she felt it was time to commit.

Except it would take forever. Days, maybe weeks, and she needed to finish this assignment by Monday. She could do the internal bit with Daniel tonight (she blushed at the thought, embarrassed and slightly thrilled that she could be so smutty while in the midst of an important MBA assignment), but she still needed information about other bookshops—share prices, analysis reports, stuff like that.

She sighed again. She'd have to go to the library. But would there be time? She wanted to get to the hospital by three and that meant leaving at two, which only gave her . . . three hours. Hopeless—by the time she got to the library and waited in line, she'd only have an hour, two at best.

Unless . . .

Her eyes fell on her father's laptop. It was bound to have an Internet connection. She frowned. No, she couldn't. Since getting back from his house yesterday she'd been so badly tempted to have a little look through his files—just to check that everything was okay, just to *reassure* herself. But it would be wrong. She couldn't do that sort of thing.

Although, if she did use it, she could get to the hospital quicker, and he did seem in quite a hurry to get ahold of it.

But it was still his computer. It would be an invasion of privacy.

Although she'd only be opening up the Internet browser, not looking at any personal files or anything . . .

She opened up the case.

Okay, she told herself. Quick analysis of the situation.

Option One: Go to library, lugging laptop, wait in line, do research, get to hospital late and flustered.

Option Two: Use laptop. Just surf Web; don't look at anything else, thereby making no infringement on father's privacy. Get to hospital early and relaxed.

Deftly, she took the laptop out of its case, plugged it in, connected it to her phone line and booted it up.

Two hours later, she was nearly done. She'd downloaded spreadsheets and reports and editorials on the bookselling industry from the *FT* and the *Wall Street Journal*, and had even found some commentary on Wyman's itself, including some very complimentary articles about Daniel when he got the job. Now all she had to do was transfer them all onto a CD and she'd be ready to go.

And she hadn't even looked at any of her father's files.

It wasn't like she hadn't been tempted, either. She'd wanted so much to have a quick search under "Axiom" to see what she could find. But she hadn't had so much as a peek—her days of spying on her father were well and truly over. If she'd learned one thing recently it was that trust was paramount.

Maybe Paul Song was working for her father as a feng shui consultant, she thought severely. He could have had a disaster with some crystals or something—that would explain the desperation in his voice.

Jen frowned. As much as she tried, she just couldn't picture her father going in for feng shui, or crystals for that matter. Okay, so maybe her mother had asked him to call, to find out how her ex-husband was. Maybe Paul had dialed a wrong number. Maybe . . . Jen shrugged.

Maybe she was just going to have to live with the fact that she didn't know and might not ever find out.

She picked up a disk and slotted it into the laptop to transfer the Web files she'd been browsing. The drive opened up in a window and she moved her files across. Then she frowned—there was an Excel spreadsheet with "2004–05 accounts" and she couldn't remember whether it was hers or not. She double-clicked on it, expecting to see the filed accounts of one of Wyman's competitors or a boring accounts spreadsheet from Bell.

But instead, the spreadsheet contained something very different, and when the file sprung up on the screen, she gasped.

❧ 22

"You!" George said again, his eyebrows raised. "Well, I really am honored!"

Harriet watched as he turned to put his pillow behind his head, wiping his eye surreptitiously as he did so. She smirked slightly.

"You know, it doesn't really suit you, looking helpless like this. I bet you're not enjoying it in the slightest, are you?"

George looked at her defiantly. "I won't be here for much longer," he said quickly. "So, what can I do for you? Need some money to bail out that firm of yours? I hear you're running out of funds, but then again that's hardly surprising, bearing in mind that you seem to have something against accepting clients who can actually afford to pay you."

Harriet smiled sweetly, trying not to let her agitation show. *He always said that*, she told herself quickly. There was no need to rise to it just because this time he'd hit a nerve.

"Unlike Bell Consulting, who will take on anyone with money, no matter how they got hold of it," she said, moving over to the window to look out. "You don't have much of a view here, do you, George. I'd have thought you'd have demanded the best view in the hospital, a man with your . . . authority."

She looked at the various tubes sticking out of George as she spoke and he narrowed his eyes.

"I don't want a view, I want to get the hell out. Now, are you just here to gloat or does your visit have a purpose? I suppose you must be needing company now that your daughter has seen through you."

Harriet glowered at him. "Oh, George Bell, you think you're so clever, don't you? But I'm on to you. Jen's so desperate for a father to love her that she's blinded by your protestations of innocence, but they don't wash with me."

"Is that all?"

Harriet sat down on the chair next to his bed. "Lost any clients over this yet?" she asked silkily.

George frowned. "Over what?"

Harriet smiled. "Oh, toughing it out, are you? I'm referring to the article in the *Times*. The . . . how shall I put this . . . truth about you and your grubby dealings with Axiom. I imagine your lawyers will be expecting a rather busy few months ahead, don't you?"

George stared at Harriet. Was this the article Malcolm was referring to? Why the bloody hell hadn't he seen it? "No one believes those bloody rags anymore," he said defiantly. "Journalists just make things up to fill space."

"Making up letters from Malcolm Bray to George Bell thanking him for his help?"

George flinched slightly. "What letter? I don't know what you're talking about."

Harriet raised her eyebrows. "I'm sure you do, if you think about it. The letter that was quoted in the article? If you don't remember it, this might jog your memory."

She took a newspaper out of her bag and passed it to George, who skimmed the story quickly.

"What the . . . How dare they!" he roared. "I'll have their guts for garters. I'll . . ."

Harriet frowned, then smiled, then laughed. "Oh dear me," she said, delighted. "Oh my word. You hadn't seen it, had you? Oh, how funny."

"It's rubbish," George said flatly. "Anyway, no one saw that letter. No one knew about it."

"One person evidently did. I just can't believe she didn't tell me about it. But then again, she always did have a mind of her own."

Harriet narrowed her eyes as she watched for George's reaction. She had no idea whether Jen had found the letter and leaked it to the press or not—in fact, she suspected that she probably hadn't. But she rather hoped that George might think she had. It didn't do to have your daughter and ex-husband too close.

George looked at his ex-wife incredulously, realizing that she was talking about Jen. "She wouldn't," he said firmly. "We talked about it, and we agreed it wouldn't go any further."

Harriet's eyes widened. "So it *was* her," she said with a smile. "I suspected as much. Oh, George, you are dreadfully naïve, you know. You really think that your daughter loves you and is on your side?"

She shook her head. "George, she hasn't seen you in years. She hates Bell Consulting as much as I do. But I'm sure you're right. No, after all that dedicated parenting you put in over the years, I'm sure she wouldn't dream of shopping you to the newspapers."

George stared at her. "She's seen through you, you

know," he said carefully. "I wouldn't play the moral upper-hand card on this one."

Harriet's eyes narrowed. "Look, George," she said eventually, deciding to extend her bluffing. "You're fighting a losing battle here. Just accept it—you lost your daughter a long time ago, you lost me even longer ago, and now you're going to lose your firm, your reputation, and all your money. And the best bit is you deserve everything that's coming to you!"

"Keep out of this, Harriet, I'm warning you," George growled.

"Oh, but it's so much fun, George," Harriet said with a little smile. "If you'd only listened to me all those years ago, none of this would have happened. But you didn't, and . . . well, here we are." She looked at her nails, pushing back a stray cuticle.

George looked at her incredulously. "You're still banging on about Axiom, aren't you? You can never just let anything go."

Harriet stood up. "Why should I, George? I told you to ditch Axiom the first time they breached regulations. They were my client and I said I wanted to terminate the contract, but oh no, not Malcolm Bray, not your old school pal Malcolm. The school pal who's been jealous of you since you were in short trousers and you never even realized? Well, you didn't listen to me then, and you're evidently not going to listen to me now, so I think I'll be off."

"You wanted me to get rid of Malcolm because you'd been sleeping with him and he finished with you," George said softly. "You talk so much about ethics, but I don't think that getting rid of a client because they've moved on to another woman is truly ethical, do you?"

Harriet faltered slightly. She hadn't expected this. "You knew?" she asked, her voice nearly a whisper.

She watched as George looked at her oddly as if concentrating hard on something, then turned as if rummaging behind his pillow for something, wiping his face and cheeks as he did so.

"I blamed myself in a way," he said in a strangled-sounding voice. "I was never there. Malcolm saw his opportunity."

"And you're still friends? After all that, you're still friends?" Her voice was wobbly now. She couldn't decide what upset her the most—the thought that George had known all along or the knowledge that it obviously mattered so little to him that he was still friends with that bastard. Malcolm had convinced her that he was in love with her. Had made her believe him. And had then walked away without a second glance. How could George remain friends with a man who had betrayed both of them like that?

"We all have our own way of dealing with things, Harriet."

Harriet paused for a moment, then smiled tightly. "Yes, George, I suppose we do." And with that, she left the room, shutting the door behind her. As she walked down the corridor she thought she could hear the sound of a man sobbing, and it reminded her just how much she hated hospitals.

Jen went white as she scrolled through the document. Payment after payment from Bell Consulting to a numbered Indonesian account. No details, no explanations. Why would a spreadsheet like this exist? And what was it doing on her father's computer? She wracked her brains, trying to ignore the little voice inside her head that kept saying "Bribes. It's bribe money," but it kept getting louder. Had her mother been right all along? Had she fallen hook, line, and sinker for her father's lies?

She didn't want to believe it. She was desperately trying to think of any justifiable reason for the money transfers. Trying to think of something her father might have said that could explain it. But she drew a blank. He had an Indonesian office, but these weren't business transfers—there was no "in" and "out"; just "out." These were payments for services rendered. Payments to make things happen. They had to be bribes.

The . . . the bastard. Her father was a lying, cheating bastard. The past few weeks had just been a ruse to get her off his case, to stop her finding out the truth. And she'd fallen for it. He was lower than low, and she . . . well, she was even worse for letting him suck her in, letting him flatter her into believing him, into trusting him again.

She was breathing quickly, her heart pounding in her chest. What was she going to do? Who was she going to tell?

She stood up and started pacing around. She should call her mother.

No. No, she needed the truth first. She was going to give her father his bloody laptop. She was going to tell him what she'd found. And she was going to make him tell her, admit the truth. She wanted to see his face, wanted him to see the hurt on hers. Wanted him to know that he would never have a daughter again, ever.

In what felt like slow motion, she sat down and transferred the file across onto her CD. Then she calmly bundled the laptop back into its case, picked up her bag, and left for the hospital, slamming the door behind her so loudly that the neighbors upstairs ran to the window to see who'd left in such a rage.

"I'm sorry, dear, you missed him."

Jen looked at the nurse blankly. "What do you mean I've missed him? He was right here yesterday. He's staying here—it's not like he could have just popped out."

The nurse looked at her strangely and Jen realized that her tone was perhaps a little on the sarcastic side.

"I'm sorry," she said quickly. "What I meant to say was, do you know where he is?"

The nurse shook her head. "Home, I expect. He checked out about an hour ago."

"Checked out?" Jen said indignantly. "This is a hospital, not a hotel. How can he just check out?"

The nurse smiled indulgently. "We're not a prison," she said. "People can leave if they want to."

Jen frowned. "But why would he want to leave? Why would he just go, when I was bringing his things round to him? It doesn't make any sense."

The nurse shook her head again. "I don't like to get involved," she said with a little shrug.

"But I've got his computer," Jen said redundantly. "He asked me to bring his computer."

"Maybe you could take it to him at home?" the nurse suggested.

Jen frowned and looked around the bare room. Suddenly she noticed something next to the bed. There, on the bedside table, was a newspaper. She walked over and looked more closely at it and discovered that as she'd feared, it was the copy of the *Times* with the story about Malcolm Bray's letter in it. Her heart sank as she realized that someone had shown it to George, that he probably thought she'd leaked it on purpose.

"But he can't have gone home," she insisted. "I need to talk to him."

The nurse nodded understandingly and Jen wondered how many loopy relatives she had to deal with on a daily basis. She'd probably be in the staff room—or whatever nurses had—that evening telling her colleagues about the crazy daughter who refused to believe her father had gone home. "Sad, it was," she imagined her saying. "Didn't look crazy, but just shows, you never can tell . . ."

"I'm sure he'd be happy to see you if you dropped by at home," the nurse suggested.

Jen felt like stamping her feet and crying out like a toddler. She didn't *want* to go to his house; she wanted her father in this bed, a captive audience, so that she could shout at him, so that she could give him the speech she'd prepared and memorized on the way here, the speech that would hound him for the rest of his days, make him realize how inadequate he was, how alone he would be in this world. He'd probably have people around him at home. And it was his territory, his power base. It just wouldn't be the same.

"Actually, I can take that."

Jen turned, startled, to see a Bell consultant at the door. She recognized him. It was the one called Jack.

"That won't be necessary," she said firmly. "My father asked me to bring this to him, and I plan to do so."

He held out his hand and smiled smoothly. "Actually, Mr. Bell asked if I'd swing by and collect it from you. Save you the bother of having to go to his house. I think you've got his phone, too?"

Jen stared at him. This was all the leverage she had, the only thing that she knew her father needed. If she gave them up, he wouldn't ever have to see her. He'd obviously read the article, obviously deduced that she'd never trusted him in the first place, that she'd run to the newspapers and betrayed him. Well, maybe that wasn't such a bad thing. Maybe that's all he deserved.

"If you don't mind?" Jack said with the hint of a smile but cold, calculating eyes.

"Fine," Jen said eventually, thrusting both at him. "But you can tell him from me that I hate him. That as far as I'm concerned, he doesn't have a daughter anymore."

And half expecting the *Dynasty* theme to start playing, she ran from the room and all the way to the tube station.

❧ 23

"Okay guys, settle down now," Jay said as Jen, Lara, and Alan filed into the lecture hall the following Monday morning. "I'd like to introduce Dr. Marjorie Pike, who will be talking to you about strategic options and evaluation. Marjorie did her MBA at Henley Management College, and her doctorate at Wharton in the U.S., and she's been lecturing there for the past five years, so we are very fortunate to have her here with us today. Marjorie, over to you."

The three of them scurried quickly to find seats as Marjorie slowly and decisively walked to the front. She was a small woman with white skin and black hair pulled into a chignon, and her eyes seemed to pierce each and every person in the room. No one made a sound.

"Options, options, options," she said thoughtfully. "Do you do an MBA or a marketing qualification? Do you work in the U.K. or the U.S.? Do you buy this house or another—or do you hedge your bets and wait to see how the housing market plays out over the next year or so? Every day, we face options and make decisions. The problem is, most times we make the wrong ones—do you stay for one more drink or go home while you're ahead? We generally have that last drink and we generally find ourselves regretting it in the morning. And while making a bad decision might be okay if it's just the wrong toothpaste that you bring home, it's not okay if you invest billions of dollars of shareholders' money in the wrong venture. Right?"

Jen nodded glumly. She knew more than she'd ever wanted to about making the wrong decision. Frankly, she felt that she was an expert in the subject.

"So what do you do?" Marjorie was saying. "You have your strengths and weaknesses set out. You've identified your threats and opportunities. How do you turn those into options, and how do you decide among them?"

More silence. Then Alan put up his hand.

"Yes?"

"Well," he said falteringly, "you develop actions that take advantage of opportunities, and others that mitigate the risks."

"How?"

"Well, if an opportunity is to . . . attract a new customer—type of customer, I mean—then you do research to find out if you've got a chance. If it's viable, I mean. And if a threat is a competitor who's also, you know, after the same customer, then you have to work harder to make sure he doesn't get her . . . get them. So, you know, you might do some heavy advertising or something . . ."

He trailed off and Jen looked at him strangely, wondering why he was sounding so gung-ho about all this. She guessed it was just his usual geeky enthusiasm for anything to do with strategy, but even so, he was getting all excited, bobbing up and down in his seat. She stared at him for a second, then lost interest as she found herself thinking about her father again. He'd certainly taken advantage of opportunities. And she'd let him walk all over her. Well, he wasn't going to get away with it. She wasn't sure quite yet what she was going to do about that spreadsheet, but she was definitely going to do something. Take it to the police, probably.

"Good. That's very good," Marjorie said briskly. "But in this situation you could also decide to consolidate, couldn't you? Buy up one or two of your competitors or maybe even your suppliers. What if you have more than one opportunity? What if you could enter a new market or rebrand your product for a new audience or focus on increasing your existing market share? What then?"

Alan frowned. "Rebranding," he said seriously. "I didn't think of that." He started scribbling frantically, and Jen rolled her eyes dismissively.

"In a textbook, strategic options are very easy," Marjorie continued. "You pick a couple of horses, see if they'll run, and bingo, you can make a decision. In real life it ain't that easy. In real life it's messy and complicated and you don't just have to consider the business imperative; you also have to consider the people and their personalities. One option might be to sell off a loss-making part of the business. But if the managing director set that business up himself and is emotionally attached to it, selling it probably won't be a viable option. Okay, someone give me an example, a company you've already analyzed and that we can look at briefly to highlight the issues."

She looked around the room searchingly and everyone looked at one another shiftily. Finally someone at the back said the fateful words, "We've already done some work on a condom company."

There were a few sniggers, although subdued ones—

somehow Marjorie wasn't the sort of person anyone fancied their chances with. But she took it in her stride.

"A condom company? Interesting. Okay, then. And presuming that you have all exhausted the humorous elements of a condom's strengths and weaknesses, what are the possible options for this theoretical company?"

"Sex toys," someone called out.

"Market penetration," someone else called out to a quick applause.

"Entering new geographical markets," shouted another.

"Okay, thank you," said Marjorie, scribbling them down on the board as people giggled. "So we're looking at market penetration, new markets, and new products, right? And how do we choose from among these options?"

"Well, it has to be a good fit," said someone in a deadpan voice. Marjorie chose to ignore the joke.

"Sure, strategic fit. But what does that really mean? You," she said, pointing at Alan, who immediately sat up straight.

"Well," he said seriously, "I suppose that you need to align yourself to your brand. Your product, I mean. Align your product to your brand." He looked slightly flustered. "So, you'd need to change your brand before you could interest a new market, like, you know, sex toys."

"Right," said Marjorie uncertainly. "I'd probably look at it the other way around; you look at your brand values and your unique selling point and don't try moving into a new market if it doesn't fit. Once you damage your brand, you may not have a company. Of course, nothing is sacrosanct—some companies change their raison d'être successfully, like IBM, who were a man-ufacturing company and are now more focused on consultancy. But you've got to be pretty confident—or desperate—to pull something like that off. So, what else?"

"Viability," Alan said. "Assessing whether you have the internal capabilities required. If you do, you might be able to . . . adapt your brand."

"Okay," said Marjorie, frowning slightly, "give me some examples."

"Like finding out what the customer wants and then trying to figure out if you've got it. What they want, I mean."

Now Marjorie was looking at Alan strangely.

He reddened and cleared his throat. "I mean, if you want to move into Europe, do you have any infrastruc-ture there?" he said quickly. "Do you speak any Euro-pean languages? That sort of thing."

"Great. This is good," said Marjorie, and Alan sat back, looking relieved. "What I'm trying to get across here is that when you get to the point of options, you might think that you've done all the hard work, but the reality is that the work is just about to begin. You need to think through everything, consider the outrageous and the mundane. You need to know what's going on in your company and out of it—and that includes the quirks of your top team and the politics of the current government. You need to consider whether an option is achievable, whether it's credible, whether it's acceptable. What are the risks? Can they be managed? So, back to our condom company. Let's think about the risks associ-ated with moving into a new market. . . ."

Jen frowned. She certainly needed to assess her own

options—she just wasn't sure that she wanted the help of a business model to do it.

"Options, you say?"

Bill was looking thoughtful.

"Yes. I've just been in a strategic options lecture, and I was just wondering how you know which way to go. When you've got no idea what to do next."

Bill stroked his beard, which was now a good two inches long. "You know, I'd like to tell you a little story, if that's okay with you."

Jen nodded.

"There was this young dude. World at his feet, just out of business school. And he's doing the rounds of the consultancy firms, industry, anything and everything, you get me?"

Jen nodded seriously.

"Okay, so he's talking to these guys and taking his CV around and they're offering him things—great salaries, perks, his own office, his own car, a mobile phone . . ."

Jen raised her eyebrows.

"So, this is a while back. When mobile phones were still a status symbol."

Jen shrugged.

"Anyway, he's in a quandary. Which way to go? What should he do? And so he went for a long walk to clear his head. Tried to work out whether the office was better than the phone, or the salary better than the perks. And as he's walking, he's realizing that he's all caught up in the frippery, the surface details. When what he should be focusing on is what he wants out of life, where he wants to be five, ten years from now. And you know what he realizes?"

Jen shook her head.

"He realizes that he doesn't want any of it. Doesn't want the money, the smart suit, or the fancy car. He wants to do something more meaningful. He wants to help people. So he turns right round, goes back to college, and he starts training all over again, this time on life coaching, not business analysis. You see what I'm saying?"

"That you're not the person to ask about business analysis?"

Bill looked hurt and Jen grinned at him.

"Oh, you're kidding. Oh, I getcha. Funny. That's funny! But seriously, what I'm trying to say is that you need to look inside of yourself. There are always options. But they're here, in your heart, not in your head. Am I right, or am I right? Huh? Huh?" Bill affectionately punched Jen's arm and she grinned at him.

"I guess you're right," she told him, realizing that she had no idea how Bill's story was meant to help her.

Daniel leaned back in his seat and looked his chairman in the eye. This was crunch time. He was going to convince Robert that cost-cutting and mindless growth wasn't the way to go. He had plans and innovations that would take this bookseller into the twenty-second century, let alone the twenty-first, and Robert couldn't fail to be impressed. *Bookselling is an art,* he would say. *It's not about piling 'em high and selling 'em cheap—it's about understanding the reader, getting inside their head, meeting their every whim.*

He smiled comfortably. The truth was that he felt excited about his job for the first time in months. His lunch with Anita had ignited a spark in him again, got him thinking his ideas were good ones. Now he just had to convince Robert.

"So you see," he said confidently, "anyone can look at financial efficiencies and trim their costs. But I think the real future for this company is in innovation. We need to get people to love reading, not desperately try and cut prices to entice them into the store. Books aren't expensive at all when you compare them with films, with other types of entertainment, and they provide hours of pleasure. We need to get inside the minds of our customers and come up with something that will knock their socks off. Get back to what the company is all about—books."

Robert Brown took his glasses off, cleaned them, and put them back on, then looked at Daniel thoughtfully. "You think the business is all about books?" he asked.

Daniel frowned. Where was Robert going with this? "Yes," he said simply, his hand reaching involuntarily to smooth his hair down. "Yes, of course it is."

"I see. It's just that from where I'm standing, the business is about its shareholders. Creating value for them. Dividends, that sort of thing."

Daniel looked at him impatiently. What was this, a lesson in business from his chairman? "Absolutely," he said with a tight smile. "And that's very important. But we do that through selling books. Get that right, and our shareholders will, I'm sure, be over the moon."

Robert nodded. "Look, Daniel. You built up a great little bookseller business. Really, you did a tremendous job. But you're working for us now. We're a big business. And we expect big profits. As do our shareholders."

Daniel swallowed, feeling his throat tighten. "You don't want to hear any of my ideas?" he asked.

"In the short term, as I've explained, the board feels that we should stick to what we know. Drive down costs, slash prices, maybe do a few more three-for-the-price-of-two deals. And in the meantime, look for an acquisition. It's all about market share, Daniel, as the board knows too well."

"The board or you?" Daniel asked bitterly, turning to look out of the window, taking in the view of London from his office. There was Buckingham Palace and Big Ben, and in the distance he could just see the edge of the London Eye. It was a great view. And it represented everything he'd worked so hard to achieve. He wasn't sure he could walk away from it.

Robert didn't say anything.

"You bought my business because of its innovation," Daniel continued. "Because we were better, faster, and more focused than any other bookseller."

"We bought it because it was a profitable business, Daniel. And because we saw more profit could be made with the right strategy."

Daniel took a deep breath in, then let it out slowly.

"Think about it, Mr. Peterson," Robert said, getting up from the table. "I have every confidence that at your presentation to the board next week you will focus on cost-cutting and price reductions. We want value-add propositions, not harebrained schemes. I hope that my confidence is justified."

As he left, Daniel turned back to his computer, opened up his presentation, and pressed delete. He was furious. He'd never been so angry. He watched as his hard work disappeared; watched the ideas he'd been so excited about turn to blank pages. And it was only when the phone rang and he reached over to pick it up that he noticed that his hands were shaking.

"Daniel Peterson," he said gruffly.

"Daniel, it's Anita. Look, sorry for the short notice, but I wondered if you were free for lunch this afternoon? I was talking to our chief exec about your branding idea and he loved it. Wanted me to get some more details . . ."

"Forget it," Daniel said despondently. "It isn't going to happen."

"But you haven't even done your presentation yet, have you?"

"Robert didn't even want to hear about it."

"So have lunch with me and we'll make it too convincing for him to reject it."

Daniel sighed. "Fine," he said. Maybe a lunch wasn't such a bad idea. If he stayed here, he might end up kicking the door in.

"Wonderful. Wolseley at one?"

"Fine."

Daniel put the phone down before Anita could even say good-bye, and went back to the delete button.

Jen wandered out of Bill's office and mooched down the corridor, bumping into Lara and Alan, who were coming the other way.

"You okay?" Lara asked concernedly.

Jen shrugged. "Fine. Just fine."

"You want to grab a hot chocolate? I usually find a sugar rush cheers me up on a Monday morning."

Jen shook her head. "No . . . I think I'm going to go for a little walk, actually."

Lara nodded understandingly. "Oh well, I suppose I should go to the library and do some work anyway."

Suddenly Alan cleared his throat. "I'd like to have a hot chocolate."

Lara and Jen turned to look at him and he reddened.

"What?" Lara asked.

"Hot chocolate. I'd like to grab one, seeing how Jen's too busy."

"Right," Lara said, looking slightly bemused. "Well, okay then. Thanks."

"You're welcome," Alan said, smiling now. "So, you like hot chocolate, do you? Are there any particular brands that you prefer?"

Lara raised her eyebrows. "Freak" she said affectionately.

She turned to Jen. "See what happens when you desert me?" she whispered. "If I end up having to talk about business process reengineering all morning, I'll blame you!"

～ 24

Jen walked out of Bell Towers and headed through St. James' Park, toward Daniel's offices. She would surprise him with a coffee, she'd decided, telling herself that it was to cheer him up, but knowing that really she just needed someone to talk to. Perhaps she should buy him a cake, too.

She popped into Pret á Manger and bought two lattes and some lemon drizzle cake. No one could turn down lemon drizzle cake, she reasoned.

She looked at her watch. Twelve P.M. What if he was at lunch? Or in a meeting? He probably spent his life locked in boring meetings and if she just turned up, he might think she was a total loon.

Perhaps she should call, she thought, but rejected the idea immediately. The point was that she wanted to see him, even if only for a few minutes. She needed to see Daniel's face, to reassure herself that some things in her life were still okay. She'd just pop in for a quick chat, and if he was busy, then she'd just come back later.

She found Wyman's easily enough—it was a large, squat building sandwiched between two gray government buildings with a large aluminum sign outside—but somehow it wasn't quite what she'd been expecting.

Even though she knew that Daniel was the managing director, she always thought of him as working above a book shop—or at least working in an old eighteenth-century building with battered wooden floors and shelves crammed with books everywhere. Which just proved how little she knew about anything, she thought to herself despondently as she signed in, and was directed to the fourth floor.

As she stood waiting for the lift to arrive, she looked around the lobby and felt a little thrill. This was virtually Daniel's company. He could do what he wanted with it, she thought to herself. There was a large vase of lilies just next to the lift, and Jen inhaled the lovely sweet smell. Maybe she'd work somewhere like this when she was done with Bell Consulting, she decided. A good, old-fashioned company that just sold books and didn't get involved in backhanders or dodgy dealings.

She arrived on the fourth floor and followed the corridor into a small open-plan area, behind which was an office. Her heart leaped slightly when she saw Daniel, sitting at his desk, staring at his computer screen, and she smiled quickly at the woman sitting outside, figuring it was probably his secretary.

"I'm here to see Daniel," she said breathlessly. "I've brought him coffee."

The woman looked at her, unimpressed. "It isn't in the diary," she said flatly.

"The coffee?" Jen asked, confused.

"A meeting," the woman replied. "Your name?"

"Jen?" Daniel appeared at his door, and the woman shrugged. "What are you doing here?"

"Coffee," Jen said immediately. He didn't exactly look pleased to see her, she noticed, and tried to ignore the anxiety that suddenly appeared in her stomach. "I brought you coffee and cake."

Daniel held his door open for her and she walked into his office.

"I was hoping you might give me a one-to-one tutorial on my dissertation," she said with a little smile. "And I'm prepared to pay you with coffee and lemon drizzle cake."

Daniel looked at her, bemused. "Now?" he said. "You want a tutorial now?"

Jen shook her head. This wasn't quite going to plan. She thought he'd have been pleased to see her—he'd been working all weekend and she thought he might have missed her. She'd certainly been missing him.

"No," she said immediately. "Of course not. I was joking. So how's the work going?"

Daniel shrugged. "I've been working on a presentation. I'm presenting to the board next Monday. . . ." He looked up at his wall calendar, on which the presentation was clearly marked. 4:30 P.M.: D-DAY.

"D-Day?" Jen said with a little smile. "So we're talking about an invasion, are we?"

"Something like that."

He seemed distracted, like he was barely listening to her, and Jen suddenly wished she hadn't come. She'd pictured this very differently—Daniel wrapping her up in his arms, listening while she told him everything that had happened, telling her with incredible insight exactly what she should do . . .

She frowned. Maybe she was just being selfish, expecting him to be focused on her when he obviously had important things on his mind.

"Don't worry about your presentation," she said as

reassuringly as she could manage bearing in mind that her own confidence was sinking fast. "You've got all those ideas you were telling me about, most of which, I have to tell you, have found their way into my assignment. . . ."

She looked at Daniel, hoping for a smile, but his face was still like thunder. "So which bits are you going to start with?" she continued, setting out the coffee and cake on his table. "The co-branding? I think that's great. Or are you going to talk about reader clubs? I tell you, they'll love all that stakeholder analysis stuff . . ." Jen trailed off as she realized that Daniel wasn't even looking at her.

"Is something wrong?" she asked tentatively. "Have you decided against the clubs or something?" She hoped he hadn't because that particular idea had been hers.

"They're all crap ideas," Daniel said dismissively. "This company is here to serve its shareholders, not a bunch of people who might or might not be encouraged to read more by setting up a bloody club."

Jen frowned. "You don't mean that," she said quickly. "Come on, talk me through that branding idea again. I was thinking that you'd maybe have to limit it to one or two big publishers, because otherwise—"

"Didn't you hear me?" Daniel interrupted. "I said they're crap ideas. They're not going to happen. What I need to do is get those bloody publishers to give me a better deal. Undercut the competition. Find some way to improve our profit margins. Maybe we shouldn't even sell books anymore—I think DVDs have a better markup now. . . ."

Jen stared at him indignantly. He was sounding just like her father. Or, rather, what she'd thought her father was like before she got to know him again. Or . . . she shook herself. Who was she kidding—she had no idea what her father was really like. That was the problem. But she did know that Daniel was talking like an idiot.

"I don't know what's up with you," she said calmly, "but the only crap around here is that stuff you're spouting."

She picked up her coffee and took a long sip. She could feel herself getting upset, and she didn't want to have an argument, not now. She'd come to Daniel for reassurance, not to have a fight.

But reassurance was not on offer. Instead, Daniel glowered at her. "You think I'm spouting crap? Oh, grow up, Jen. I thought you were the one doing an MBA."

"Grow up?" Jen was angry now. What right did he have to talk to her like that?

"You heard me. Oh, what's the use. Do your assignment, Jen. Write up all those lovely ideas—they're perfect for an MBA. They're just not going to work in the real world, okay?" He walked back to his desk and sat down at his computer.

"You're not a managing director, you're a bloody tyrant," Jen said hotly. "I thought you were a nice person. I thought you were interesting and funny, and all the time you were just . . ."

"Just what?" Daniel asked, still staring at his computer. He was really angry now.

"Well, actually, you're just a prick," Jen said, standing up and pushing her coffee away. "You're not the Daniel I know, and I don't actually want to be here with you if that's okay."

"Fine, fuck off, then," Daniel said angrily, his eyes

flashing. "Go and lecture someone who actually gives a damn."

"You know, Daniel, I thought you did. I actually thought you did," Jen said, storming out of his office and trying to ignore the amused look on his secretary's face.

She decided against the lift, running down the stairs instead, and tore out of the building as fast as she could. *What had happened in there?* she wondered, stomping down the street as she tried to make sense of Daniel's reaction. Did he suddenly turn into an ogre when he was in the office or was he angry with her? Had she said something to annoy him?

She pulled out her mobile phone and stared at it for a few minutes, hoping that he'd call and apologize, but it remained steadfastly silent. *Maybe it is me,* she suddenly thought. *Maybe he's bored of me, irritated by me. I didn't see him all weekend and maybe that was a sign . . .*

Jen shook herself. No, it was impossible, she wouldn't believe it. Daniel wasn't like that. Although she hadn't thought he was an argumentative prick either, and she'd been wrong about that.

Gradually calming down, Jen decided to go for another coffee. She hadn't had a single bite of her lemon drizzle cake, and when Daniel came to his senses and called to apologize, she wanted to be nearby.

❧ 25

An hour later, Anita walked into the Wolseley and raised her eyebrows when she found Daniel staring despondently out of the window.

"Daniel, there you are. You know, I'm so pleased you were free today. I had such an interesting conversation the other day . . ." She trailed off as she realized that Daniel wasn't even smiling. "Things really that bad, then?" she asked seriously, putting her hand on his.

"Worse."

"You want to tell me about it?"

"I told Jen to fuck off."

"Okay, that's pretty bad. What did she do to deserve that?"

"Told me that bookselling isn't all about huge profit margins."

Anita frowned. "Huh? I thought you'd have agreed with her."

Daniel put his head in his hands. "Of course I agree with her. I'd just said the same thing to my chairman, who told me that unless I changed my story when I presented my five-year strategy to the board next week I could forget my job."

"He said that?"

"No. But I know that's what he meant."

Anita called the waiter over and ordered some wine and olives. "And you took it out on your girlfriend? Clever."

"I was miserable, she got all indignant on me, made me feel even worse, and I . . . I just lost it slightly. Jesus, Anita, everything is suddenly so hard."

Anita shook her head. "It isn't suddenly so hard; you've just found a hill that it isn't so easy to climb. Daniel, you've had an amazing career, you've been very successful, but maybe it's made you think that it's too easy. If you want something, you have to fight for it."

"Are you talking about Wyman's or Jen?"

"Both, probably, but I think I'm probably on safer territory on the Wyman's front. . . ."

"I feel so helpless." Daniel shrugged. "I feel . . . impotent."

Anita raised one eyebrow. "Okay, definitely straying into new territory here. Daniel, you really want my advice?"

He nodded.

"Stop the self-indulgence," Anita said firmly. "Tell it like it is, and be prepared to walk away if they won't listen. But first you should probably apologize to your girlfriend." There was a long silence, then Daniel reached over the table and kissed Anita on the lips.

"Suicide watch over," he said seriously. "As always, you've cut to the chase and told me exactly where I'm going wrong. And as always, I am in your debt for it."

Anita smiled. "And as always, you can buy me a nice lunch to repay your debt, and let me tell you about a new book we've got coming out next fall that I just know you'll want to buy several thousand copies of. . . ."

* * *

Jen stared at her empty coffee cup. An hour and twenty minutes had passed, and still no phone call. This wasn't just confusing—it was totally weird.

Was he angry at her? She shook her head. How could he be angry at her? All she'd done was tell him the truth—that he was behaving like an idiot.

Jen cringed slightly. Maybe she had been a little over the top—but then again, so had he. She'd been so humiliated when he shouted at her like that. It was like he'd turned into someone completely different.

Maybe he *was* someone different, she mused. Maybe she just didn't know him that well after all.

No, impossible. She was going to call him and have it out with him. There had to be some explanation. Had to be a really good reason for his outburst.

Jen sighed. She couldn't call him. He was the one who should be calling her. If she picked up the phone, it would be like she was apologizing. And she had absolutely no intention of doing that, particularly when he couldn't even be bothered to call her.

Glumly, Jen checked her phone again to see if the signal was working. It was. *Fine,* she thought to herself irritably. *Absolutely fine. If that's how he wants to play it, I'll just go back to Bell. Do something useful with my time.*

She started stomping down Piccadilly toward Bell Towers, muttering under her breath as she walked. *Bloody men,* she fumed crossly. *They're all the same. You think they're nice, and then they turn out to be like the rest. Selfish, that's what they are. Totally and completely sel . . .*

Suddenly Jen stopped. She was right outside the

Wolseley, one of her favorite restaurants, and someone who looked just like Daniel was sitting at a table with an amazing-looking blonde.

She frowned. It couldn't be him. Could it?

Hoping that the doorman wouldn't think her too strange, she edged closer to take a proper look. It was him. She opened her mouth in shock—for more than an hour, she'd been nursing a coffee, waiting for him to call, and all the time he was out having lunch? It was unbelievable. Unbearable.

She edged backward so that he couldn't see her at the door, and watched in horror as the two of them talked. The woman had her hand on his, and they looked . . . intimate. Suddenly Jen felt sick. She wanted to walk away, but couldn't. Instead, she was forced to watch the woman smiling indulgently at Daniel, and then watch Daniel reach over and kiss her right on the mouth.

Shocked, Jen reeled back. So that was why he'd been so agitated, why he'd been so keen to get rid of her. He was seeing someone else. For how long, she wondered bitterly. And just when had he been planning to tell her?

As Daniel sat back on his chair, his face one big smile, Jen turned abruptly and started to run. She needed to get away, as far away as she could.

When will I learn, she asked herself, big fat tears wending their way down her cheeks as she ran. *When will I realize that life is not about happy endings? It's horrible and cruel and people are bastards and everyone lies about everything, even the people you love . . .*

After a few minutes, she slowed down a bit, her breathing heavy and her throat sore from crying. She was close to Bell Consulting now, but somehow she didn't want to go in. She looked dreadful for one thing, but more important, she didn't feel like it. She wanted to climb into a big bed and pull the duvet over her head until the pain went away. You couldn't depend on anyone, she thought miserably. As soon as you trust someone, they let you down and trod on your heart. Well, she wouldn't trust anyone again. That was the only way to go.

So what if I've got lectures, she thought to herself. *Doesn't mean I've got to go. Why should I? I hate Bell Consulting. I hate them all.*

Sticking her hand up, she flagged down a cab, got into the back, and just managed to give the driver her address before crumpling into a heap on the backseat.

When she got home, Jen made herself a coffee and decided to drink it in the garden. She stepped outside, shivered slightly, and wrapped her cardigan around herself tightly.

Her little garden was icy cold, and yet in spite of the cold weather, it was defiantly acting as though it were spring—little buds appearing, everything becoming greener after the bleak, bare winter months. Jen looked around wistfully. It looked so full of expectation, so optimistic, and whereas usually this would be enough to cheer her up, right now it just reinforced her own gloom. The fact of the matter was that she didn't want to be optimistic. That was what had got her into trouble in the first place.

As she sat down, she heard her doorbell ring, and her heart leaped. Was it Daniel? Was he going to be here with some really good explanation for that kiss? Was he going to apologize and make things okay again?

Quickly, she ran to the door and opened it. But she

was soon filled with a mixture of despair and relief when she saw that it wasn't him.

"Gavin," she said with a sigh. "What are you doing here?"

"All right, gorgeous," Gavin said affably, giving her a quick kiss. "I got some crazy voicemail messages from someone who sounded just like you. Ring any bells?"

Jen frowned. "You'd better come in."

She made them both tea and they sat down at the kitchen table.

"Thanks, Jen. So look, do you mind telling me what the hell those messages were all about?"

Jen rolled her eyes. Her anger at Gavin seemed a lifetime ago and she could barely muster the energy to explain now.

"It was about the letter," she said miserably, stirring a spoonful of sugar into her tea.

"What letter?"

"You told the *Times* about the letter I showed you, that's what my problem is. Not that it matters anymore." Her voice was deadpan, unenthusiastic.

Gavin looked at her, confusion on his face. "What?"

"The letter, Gavin," Jen said impatiently. "It was in the *Times* over Christmas. Look, it's fine, I'm over it, I just . . . well, I thought I could trust you and evidently I was wrong. . . ."

He put down his tea. "Jen, I have no idea what you're talking about. I've been in Scotland. Haven't talked to a single journalist."

Jen sighed. "Look, I don't know why you're lying, because it doesn't matter anymore."

"It does matter because I'm not fucking lying!" His voice had gone up several octaves and Jen frowned.

"Really? It really wasn't you? But who else could it have been?"

"I've got no idea. Jesus, I'm not coming to stay with you again if this is what I get. How many times do I have to tell you it wasn't me? Must have been one of your other boyfriends. . . ." He looked at her as he spoke, watching for a reaction.

"I don't have a boyfriend, actually," she said sadly, testing out the words and realizing too late that she wasn't over the whole crying thing.

Gavin jumped up and put his arms round her. "Come on, sweetheart, come on, it's okay. I'm here now. . . ."

Jen allowed herself to relax into his embrace for a few seconds. All she'd wanted earlier was a hug, a kind word, and instead, Daniel had shouted at her. Gavin wasn't exactly who she wanted comforting her, but he'd do.

"It's not okay," she said balefully. "Nothing's okay. I fought with Daniel, and Dad . . . well, I thought I could trust him, and, *ohheeuugghh*."

She sobbed on Gavin's shoulder and he stroked her hair gently. "Don't worry about them," he said soothingly. "That Daniel bloke was never right for you anyway."

"I was falling in love with him." Jen sobbed, suddenly unable to hold in anything anymore. It felt good letting her tears flow.

"No, you weren't. You just thought you were. Everything will be fine, you just wait and see."

Jen allowed herself a few more sobs, then pulled herself away. "You seriously didn't tell anyone about the letter?" she asked, sniffing loudly.

"I swear."

"Then who did?" Her question was rhetorical, but Gavin didn't seem to notice.

"That idiot you were going out with? Or what about your mum?"

Jen shook her head. "I didn't tell either of them about it."

Gavin looked pleased when he heard that. "Good thinking. Just tell people you can trust."

Jen raised her eyebrow at him.

"Look, Jen," he said seriously, taking her hand. "Let's forget all the bullshit, shall we? We're good together, you and me. If that other jerk's off the scene and you've finished playing private detective, we can go back to how we were, right?"

Jen looked at him slightly less warmly than before. "Playing private detective?"

"Oh, you know, this whole corporate thing, playing around, spying on Daddy. I didn't want to say anything, but it was a bit sad, wasn't it?"

"Spying on Daddy? Is that what you think I was doing?"

Gavin looked confused. "That was what you were doing, wasn't it?"

Jen shook her head. "You know, for a moment there, you almost had me," she said with a sad smile.

"Almost?" Gavin said hopefully.

"Bye-bye, Gavin. Time to go now, I think."

Gavin took her hand. "Look, I didn't mean it about the private detective," he said seriously. "Come on, Jen. You and me—we made a good team, didn't we? We had a good time. I miss it."

Jen looked at his hand and shrugged. "We did make a good team," she agreed. "But not anymore."

"You're just saying that because of that bloke, aren't you?" Gavin persisted. "Look, he's out of the picture now. You were in love with me too, remember?"

Jen frowned. She supposed he had a point. But somehow she couldn't remember being in love with Gavin. Couldn't remember feeling this desperate at the thought of losing him.

"Gavin, don't," she said softly.

He looked at her intently, then took his hand away and smiled lightly at her. "No chance of a good-bye shag, then?" he asked jovially.

Jen raised her eyebrows at him.

"Well, call me if you change your mind."

He gave her a good-natured wave as he left her building, and she watched as he disappeared around the corner. If he was telling the truth about the letter, then who had leaked it, she wondered. And more to the point, who on earth could she trust now?

A few minutes later, Jen was stripping off for a bath. She filled the tub, lit candles, and put on a Groove Armada CD, then slipped into the welcoming water and felt her body relax.

She shut her eyes and tried out a relaxation technique Angel had taught her—you imagine yourself in your favorite place, letting all your senses explore it, and you convince your mind that you're actually really there. Angel called it the thirty-minute holiday.

Jen imagined herself on a beach somewhere, feeling soft, warm sand between her toes. Walking into the bluest sea and feeling the sun warm her bones. Then she was building sandcastles, putting the sand in her bucket meticulously and turning it upright, carefully removing it so as not to disturb her masterpiece. She would have a moat, four turrets, some servants' quarters. As she built, the sea began to come in, so she started to up her pace— but it was coming in too quickly, ravaging her castle and tearing down one side of it. Frantically she tried to build more, but the sand had become waterlogged and wouldn't hold its shape. Her parents were both shouting advice to her, but she couldn't hear them properly because they were both talking at once, and when they saw that it was ruined, they both walked away.

Jerkily Jen sat upright. A loud ringing noise had woken her up. Quickly she jumped out of the tub and pulled a warm terry-cloth robe over her. Slipping her feet into sheepskin slippers, she made her way to the kitchen where her mobile phone was vibrating furiously and the name MUM was flashing on the screen.

Jen's heart sank. She'd been building up to a conversation with her mother, had planned it meticulously, and put it off effectively for days. Now the mountain had come to Mohammed and she'd forgotten everything she wanted to say.

"Mum?" she said, wishing she'd stayed in the bath.

"Oh, so you still remember who I am, then?"

"Yes, Mum," Jen said with a sigh, wondering guiltily whether amnesia might not be rather an attractive option right now.

"I'm really sorry."

"Jen, I wanted to say I'm sorry."

"Jen, look, about this afternoon. I overreacted and I wanted to apologize . . . ," Daniel muttered to himself as he came out of the tube and started to walk the twenty-minute journey to Jen's flat, trying to work out the best opening line. He'd thought about phoning, but it seemed so impersonal and anyway, you couldn't make up on the phone; everyone knew that. Firstly it was fraught with difficulties—not seeing someone's face made it very difficult to judge whether you could start cracking jokes yet; and secondly the best you could hope for at the end was the promise of a future meeting, whereas when you made up in person you could really . . . consolidate things.

Easy, Daniel, don't walk before you can run, he warned himself as he began to get carried away with images of him and Jen consolidating their relationship again and again. First he had to convince her that he wasn't a total asshole.

"Ow!"

He yelped as someone walked into him. *Bloody people not looking where they're going,* he thought, looking up to see a face he almost thought he recognized, but rejected the thought immediately because he didn't know anyone who looked like he'd been sleeping rough for several weeks.

"You want to keep your eyes open," the face said, to Daniel's indignation.

"Me?" he said incredulously. "You're the one walking into people."

The face looked at him curiously. "You're Jen's ex, aren't you?"

Daniel frowned. Of course. It was the ex-boyfriend. The tramp. "Think you're a bit confused there," he said quickly, deciding that he really didn't want to engage in conversation with this guy. "You're the ex. I'm Jen's current boyfriend."

"Not the way she describes it."

"You've seen her?" Daniel kicked himself as he spoke. He didn't want to know if this tramp had seen Jen. Didn't want to encourage him.

The tramp looked at him, a little mocking smile playing on his lips. "Look, mate," he said as if letting Daniel into a big secret, "the thing is, me and Jen . . . well, there's more to it than just, well, me being her ex-boyfriend. We're still close. And as far as she's concerned, she doesn't want to see you again."

Daniel's eyes narrowed. "Well, in that case, she can tell me to my face," he said firmly.

The tramp grinned. "You've got more balls than me, I tell you. Don't think I'd fancy going to her flat just to be told to go to hell, but I suppose it takes all sorts. The thing is, mate, you missed the bus, so to speak. And I've . . . well, hopped back on, if you catch my drift."

Daniel stared at him. Jen was going out with someone who referred to her as a bus? Anyway, it was impossible. He'd seen her a couple of hours ago and she hadn't said anything about this joker.

"Still, I'll just be on my way," he said and the tramp shrugged.

"Fine with me. I'll see you in a bit, then."

"What?" Daniel asked sharply.

"I'm just popping out for some wine, so I'll be with you in a few minutes. You'll probably need a drink, come to think of it."

"You're going back round to Jen's?"

The tramp nodded. "We're celebrating the fact that we're getting back together," he said firmly. "Actually, mate, you did me a bit of a favor arguing with her like that. Made her see sense about me and her. I appreciate that."

Daniel suddenly felt a bit sick. What had he done? Jen was back with this . . . this idiot, and he couldn't even blame her. Who'd want to go out with someone who flew off the handle when you popped in to see them at work?

"It seems my timing is rather off," he said quietly.

"Like I said," the tramp said with a shrug. "You've missed the bus, mate."

Slowly, Daniel turned around and walked away, the bouquet of flowers he'd bought hanging limply at his side.

Gavin watched him walk away, then turned back round. He was doing Jen a favor, he told himself. Sometimes you needed to protect your friends—from other people, but also from themselves.

"Well, I have to say that I've rather been expecting you to call and apologize. But seeing that you haven't, I thought I better call you instead."

"You don't think that you owe me an apology?" Jen asked, managing to keep her voice steady. "For lying to me?"

"I explained all that," Harriet said irritably. "I was protecting you, that's all. That's what mothers do, you know."

"I didn't want protection, I wanted the truth."

Harriet sighed. "You didn't know what you wanted, and I'm not sure you do now, either. So anyway, I just wanted to tell you that your little leak to the press got your father very rattled. Very rattled indeed. Which makes me think he must be vulnerable. Maybe he's worried you know more than—"

"How do you know?"

"Know what, darling?"

"That he's rattled. And about the letter, which I never even mentioned to you? How did he find out about it, and how do you know that Dad's rattled?"

Harriet sighed. "Oh, that. You always were a detail person, weren't you? Well, I assumed it was you because I couldn't think who else it would be. And when I mentioned the article to your father, he confirmed that it had to be you that leaked it. Really, darling, to think I was worried you had fallen for his charm. I was rather proud, you know—"

"You told him?" Jen interrupted. "When?"

"I wish you'd stop butting in like that, darling. I went to see him in the hospital. A major sacrifice, incidentally, because you know how much I hate those places, but I have to say it was worth it. His face . . . well, it was a picture . . ."

Jen felt herself getting indignant, hot angry words welling up in the back of her throat. But instead of letting them erupt as she usually would, she forced them down, tried to ignore them. She'd had enough of arguing. She needed to tame her temper. And anyway, what did it matter if Harriet had spilled the beans? He would have found out at some point, and since it looked like he was the corrupt bastard her mother had made him out to be after all, it was probably a good thing that she had.

"Great," she said unenthusiastically.

"So?" her mother asked expectantly.

"So?"

"So what else have you found out? There was a news

report earlier this afternoon, and the police in Indonesia have drawn a blank—they can't find any evidence of any corruption, which is hardly surprising because no one's exactly going to admit to taking a bribe, are they? The thing is, Jen, if we don't get to the truth, no one will."

Jen thought for a moment. If she told her mother everything, it would make things much easier. Harriet would know what to do with the spreadsheet. She would know what to do, full stop.

So what was stopping her?

"Well, there are a couple of things," she said eventually. "But I need you to promise you won't tell Paul."

"Paul? What do you mean, darling?"

"I mean, promise me you won't tell him what I tell you."

Harriet sighed. "So it *is* true. Paul warned me about this."

"Warned you about what?" Jen asked immediately, her hackles rising.

"I know you've never liked Paul, but I will not have you demonize him," Harriet said angrily. "This is nothing to do with Paul. He's about the only person I can trust nowadays now you've got so cozy with the enemy."

"You can trust me!" Jen said indignantly. "You barely know Paul, and when you hear what I've got to say—"

"I won't, Jennifer. I won't hear it, do you understand? He wondered if you were the right person for this job, and I should have listened to him."

Jen frowned. "You discussed me working at Bell Consulting with Paul?"

"Of course, darling. We tell each other everything."

"I doubt that very much," Jen said sarcastically, thinking of the phone call at her father's house.

"Jen, until you can be civil, I really don't think we have anything to talk to each other about."

"Fine," Jen said hotly. "I couldn't agree more."

Angrily she hung up the phone and slumped down on a chair. This had to go down as the worst day of her life, she decided. And she had a horrible feeling that things weren't about to get much better, either.

❧ 26

Angel's skin was glowing and her eyes were shining.

"I thought you said you were hungover," Jen said as she joined her for brunch, peering at her friend closely for signs of bloodshot eyes or gray skin.

"I am," said Angel, looking for all the world as if she had just returned from a relaxing week at a spa. "I look dreadful."

Jen raised her eyebrows and picked up the menu.

"Although to be honest, Jen, so do you. What's up?"

Jen put the menu down. "How is it," she asked, "that your life can change so dramatically, and so much for the worse, in the space of about two days? I just don't get it."

Angel frowned. "Your life is worse? How? It isn't your father, is it?"

Jen looked at the table in front of her. Angel would never say "I told you so"; would never tell her that had Jen listened to her, and protected herself a little more, instead of jumping straight in and allowing herself to get carried away by the idea of having a father again, she wouldn't be in this pickle now. But it would still hang in the air.

"You were right," Jen said simply. "He isn't what I

thought he was. Or rather, he is what I thought he was, before I convinced myself that he wasn't."

Angel wrinkled her nose in confusion. "Would you like to explain that?"

Jen sighed. There was so much to explain. About her father and the spreadsheets; about her mother and Paul Song; about Gavin; about Daniel and that woman . . . As she reviewed the list, she felt the familiar prick of tears, but blinked them back. This was not the time to feel sorry for herself. This was the time to do something about it.

She started talking, and watched as Angel's eyes widened in amazement. Every so often she would exclaim "no!" or "he didn't!" or "you didn't!" and Jen would nod sagely and confirm that yes, it did happen and he or she did do that.

Eventually, she finished and sat back. Angel was silent for a few seconds as if processing all the information. Then she looked up at her friend.

"And what are you going to do about it? Who are you going to tell? And why haven't you gone to box that Daniel's ears yet?"

Jen found herself smiling slightly at the image of herself pitching up at Daniel's office and threatening to punch him.

"To be honest, I don't know," she admitted. "I tried telling Mum, but as soon as I mentioned Paul Song she got really defensive."

"Do you really think he's involved?"

Jen shrugged. "I really hope not, for Mum's sake, but it doesn't look good, does it? I mean, why would he be calling my father at home? And that stupid wooden block that he said was from China, and that was actually from Indonesia . . . it just seems too much of a coincidence."

"Do you know what the payments were for yet?"

Jen shook her head. "No, but come on. Money going into numbered accounts and Axiom's name dotted around . . . I've looked at that spreadsheet a thousand times and I can't come up with any explanation other than bribery."

"So then you should go to the police."

"I know."

"But?"

Angel's eyes were boring into Jen's and she shifted uncomfortably. "I will," Jen said evasively. "I just . . . don't know what I'd tell them yet."

"Have you spoken to your father?"

Jen shook her head.

"Don't you think maybe you should?"

Jen shrugged. "Maybe. I just haven't had the energy really. And I'm still so angry with him."

"That's a good thing. Talk to him while you still have fire in your belly. Come on, Jen. You have to do this."

Jen sighed. Angel was right. She'd been procrastinating for days now, somehow unable to muster the energy to actually do anything. All she wanted to do was hide, pretend that none of this had happened, convince herself that it wasn't her responsibility. It was so unlike her—usually she rushed straight into things without thinking twice—and she was letting it get the better of her.

"I guess you don't want to lose your father again," Angel continued thoughtfully. "But if what you say is true, then I think probably you've already lost him."

"And Mum. And Daniel," Jen said dolefully. "But

look, I've had enough of my problems for the time being. What about you? How's the wedding going?"

Angel's face brightened visibly. "It's the most ridiculous ceremony," she said, rolling her eyes. "Everyone is spending far too much money, the outfits are crazy, and both sets of parents are so wound up they're about to snap. Tell me, how easy do you think it would be to get an elephant to a wedding in London. Pretty hard, no? We're going to have two . . ."

As she talked, Jen found herself listening enviously to Angel's tales of her large, extended family. Everyone knew everyone else's business; everyone was expected to pull together. And even though Angel complained, Jen could see that she didn't mind really. *How reassuring,* she thought to herself, *to be part of something so solid. How nice to know that whatever happened, you had a tribe of family around you to support you, nag at you, and tell you where you were going wrong.* If she was right in her suspicions, she'd probably never speak to her father again and her mother would lose Paul Song and might never forgive Jen for it.

". . . and so I had to climb down the drainpipe. It was so exciting—like being a teenager again."

Jen frowned. Had she just missed something interesting? "You climbed down the drainpipe?" she asked.

"Yes! Well, I could hardly have my family knowing that I was going out on a date with the man they want me to marry!"

"You were going on a date with the man they want you to marry, and you wanted to keep it a secret? I'm confused."

Angel rolled her eyes. "Jen, keep up, will you? He's a very gorgeous man, and I like him. The last thing I want is for my parents to get the idea that they can set me up in an arranged marriage with him."

Jen frowned, then shook her head. "And you think that *I* like to make things complicated," she said with a little smile.

The following morning, Jen found herself back in Bill's small office, sitting upright, ready to go. She had a plan, which she'd developed the night before after her brunch with Angel, and now she was ready to kick things off.

Number One: Leave Bell. She didn't want anything to do with Bell Consulting anymore, and didn't want an MBA if it meant turning out like Daniel.

Number Two: Tell her father exactly what she thought of him, and make it clear that she would be telling everyone else, too, including the police.

Number Three: Tell her mother about Paul Song, in no uncertain terms. Harriet would simply have to listen, whether she liked it or not.

Number Four: Have it out with Daniel. Let him know that she saw him in that restaurant, that she knew what he'd been up to, and that she wasn't going to stand for it.

Of course, Number Four was the bit she was most dreading, the one she hoped that she wouldn't get to any time soon. It was one thing shouting at her father, but it was quite another thing to confront the man she loved. Or thought she loved. Particularly since he didn't appear to love her back. Still, she'd cross that bridge when she came to it. Right now, she was focusing on Number One.

"So, how's Jennifer today?" Bill asked with a big smile. "And how are your studies going?"

Jen looked Bill in straight in the eye. "Actually I haven't really been here much for the past couple of days. I'm . . . I'm thinking about quitting the course."

The smile disappeared off Bill's face and was replaced by a look of concern.

"Quit the course? But you're doing so well! Is it the assignments that are freaking you out, because you really don't have to worry. I can help you through the research . . . it's a piece of cake, really."

Jen smiled. "Thanks, Bill, but it's not the work. It's . . . well, it's just that I don't think I really want anything to do with the business community or Bell Consulting."

Bill looked worried and stroked his beard. "I see. That's quite a strong position you have there. Any reason you'd like to share?"

"As far as I can see, all businesses do is try to extort money out of people, and I don't want anything to do with it. And as for Bell . . . well, let's just say I don't want to be a consultant either."

Bill nodded. "Sure," he said. "Business is a terrible thing. All those people working hard and providing goods and services that people need. Dreadful, I agree."

Jen frowned as she realized Bill was making fun of her. "They may make goods and provide services, but they're only doing it because it makes them money," she said firmly.

Bill frowned.

"Sounds like a pretty naïve view of business if you ask me," he said seriously.

Jen arched an eyebrow at him. "Naïve?" she asked indignantly. "I hardly think so." She'd been thinking that she was becoming too cynical if anything.

Bill stroked his beard. "Okay, then let me ask you something. Let's take a drug company. What do they do?"

Jen sat up straight. "Easy. They develop drugs which they then sell at a huge profit and convince governments to stop other companies producing these drugs cheaper, even if they could save lives all around the world. They're hideous companies. Really awful."

Bill smiled. "Okay, so you think that once they've developed a drug they should give it out for free?"

"They should sell it at the price it costs to make it. Not charge people an arm and a leg."

"But wouldn't the price include the research and development costs, which can mean years of scientists conducting expensive experiments?"

"Yes, but . . ."

"But?"

"But they still make huge profits."

"Which makes people pleased to invest in them, which means they have more money for research."

"They're only interested in drugs that can make money for them," Jen said sullenly.

"And if they didn't make a profit, do you think there would be the same level of investment?"

Jen frowned. "I guess not . . ." she started, then stopped.

"Business itself isn't bad," Bill said gently. "You need rules, codes of conduct. But making money isn't in itself a bad thing. Motivates some people more than others of course. . . ."

"What about corruption?" Jen demanded. "Businesses are rife with it."

"Not as rife as a lot of governments."

Jen sat still for a few seconds. What would he say if

she told him about the spreadsheet she'd found on her father's computer, she wondered. Would he think corruption wasn't rife then?

"Jen, don't quit. Not now. If you feel strongly about these things, do something about it—don't just walk away. You always struck me as more of a fighter. . . ."

Jen stared at him. "But . . . ," she said, leaving the word hanging in midair.

"*But* is a great word if you want to divorce yourself from a situation. Is that what you want to do?"

Jen nodded, then shook her head. That was the last thing she wanted to do. But stay at Bell? That would be impossible. Wouldn't it? She frowned, and noticed Bill looking at her, hopefully.

"So you'll keep at it?" he asked, as Jen wrestled internally. Maybe he was right. Maybe walking away was the cowardly option.

"I don't know," she said slowly, wondering where this left her action plan. "But I'll definitely think about it."

"Okay, but while you're thinking, you probably want to crack on with your research. And don't you have an assignment due in?"

Jen smiled slightly. "I still hate business," she said defiantly.

"Glad to hear it. See you next time?"

Jen nodded against her better judgment. If the second item on her list went as planned, she'd probably be kicked out anyway.

"So you see, Mrs. Keller, our position is very difficult. In these circumstances we are forced to request additional collateral or suggest that the firm seek alternative financing arrangements . . ."

"Ms. Keller."

"I'm sorry?" The young man in the suit shifted awkwardly in his chair. He hated these conversations. Didn't see why his boss at the bank couldn't have made this meeting. All right for him, crying off at the last minute, blaming a more important meeting elsewhere. He was probably drinking coffee in a Starbucks somewhere feeling all pleased with himself for dumping this on someone else.

"It's *Ms.* Keller. You called me Mrs. Keller."

"Right. Right. Sorry about that." *You'd have thought she had more important things to worry about,* he thought, wondering to himself how much longer he'd have to be here.

"So, what sort of additional collateral are we talking about here?"

"Oh, you know, property. Other valuables—the odd Grand Master tucked away, that sort of thing." He looked at Harriet and mentally kicked himself. Bad time to be having a laugh, making little quips. No, keep it serious. Like an undertaker.

"My house, I believe is . . ."

"Already mortgaged, yes."

"And our revenues aren't . . ."

"Not enough to guarantee future repayments, Ms. Keller, no. That's the problem we've got here. You see, banks aren't like venture capitalists: They don't benefit from your success. We just get our regular payments with interest. If you do twice as well as you expected, we get the same amount. We don't like taking risks, that's the thing. So unless you can find some alternative financing arrangement . . ."

"You mean I have to sell my business?"

The young man shifted uneasily. "Like I say, you've got a few days to decide what to do. You can sell up, or you can find someone to invest some money, or . . ." he trailed off. *Or you can file for bankruptcy* wasn't something that just tripped off the tongue. "Only, if the decision is to pull," he continued, deciding that there was no need to actually spell it out for Ms. Keller, "that won't give you much time, so you'd be better off, you know, working out your options."

Harriet glowered at him and he shrank back slightly. "Please go now," she said softly, and he grabbed his papers and crammed them in his briefcase, not caring that it wouldn't shut properly, and then bolted for the door.

Five minutes later, Harriet left her office and ran into the café across the road. As she came out, she wrapped her coat around her and clutched her free-trade organic coffee. She hadn't been out of the Green Futures building during daylight in days, she realized—not even to buy a sandwich—and it was rather nice to have a cool breeze on her face.

She looked up at her building and sighed. She didn't feel like going back in, not just yet. She was too tired, too battle-weary. She felt like she had been singlehandedly fighting a war—and she didn't know if she wanted to do it anymore.

She turned round and walked down the road until she found a bench. How long had it been since she had just sat and watched people walk by? Far too long. Years, probably. There was always something pressing to do, always someone to talk to.

She sat down and took a sip of her coffee, which was deliciously creamy.

Then she frowned. There wasn't always someone to talk to, actually, not when she thought about it. At work there was—people always wanted her time, her opinion, her vote of confidence. But increasingly she was finding that outside work she didn't have many people to talk to at all. Jen was so difficult these days, so prickly all the time, and Paul kept disappearing off to talk to clients or whatever it was he did when he wasn't with her.

It was all George's fault, she thought to herself bitterly. She should never have married him; should never have allowed him to convince her to fall in love with him.

She closed her eyes and remembered with a shudder what it had been like being married to George. Never knowing when he would be jetting off on one of his business trips without even telling her. Never being taken seriously. And Jen, so in love with him. So convinced that he was wonderful. It had been too much to bear.

Could anyone blame her for having an affair, for succumbing to the first person who gave her any attention? Harriet sighed. Of course they could blame her. She blamed herself. Had blamed herself ever since. That bastard Malcolm had used her. And when she'd found out what he was up to, George wouldn't even listen to her. *He chose Malcolm over me,* she thought bitterly. *He chose business and profit over love and ethics.* And he was still doing it now.

Well, she wouldn't allow it, Harriet resolved. George would get his comeuppance if it was the last thing she did. And as his and Malcolm's profit-obsessed businesses crumbled into the ground, Green Futures would be on the ascendancy once more. She was going to fight back. Somehow or other she was going to save her firm. There had to be some money somewhere; someone who'd give her a loan, tide her over for a little while.

She gulped down her coffee and looked at her watch. Time to go back to the office.

But as she was about to stand up, someone sat down next to her. She turned round and her eyes widened.

"Malcolm. What . . . what are you doing here?"

Malcolm Bray smiled. "Good to see you Harriet. I wonder, do you have a few minutes?"

"Can I help you with anything?"

Jen looked at the sales assistant vaguely and shook her head. She'd taken advantage of a free hour in her timetable to come to Books Etc. to have a look around, partly because it looked like she might have to finish her assignment now, and partly because she wanted to do something to irritate Daniel, even if he didn't know about it. Frankly, she never wanted to go into another Wyman's again. And when she'd written her assignment, she would send it to another bookseller, just to spite him. Someone had to implement the ideas they'd talked about, and if it wasn't going to be him, he deserved his competitors getting one over on him.

She wandered around aimlessly for a while, trying to think up good reasons why self-improvement books should be on the left-hand side of the store and cookery books on the right, but after a while she gave up. Perhaps it had been a little ambitious, she acknowledged, to think that she could focus on her stupid assignment when so much else was at stake. She'd planned and rejected a million times what she was going to say to her father. And every time she even thought about it, her heart started pounding madly in her chest. She looked at her watch. It was eleven A.M., which meant that she had three hours until the meeting. At eleven-thirty she had a lecture, which would hopefully keep her occupied until twelve-thirty P.M., and then she'd have to wait an hour and a half, her stomach in her mouth.

Jen noticed the sales assistant looking at her oddly, and decided that it was probably time to leave. She could grab a coffee on her way and take a leisurely stroll back to Bell Towers. But as she turned to go, a book caught her eye. Or, rather, not a book but a book jacket. On it was a photograph of a man she recognized, a man whom, she realized after frowning in concentration for a couple of seconds, she'd seen with Paul Song at the charity dinner all those months ago.

Quickly she walked over to what turned out to be the biography section, and picked up the book with interest. And then she started. The book she was holding was the biography of a successful entrepreneur. And his name was Malcolm Bray.

𝒮 27

Jen made her way to her usual seat in the lecture hall, next to Lara and Alan who were talking quietly to each other.

"How's it going?" Lara asked with a grin and Jen smiled, relieved that she'd managed to stop herself from calling Lara the minute she'd decided to quit the MBA. She was gradually learning about restraint and not rushing into things, and now she didn't have to explain why she was back at lectures, she thought, feeling very pleased with herself.

At that moment, Jay walked in and everyone gradually hushed.

"So," he said dramatically. "I'm sorry to tell you that today, you get me. This section of the course is entitled 'Conclusions,' and this is the last series of lectures on strategic analysis. Next term you'll be focusing on your electives and writing your dissertations. But right now I want you to ask yourselves: What conclusions can we draw from a strategic analysis? What conclusions have you drawn from the course? And what conclusions have you drawn about yourselves?" Jay looked around the room and silence descended.

"Guys, guys, don't shout out all at once," he said playfully. "Okay, so no one wants to share their conclusions. So let's think about this for a moment, shall we? The thing about conclusions is that they are difficult to formulate and they're also very changeable. Let me explain. You've done some analysis on a company—someone give me a company . . ."

"Durex," shouted out someone. "Mates," shouted out someone else. Jay shrugged.

"Well, I walked into that one, didn't I? Okay, so we'll take your precious condom company. So you've done your analysis, you think you understand its strengths and weaknesses, you've identified its opportunities and threats. You develop some strategic options, and then you come to your conclusions—or perhaps you might call it your recommendations. Either way, at this point you are basically putting yourself on the line. You're saying 'go this way' or 'go that way' or 'stand still' or 'stand on your head'—whatever it is, it's the right thing to do in your opinion based on your analysis. And you might be right. You might have the perfect answer. But then what happens—the day after you've finalized your presentation, made it all pretty, given it to the managing director with a nice plastic cover, someone finds a cure for AIDS. Or someone invents a new barrier device that threatens to destroy the condom market. A competitor goes out of business. The managing director is fired for an impropriety and the new guy wants a whole new approach. Things happen. All the time. And the moment you have your conclusions ready, they're out of date.

"So what does this mean—that there's no point coming to any conclusions? No point doing anything because everything's going to change anyway? No. Not at all. Managing directors aren't fired most days. People don't find cures to terrible diseases most days. Mostly, you pick your course, you pick your lane, and you just do the best you can. But what you cannot afford to do is to think that your conclusions will necessarily still be valid next week, next month, or next year. People change, businesses change, environments change, customers change. You have to keep picking up your analysis and looking over it again—have you missed anything? Does it all still ring true? If not, do you need to tweak your strategy?

"But, okay, that caveat understood, what are we looking for in our conclusions?"

Jay looked around the room and Alan put up his hand. "An action plan?" he suggested.

"Great," said Jay. "But not always. Action plans might come later. What else?"

"Recommendations," shouted a guy at the back.

"Exactly," said Jay triumphantly. "I gave you a bit of a clue earlier, didn't I? So, recommendations. What you're saying is 'this is the way things are, and I recommend that in order to build your brand, grow your profits, cheer your shareholders up, you buy company x or move into market y.' No one wants a report that says 'yeah, things are okay, and you've got a few options and they all look pretty good to me.' No one will pay you for that. They want your advice. Sure, you put in as many caveats as you can—you'd be a fool to say 'buy company x' without listing all the assumptions you've made and the requirements of such a move. But don't just sit on the fence. Too many consultants sit on the fence and it gives the profession a bad name. At Bell we want people who say what they mean, who aren't afraid to pick a side. Okay?"

Jen sat back and frowned. She certainly wasn't afraid to pick a side. She just seemed to pick the wrong one on a regular basis.

"And it isn't always going to be clear-cut, either," Jay was saying. "Maybe there will be two very different options on the table and both have strong advantages and a number of disadvantages. So how do you pick between them? Well, you weigh up. You assess the risks. You think about the people involved and consider which option they'll do the best—sometimes you may choose the more risky option because you think that it's best suited to the current top team. And every so often, when there's really nothing to help you make a decision, you just have to look deep down inside yourself and see what your gut says. It isn't particularly scientific, but gut feel is a powerful thing, not to be ignored."

Jen took a deep breath. Her gut feel couldn't be more clear. Now she just had to do what her gut was telling her to do.

At two P.M. on the dot, Jen arrived at her father's office.

"Jen," he said as she walked in, and the two of them eyed each other warily.

"Would you like to sit down?" he asked. Jen thought for a moment, trying to work out whether she'd feel more comfortable standing or sitting, and eventually took the seat her father offered her.

"Thank you for my laptop and phone. And sorry I couldn't be there in person—I had . . . well, things to take care of. I take it this is about the newspaper article," George continued, dismissively. "And I have to admit, I was disappointed."

Jen looked at him sullenly. "Cut the bullshit," she said,

and then regretted it when she realized that she wasn't Bruce Willis and that she sounded faintly ridiculous trying to sound all tough.

George raised an eyebrow.

"The newspaper leak wasn't me, although I wish it was. I'm here because I saw the spreadsheet," Jen said quickly. "The one with all the payments to Indonesia. You promised me you had nothing to do with it. . . ."

Her voice was beginning to catch with stress and emotion, and she forced herself to swallow.

"You looked at my personal files?" George asked, his voice cold.

"Yes. Not on purpose, but I still saw them. I was doing some research on the Web and used your computer, and there was this file that I thought I might have downloaded . . ." Jen paused. Why was she defending herself? She wasn't the one involved in a corruption ring.

"It doesn't matter how I found it," she said firmly. "What matters is that you are a liar and a cheat and . . . how could you do it? How could you help that bastard Malcolm Bray win those contracts?"

George looked at her for a moment, then looked away. "Jen, do you remember what I told you about trust? About how important it is to trust people?"

Jen nodded silently.

"Well, I think you should just trust me on this, don't you?"

Jen frowned. "Why should I? What have you done to win my trust? I know what I saw. . . ."

"You saw a spreadsheet, Jen, and you have no idea what it means. I think it would be best for everyone if you left well enough alone."

"That's it?" Jen asked indignantly. "You're not going to tell me what's going on? Apologize? You're just expecting me to walk away and keep my mouth shut?"

"That's exactly what I expect. Now, is there anything else?" His voice had a warning note to it, and Jen found herself getting angry.

She stared at her father, looked at his impenetrable blue eyes and searched for a flicker of something—guilt, perhaps—but there was nothing.

"No," she said eventually. "I think that covers it."

She walked out of his office, unsure whether to cross Number Two off her list. She had expected many things—an argument, threats, pleading—but not an evasive "you should trust me" platitude. And certainly to be told, in a patronizing tone, to keep out of his business.

Well, sod that. She wasn't going to keep quiet about this any more than her father was going to convince her that that money moving into Indonesia was anything other than bribes. She was going to crack on with her action plan. He'd regret dismissing her like that, she thought bitterly. George Bell was going to find out just what he was up against.

Quickly she took out her mobile phone and called her mother's number. Harriet had to listen to her this time—had to know the truth, not just about George, but also about Paul and his clandestine meeting with Malcolm Bray.

"Hello, Harriet's phone."

It was Hannah. "Hi, Hannah, it's Jen here. I need to talk to Mum."

"Yeah, no can do, I'm afraid. She's in a meeting and no one's allowed to disturb her."

"What kind of meeting? Who with?"

There was a pause. "Actually it's a bit weird, Jen. This guy turned up with her an hour ago and they've been in her office ever since. And Geoffrey says he recognizes him. Says he's called Malcolm Braid or something. Poor Geoffrey keeps hovering around the door hoping your mum'll invite him in to the meeting, but she's just ignoring him. . . ."

Jen took in a sharp intake of breath. "Are you sure? She's with Malcolm Bray?"

"Look, I dunno, do I? But that's what Geoffrey says. Do you want to speak to him?"

"No," Jen said vaguely, her mind racing. What possible reason could her mother have for meeting with Malcolm Bray? What was going on? "No. But is Paul there?"

"Paul Song? No, haven't seen him all day."

"Fine," Jen said decisively. "I'm going to come over."

"Suit yourself. Bye, Jen."

Jen shut off her phone and felt someone's eyes on her back. She turned round to see her father, who'd come out of his office and was frowning at her.

"What now?" she asked irritably.

"Jen, I'm sorry, I wanted to . . . did I just hear you mention Malcolm Bray?"

Jen looked at her father with disgust. "Yes, you did. He's in a meeting with Mum for some bizarre reason. I tell you, if she gets mixed up in anything because of you, I will never forgive you."

"We need to get over there," George said urgently.

"What do you mean 'we'?" Jen asked. "I think you've done enough."

"Jen, this is important. We'll take my car—if that's okay with you?"

Jen frowned. Her father looked more agitated than

she'd ever seen him before—but what was worrying him? Was he worried about Harriet, or, more likely, was he worried that Malcolm might be telling her more than he'd like? Either way, there was only one way to find out.

"Fine," she said haughtily. "But I think we'd better get a move on, don't you?"

❧ 28

Harriet looked out through the glass walls of her office. She used to get a kick out of the view out over the open plan, seeing her staff working, her dreams becoming a reality. But now all she saw was the beginning of the end. Malcolm had given her an hour to make a decision—the time it took him to go and buy himself a coffee and read the newspaper. Two mundane acts which had now been completed, and she was here deciding the future of her firm.

She picked up her accounts and stared at them desultorily. Green Futures owed . . . well, as far as she could make out, they owed more than they could hope to make in five years. Perhaps Dashed Hopes would be a more suitable name for the firm. Or even No Futures. How had she convinced herself that everything was fine? And where was Paul when she needed him most? He'd barely been here lately—probably deserting a sinking ship, and who could really blame him?

Harriet smiled ruefully. She felt suddenly older as she experienced the hindsight that one has when something is over. What had she wanted to do when she started out—save the world? No, that's what she'd told herself and everyone else, but in reality it was more basic than that. And far less noble. She'd wanted to prove a point. She'd wanted to show George just how wrong he was.

Harriet sighed. She had been so in love with George back then. He had been . . . dazzling. Exciting. And she'd loved working with him, even though he was the most pigheaded man. They'd disagreed constantly, of course, but she hadn't minded that; it meant they'd enjoyed big arguments, debates that would last for days, making her feel alive and part of something.

What she couldn't take was when George stopped arguing with her and ignored her instead. Not long after they were married, she found out about meetings that she hadn't been invited to. Then, when she came back from maternity leave, she found her number of clients dwindling. George had said it was because of Jen; Harriet was a mother now and she was needed at home. But Harriet hadn't wanted to be at home, stuck with a bunch of nappies and awful women who thought that just because she had a baby, she wanted to spend her time talking to them about the joys of breast-feeding. She couldn't bear being left on her own night after night while George went out entertaining clients, meeting his friends for drinks. She couldn't take his looking through her, the suspicion that he was no longer truly in love with her.

And then Malcolm Bray moved onto the scene.

Harriet turned and stared out of the window. Malcolm had been the opposite of George. They might have gone to school together, but that was the only thing they had in common. Where George was brash and loud, Malcolm was quiet and thoughtful. Where George was impulsive and decisive, Malcolm was methodical and took his time. And where George spoke his mind, Malcolm was secretive—not that Harriet had realized at the time, of course. It had taken Malcolm two years to seduce her, two years to play on her emotions, convincing her that George was having an affair himself; that if he truly loved her, he wouldn't leave her alone night after night.

Harriet shook her head at her stupidity. Two years to seduce her and two months to break her. Then he'd walked away, telling her he had no use for her anymore. He'd got what he wanted—he'd metaphorically screwed his old school friend, the one he'd been jealous of ever since George was made head boy and got into Cambridge in spite of breaking half the rules of the school and barely looking at his books, while Malcolm, the one who worked hard and did everything by the book, achieved neither.

"Harriet?" Malcolm said irritably. "Have you been listening to a word I've said?"

Jen and George walked silently down the stairs into the basement car park where his Jaguar was waiting for them.

They got in and George started the engine, negotiating his way around the car park and emerging into the bright sun of St. James.

"Paul Song," Jen asked flatly. "Why was he calling you?"

George put on the radio.

"I said, why was Paul Song calling you?"

"He called me, did he? That's interesting."

Jen rolled her eyes in irritation. "You say you want me to trust you, but I don't. And the reason I don't is because you lie, you keep secrets, and you don't even seem to be embarrassed about it." She stared ahead as she spoke, feeling stronger without her father's eyes boring into her.

"That's the point of trust," George said, his voice full of tension. "If I told you everything, you wouldn't need to trust me, would you? Trust involves taking a risk, suspending disbelief. Wouldn't you say?"

Jen turned to look at him. He was staring ahead, and a vein in his forehead was throbbing violently. "I don't know why you're coming," she said after a short pause. "Unless, of course, you're worried that Mum's getting close to the truth." She looked quickly at her father to check his reaction, but there was no sign of any emotion on his face.

"Right," he said eventually. "Well, here we are."

Jen nodded as they pulled up outside the building. "You can't park here," she pointed out. "You'll get towed away."

George looked at her. "Let's consider it expensive valet parking, shall we?"

He turned off the engine, and they both got out, George pulling out his mobile phone as they did so.

"Paul," Jen heard him say. "Yes, we're outside Green Futures right now. About to go in. You'll make the calls? Good, see you shortly."

Jen opened her mouth to ask a question, then thought better of it. She had an uneasy feeling that she was going to get her answers soon enough.

Harriet was trying to stay detached, to act professionally. This was a business deal, she kept telling herself. It was the only way.

But even as the words ran through her head, she felt

herself want to shout "No!" This wasn't how things were meant to turn out. She'd never be able to live with herself if she went ahead and signed her soul over to the devil—or, rather, to Malcolm Bray. But what choice did she have? It was do or die, and Harriet wasn't entirely sure which was preferable.

She looked at Malcolm and shivered slightly.

"You know what our brochure says?" she asked.

Malcolm shook his head.

"It says that Green Futures will only work with companies with the same goals and aims as ours. To build a better world. To work with stakeholders instead of against them. To be fair in our dealings, to be a positive force in the community . . ."

Malcolm nodded sagely. "And that's why we're so keen to work with you. To . . . support you."

There was the hint of a smile on his face, and Harriet wanted to throw something at him.

"I thought that the subtext to your mission statement was 'to get back at Bell Consulting' anyway," Malcolm continued. "Let's just file this little contract under that heading, shall we?"

Harriet stared at him coldly. The worst thing was, he was right. She had wanted to get back at Bell, to get back at George. But now she wasn't even sure about that anymore. She wasn't sure about anything. And she was running out of time.

"Look, Harriet, let's not worry too much about out-of-date strategies," Malcolm said amiably. "Let's just sign the contract. Axiom will pay off your debts, your firm will be saved, we'll tell the world that we've realized what an error it was to work with an unethical and ruthless company like Bell Consulting, and we'll have a nice press conference where you can tell all the papers about our rebuilding program." He motioned at the pen Harriet was holding.

"And you really think they'll believe you knew nothing about it?"

"They want someone to blame, and they'll have Bell Consulting. That'll keep the papers full for months."

"But . . . ," Harriet said, her hand trembling, "but what if *I* don't believe you . . ."

Suddenly Malcolm's jovial veneer evaporated. "Harriet, my dear, I would be very careful what you say from now on. This contract, this deal, is being offered on the basis that you fully accept our position. That Bell Consulting, without our knowledge, orchestrated a number of illegal and immoral deals last year on our behalf, but without our knowledge, following the tsunami tragedy. That they have subsequently been paying off officials in order to keep these deals a secret because they discovered that we weren't interested in any work that wasn't rightfully ours. That we are as angry and upset as everyone else, now that we know the truth. That we have turned to Green Futures because we cannot continue to work with an unscrupulous man like George Bell."

"And the buildings that fell down? The regulations that weren't followed?"

"A tragedy, for which people will lose their jobs. I think we can probably pin that on Bell, too, if we really put our minds to it."

Harriet closed her eyes briefly. What they were doing would destroy George. But he deserved it, surely? She'd have liked George and Malcolm to go down together, but surely one was better than none? She was doing the right thing, she told herself. If only she could get rid of the feeling of nausea.

"But how do you know the truth now?"

Malcolm smiled. "We have a source in Indonesia who will testify to the fact that Bell Consulting has been bribing him. Don't worry, Harriet, I've taken care of all the details."

"And . . . what if I don't sign? What if I don't believe you had nothing to do with it?"

Malcolm looked at Harriet coldly. "You wouldn't be so stupid," he sneered. "You wouldn't risk George Bell watching you go under, proving him right all along. And anyway, if you don't sign, you could just find yourself implicated in this whole business."

Harriet frowned. "Don't talk rubbish, Malcolm."

Malcolm smiled again. "You mean you don't know, Harriet?"

She shook her head and narrowed her eyes.

"I thought you would have realized," Malcolm said smoothly, "that one of your employees has been the conduit for the various bribes that have moved from the U.K. to Indonesia. Your friend Paul Song has, I believe, been very helpful to George, moving money around, introducing him to the right officials. Of course, now he's happy to testify on our behalf, but if you prefer, I'm sure he could point the finger at you . . ."

"Paul . . . ?" Harriet gasped.

Malcolm laughed. "Yes, Harriet, Paul. And this from the woman who thinks she's such a good judge of people!"

"You're lying," Harriet spat. "You are lying to me."

Malcolm shook his head. "Nice chap, I thought. Met him in Indonesia more than a year ago. Very helpful and *very* well connected. It was my idea that he come to you, actually. I rather liked the irony of our contact working for Harriet Keller."

He was chortling now, his face full of self-satisfaction, and Harriet was white.

"I don't believe you."

"You know, I don't really care if you do or not. Let's just get on with it, shall we?"

Harriet slumped back in her chair. Not Paul. Not her confidant. It was too much to take in at once. She had failed so spectacularly at running her business, and now it turned out that the only person she truly trusted was the person she should have despised.

If only she'd done things differently, she thought desperately. If only . . .

Slowly Harriet looked up and faced Malcolm. She was hemmed in; she was in checkmate. If she signed, she would save her firm, but she would lose everything else including the ability to sleep at night. If she didn't sign, the firm would be dissolved, she'd have nothing left. . . .

She sighed and steeled herself. George was right, she told herself. Business was about making money. By ignoring that little fact, she'd ended up here, doing the very thing she had gone into business to avoid.

"Well, then," she said eventually, her spirit broken. "Let's get on with it, shall we?"

"Which floor?" George asked as a bemused receptionist watched him and Jen approach the lifts.

"You'll need to sign him in," she said to Jen, pointing at George. "You can't just . . ."

But, too impatient to wait for the lifts, they had already opened the door to the stairwell and disappeared behind it.

"Right, so you need to sign here on the front page; initial the paragraph on page three, and then sign here, here, and here. Oh, and we'll need a couple of witnesses."

Malcolm got up. "Shall I get your secretary to be one?" he asked.

Harriet nodded. *This isn't really happening,* she told herself. *It's all just a terrible dream.*

She took the pen that Malcolm was holding and started to write.

❧ 29

"I wouldn't do that if I were you."

Jen, positioned behind her father, saw Harriet's face look up in shock as the door flew open and her ex-husband appeared in front of her. "What . . . what are you doing here, George?" she asked, her face going white. "Jen . . . what . . . I don't understand."

Jen opened her mouth to speak, but George got in there first.

"I was rather thinking of asking my friend Malcolm what *he* is doing here," he said sternly, walking into the room.

Jen followed, and perched on a chair. The tension in the room was electric—Malcolm staring angrily at George, her mother looking as if she was about to throw up, and her father prowling around the room like a caged tiger about to pounce.

"Signing something, Harriet?" he asked, his eyes falling on what looked like a contract.

Malcolm carefully picked up some papers and edged them across the table so that they partly covered the pages in front of Harriet. "Nothing of any interest to you, George," he said with a little smile. "Just a little bit of business. How are things, by the way? We must do lunch sometime . . ."

"Lunch. Yes, of course," George said thoughtfully, then he shook his head.

Jen looked at him with disdain, and then at her mother. Whatever was going on here made her sick to her stomach. As far as she was concerned, they all deserved one another, and a lot more. Was all business conducted in this way, she wondered—dodgy deals behind closed doors, threats and promises issued like banknotes?

"You see, the trouble is, Malcolm," George continued, "I'm not really the sort of person who can have lunch with a double-crossing bastard like you."

Jen frowned, surprised, and Malcolm looked up quickly. "George," he said in a warning voice. "Not here."

"Oh, I think here is the perfect place and time, don't you?" George said quickly as Jen and her mother watched in silence. "Let me guess what's going on here. Harriet, you're broke and Malcolm here is desperate. I smell a deal. . . ."

Jen stared at him. "Don't be ridiculous," she said irritably. "Mum would never do a deal with someone like Malcolm Bray. If anyone round here is doing a deal with him, it's more likely to be you . . ."

She looked at Harriet for support, but noticed that her mother was staring firmly at the table in front of her. Then she noticed the pen in her hand.

"Mum?" Jen said quickly. "Mum, tell him it isn't true . . ."

"I just wanted to save my firm," Harriet said quietly. "Your father had dug his own grave, and I saw an opportunity . . ."

"You were going to do a deal with Malcolm Bray?" Jen asked incredulously.

"*Is* doing one," Malcolm said immediately, standing up. "Look, George, I don't know what kind of a circus you're trying to create here, but it's too late. I've already tipped off the authorities that you were orchestrating that terrible corruption scandal—and Harriet has agreed to take us on as a client now that Axiom obviously wishes to distance itself from Bell Consulting. If I were you, I'd be worrying about my own future, not interfering in our business."

Jen stared at Malcolm, then at her father. "So it is true," she gasped. "You were behind it. You . . . you bastard."

George's face remained stony. "Harriet, put down that pen."

Harriet looked at him defiantly. "Don't tell me what to do, George. Don't ever tell me what to do."

"Please, then. Please put down the pen. Don't let yourself down, Harriet. Don't let everything come to this."

Harriet's hand moved slightly toward the contract. "I don't have any choice, George," she whispered. "There's nothing else for me to do."

He frowned. "There's always an alternative. We'll bail you out if you need funds. Jesus, you don't sell your soul to the devil the minute things get tough."

"Maybe Dad could pay some bribes for you," Jen said caustically. "Couldn't you, Dad?"

George turned and stared at her. "You really hate me, don't you?" he asked sadly.

"I don't hate you, Dad, I despise you. For letting me believe you. For letting me think I had a father again. I trusted you."

"And could you trust me again? If I asked you to? Now, I mean?"

Jen frowned. "Why should I?"

"Just because. Do you?"

Jen hesitated, taking in her mother's hesitant hand, her father's serious face. She had no idea what she thought of anything anymore. But deep down, she did want to believe that her father wasn't involved, that there was some perfectly reasonable explanation. Even though she knew it was highly unlikely, her heart wanted to trust him.

"Fine," she said quietly. "But if you let me down . . ."

George nodded. "Malcolm's right, I was behind it all," he said slowly as Jen watched him like a hawk. "Or, rather, I was behind the latest string of deals. I was rather baffled as to how Axiom kept winning contract after contract in Asia, when I knew just how shoddy their work was, and when I heard on the grapevine that there was money changing hands I was . . . well, I was intrigued."

Malcolm was looking at George with suspicion, but it was Harriet who spoke.

"I knew it," she said suddenly. "I knew it was you. And you knew Paul was involved all along and you let me work with him, let me trust him—"

"Paul?" Jen interrupted. "What's Paul got to do with it?"

"Ask your father," Harriet glowered. "He's the one who enjoys playing with people."

Jen looked at her father expectantly, and George smiled broadly.

"You're right again," he said. "I do like playing with people. And as for Paul, well, he's very good at what he does. Abysmal feng shui expert, but I suppose you can't have everything."

"How dare you!" Harriet shouted. "You've ruined my life once, and now you're trying to do it again."

George raised his eyebrows. "If I know Malcolm," he said archly, "and I think I do, I expect you were just about to attempt to ruin my life, so I suspect we're even. Anyway, I have never ruined your life. I made one mistake I accept, and that was to trust Malcolm. I thought that you should take the word of your old school friends, and that's what I did. But I regret it. Believe me, I regret it."

Jen frowned. "What are you talking about?" she demanded. "When did you take his word?"

"When he told me that his company was all above-board, many years ago. Your mother was trying to convince me to sever all ties with him, and I refused. Took his word over hers, which was, I can see now, a big mistake. A mistake for which we're all paying now, in many ways."

Jen frowned. "What do you mean?"

"He means that I divorced him over it. That and . . . other things," Harriet said, darkly.

Malcolm raised his eyebrows. "I'm glad I've made such a difference to your lives," he said sharply. "Now, Harriet, perhaps you could ask your family to leave and we can get on with our meeting?"

"I'm not going anywhere," Jen said firmly. "I want to know what's going on here."

George chuckled and looked at his watch. "Let me tell you," he said calmly. "What's going on here is that Malcolm Bray is about to get what's coming to him."

Malcolm frowned. "George, just bugger off, will you?" he said angrily.

"Oh, I intend to," George said affably. "But not before the police arrive."

Malcolm and Harriet looked up sharply.

"I don't want the police here," Harriet said quickly. "Paul isn't even here. He's—"

"Going to be here in about five minutes," George interrupted. "As are the police. I'm sorry, Malcolm, but it's not looking too good for you, old chum."

Malcolm shook his head. "George, I don't know what you're trying to prove, but getting the police here is just going to speed your journey to prison. You organized the bribes; you transferred the money. Bell Consulting will never survive this. . . ."

"Ah, now that's where you're wrong," George said. "You see, when you thought that I was bribing government officials for you, via our friend Paul, I was actually paying compensation to the poor buggers whose houses you built—if *built* is the right word for those pathetic imitations of houses your company put up."

Malcolm stared at him. "If this is some ridiculous ruse to cover your tracks, George, it won't work. . . ."

"No ruse," George said, then paused. "Actually, that's a lie. There was a ruse. It's just that it was aimed at you, not me. You see, our friend Paul may be a rather poor feng shui consultant, but he is a first-class undercover detective. One of Indonesia's finest."

He turned to Jen. "You can imagine that the Indonesian government were very keen to get to the bottom of any suspected corruption, can't you?"

She nodded silently.

"Well, Paul has been following your every move over the past few months, Malcolm. Every bribe, every lie. Sadly we haven't been able to trace any of the bribes you paid to get the tsunami construction work in the first place, but Paul and I have a rather good body of evidence for your subsequent attempts to bribe the officials who were investigating you. And the threats, of course. Nothing like the carrot and the stick to get results, eh, Malcolm?"

Malcolm regarded George stonily.

"I only realized today that it was you that leaked that letter to the *Times* over Christmas, though. That was stupid of me. But as soon as I did, I imagined you might pull something like this."

Jen watched as Malcolm's eyes narrowed, and her father winked at her.

"Face it, Malcolm, the game's over. You robbed me of my wife and you've tried to rob me of my firm, and now I like to think that I've partially got my own back."

Jen was looking at her father in shock. "You . . . you . . ." she stammered, unable to string a complete sentence together.

"I'm not going to sit here, listening to this," Malcolm said quickly, gathering his papers together and making for the door. "I've had enough of the two of you to last me a lifetime. Harriet, the deal's off. And George . . ."

But before he could finish his sentence, Paul Song appeared at the door, flanked by two uniformed policemen. He smiled politely at Jen, bowed to Harriet, and pointed out Malcolm, who was swiftly handcuffed.

"You're a bastard, George," Malcolm said bitterly as he was led away. "I've always despised you, you know."

"So it appears," George said in even tones. "And you, Malcolm, deserve everything that's coming to you."

*   *   *

"So you slept with Malcolm? Eeuurgh."

They were sitting in a pub round the corner from Bell Consulting, and Jen was staring at her mother incredulously, cradling a gin and tonic in her hands, while George was up at the bar buying a second round of drinks. Jen was still getting over the shock from the revelation that her father was the good guy after all, and Harriet was still having problems coming to terms with the fact that her feng shui adviser and confidant was actually an ex-militia policeman who'd bought her crystals from Woolworth's. All in all, Jen felt that they were handling it pretty well.

"It was a long time ago," Harriet said dismissively. "A lifetime ago."

"But Malcolm Bray?"

Harriet shot her daughter a warning look. "Enough, thank you."

"Sorry I took a bit long—bumped into a client at the bar," George said, appearing with a tray of drinks. "Enough of what?"

Harriet looked at him guiltily. "Nothing, George," she said quickly. "Nothing at all."

"I still can't believe you didn't tell me," Jen said, looking at her father accusingly. "All that time you let me think you were involved. Why didn't you trust me?"

"You didn't trust me," he said with a little smile. "And I didn't want you involved. Anyway, haven't you heard of the phrase 'a means to an end'?"

"Oh great, so I was the means?"

George shook his head. "Of course not. In spite of your mother's best attempts," he said, smiling.

"I still don't fully understand," said Harriet, shaking her head, trying to make sense of the situation.

"It's simple really," George said dismissively. "When Axiom got the deals in Indonesia, we were shocked, frankly. I saw the tender documents and they were uncompetitive and patchy at best. But I didn't think too much of it, until rumors started circulating about bribes and underhanded dealings. I dislike underhanded dealings, particularly when they're too close for comfort to my firm, so I did a little bit of digging. That's when I came across Paul, who was doing a bit of digging of his own. We hatched our little plan—I offered to help Malcolm out of a difficult situation by introducing him to Paul, who pretended to be a corrupt government investigator. Malcolm insisted on arm's-length deals—he's a clever man, I'll give him that—so I was supposed to pay Paul through our Indonesian office."

"But you didn't," Harriet said. "Yes, I kind of got that. But why did it take you so long to pin it on him? And why did the newspapers keep saying there were no leads?"

George shrugged. "My fault, I'm afraid. I didn't want Malcolm to suspect anything. We needed solid evidence of the initial bribes, so I sent a consultant out to Indonesia to see what he could find. Of course it was too late. And then we realized what Malcolm was doing—his plans to make it look like we were the ones behind it all along. Bloody man. If only I hadn't been in hospital over Christmas, I'd have worked it out sooner."

Jen reddened slightly as she remembered her attempts to keep him away from the news and away from work. "Still," she said quickly, "you've got him now."

Harriet bristled. "I hope Paul's got enough evidence to put him away for a long time," she said passionately.

George nodded sagely. "And to ruin his firm and put shockwaves through the industry."

They sat in silence for a few minutes, Jen watching how, together, her parents seemed different somehow. Her mother seemed more open—softer, but in a good way. A way that admitted she had vulnerabilities. And her father—well, she'd never seen him so cheerful. Although she suspected that had more to do with Malcolm Bray than either of them.

After a while, George turned to Jen. "So, how's the MBA going?"

She looked at him in disbelief. They'd been through all this, and he still wanted to know that she was working?

"Put it this way," she said, rolling her eyes, "this morning I was all ready to give up, and now I'm not so sure. But to be honest, I've had my hands a bit full lately"—she looked at her parents meaningfully—"so I'm not exactly ahead on my coursework . . ."

"You can't give up," George said immediately. "Don't be ridiculous. What's your latest assignment on? We'll help you, won't we, Harriet?"

Harriet paused. "Well, I suppose I might be able to help a little bit, although you know how I feel about MBAs . . ."

"You made me do it," Jen said incredulously.

"Come on, then, what's the assignment on?" George said impatiently.

"Bookselling," Jen said, suddenly feeling slightly less elated. She didn't want to write about bookselling anymore. She'd rather lost her enthusiasm for it.

"Bookselling?" said Harriet. "What an odd subject to choose. I'd have thought something about corporate social responsibility would be much better. Darling, you're so clever, you should choose a subject that really demonstrates your ability, don't you think?"

Jen looked her mother in the eye. "Mum, stop manipulating me. I'm doing bookselling."

Harriet sighed. "Well, if *you* think it's a good idea . . ."

"Of course it's a good idea," George said cheerfully. "In fact, the client I just met over there is in the book industry. She's in publishing, not sales, but she knows the book world better than anyone I know. You should meet her. Why don't I introduce you?"

Jen nodded vaguely. "Sure. Give me her number," she said.

"Rubbish, I'll introduce you now. You've got to grab opportunities when they present themselves, Jennifer. Don't ever leave till tomorrow what you can do today."

"I'm tired, Dad." Jen groaned. "Let me just have a drink, please?"

But her words fell on deaf ears, and George was already on his feet. "Come with me," he commanded.

Reluctantly, Jen followed her father to the other side of the pub, where she saw a glamorous blond woman sitting with three middle-aged men.

Her eyes flickered up and met George's with a smile, then she turned to Jen, who was frowning.

"Anita, this is my daughter, Jen. She's doing an MBA at Bell and writing a dissertation on bookselling. I thought the two of you should get to know each other. What do you think?"

Anita flashed a smile at Jen. "Love to, George. Hi, Jen. So you're interested in bookselling, are you?"

Jen stared at her, scowling. She was the woman from the restaurant, the one whom Daniel had been all over.

"Actually, I'm not sure my dissertation is going to be on bookselling anymore," she said quickly, her stomach starting to churn. Anita was the last person in the world she wanted to talk to. In fact, she didn't want to have to look at her for one more minute.

"What are you talking about?" asked George, bemused. "You just said—"

"I said I was thinking of bookselling. I've changed my mind," Jen said firmly, adding, before she could stop herself, "I've had enough of booksellers and bookselling."

Anita stared at her, then her eyes widened. "You're not Jen as in Daniel's Jen, are you?" she asked.

Jen's eyes narrowed. "I was," she said pointedly as her father looked at her, confused. "Before he decided to drop me for you."

Now Anita was looking confused. "Drop you for me? What the hell are you talking about? Daniel's crazy about you," she said, eyes wide.

"I saw you in the restaurant," Jen said angrily. "Look, it's fine, really. Have him."

"But I don't want him," Anita said, her face incredulous. "We were having lunch, that's all. Why would you think otherwise?"

Jen tried to keep her voice level but was struggling. The last thing she wanted was to come across as the petulant girlfriend in front of the glamorous Anita. And her father.

"He kissed you. And he hasn't called me. He was shitty to me when I last saw him and as soon as I left he went running off to have lunch with you . . ."

So, not doing so well at not sounding petulant, she thought to herself.

But Anita was smiling, not staring at her as if she were a sniveling child. "I was giving him advice, Jen. He was feeling terrible about the argument you guys had. He told me he'd behaved like a total prick and he didn't think you'd ever want to see him again."

Jen noticed her father wince slightly. "He did behave like a total prick," she said with a little smile.

"And when he told me what he said to you," Anita continued, "I totally agreed with him. But I said that if he apologized for a week, you might just forgive him."

Jen nodded, and her smile grew a little bigger.

"Anyway, he only kissed me to say thank you before running off to find you. He even called Bell Consulting and discovered you weren't there, so he was planning to go to your flat. That's the last I heard, anyway. So didn't he find you?"

Jen frowned and shook her head. "He never came," she said, her heart quickening its pace at the news that Daniel wasn't sleeping with Anita. That he'd felt bad after the argument. But why hadn't he come over? What had stopped him? "Maybe he changed his mind," she suggested, in a faltering voice.

Anita shook her head. "No, he was definitely going over."

Jen racked her brain desperately. Had she been out? Had she been in the bath? Had she . . .

Suddenly she looked at Anita and took out her phone. "Gavin," she said frantically. "Gavin was there."

Anita nodded, humoring Jen as if she knew exactly who Gavin was.

Jen dialed a number and waited, her face gradually getting hot. She heard Gavin's voice as he picked up.

"Yeah?"

"Gavin," she said. "Did you bump into Daniel the other day? When you left my place, did you bump into Daniel? And if you lie to me, I swear I will skin you alive."

There was a pause. "I might have done."

Jen sighed loudly. She could feel the adrenalin sweeping through her body. "And did you, by any chance, say anything to him that might have made him turn around?"

Another pause. "Look, Jen, I might have told him that we were kind of back together. And that you never wanted to see him again. But I was only thinking of you. I was just working on the basis that if he wasn't on the scene, you and me might . . ."

"You . . . you bloody imbecile," Jen shouted. "You stupid, idiotic . . ."

"Bastard?" offered Anita.

"Bastard," confirmed Jen, quickly hanging up the phone. "Dad, I've got to go," she said breathlessly, turning to Anita and smiling. "Thanks. And sorry about the whole thinking you were sleeping with him business."

Anita smiled. "No problem. Maybe we could have lunch sometime to talk about your dissertation. Make Daniel jealous instead?"

Jen nodded gratefully, gave her dad a quick kiss, and ran out of the pub, stopping only to tell her mother that she was going, and refusing to listen to Harriet's suggestion that she do something else entirely.

༄ 30

Daniel wiped his hands on his trousers and looked at his watch. In just five minutes, the other board members would arrive and all eyes would be on him. He would tell them about his cost-cutting plans; about his plans to wage a price war with children's fiction. And then he would go and kill himself.

Daniel frowned. No, he corrected himself, that's not what he'd do at all; he would go and implement the plans. He was a managing director and he had to start behaving like one. It wasn't like he had much else going for him, he thought ruefully.

Suddenly he got the urge to call Jen, to ask her why she was with that ridiculous tramp of a boyfriend, to ask her to run away with him to Borneo or somewhere equally far away. But he dismissed the idea as soon as he'd had it. Focus on the here and now, he told himself. Focus on what you've actually got, not on pipe dreams.

He checked his watch a second time and decided he had time to nip to the men's room.

Jen pushed open the doors to Wyman's tentatively, trying to work out what she was going to say. "I'm sorry" didn't really seem to cover it sufficiently; "I'm sorry, and don't worry, I'm going to detach Gavin's limbs from his body" seemed a little over the top. And what if he just looked at her like she was mad? He might not have cared when Gavin told him that she'd got back with him. He might have been relieved.

She shook herself. Of course he wasn't relieved. This was going to be one of those great reunions, she just knew it. Maybe she should have brought flowers.

The receptionist was busy chatting to someone at the desk, and Jen decided not to risk being asked if she had an appointment, heading straight for the elevator instead. Then she thought of something. Pausing briefly, she reached for the flowers that were still sitting right there. So, the lilies were a bit old—they were still better than nothing. She tried taking out one or two stems, but they were all tied up together and after grappling for a moment or two and worrying that the receptionist was going to say something, she picked up the entire vase and jumped into the elevator.

A minute later, the doors pinged open on Daniel's floor and Jen stepped out, wondering again what on earth induced her to take an entire vase of flowers from the reception area. It was so big it nearly covered her face. Which, she conceded, wasn't such a bad thing—at least it gave her camouflage as she walked down the corridor, even if she did look faintly ridiculous.

As she approached Daniel's office, she saw that the door was open and that no one was inside. A middle-aged woman, presumably his secretary, was sitting outside.

"Those for the board meeting?" she asked vaguely, peering at her computer screen as she spoke.

Jen thought for a moment. If there was a board meeting, Daniel would be there.

She nodded.

"Down the corridor," the woman said, pointing left.

Jen obediently followed her directions, trying to shift the vase in her hands so that she could see where she was going. She would just grab Daniel before he went in, she thought to herself. Quickly tell him that Gavin was a lying idiot and that if he was free later, perhaps they could meet up and talk. And if he said no, well, that would be fine. She would simply hand him the flowers, and walk away, dignity intact.

Or not, she thought with a shrug. But, then again, if she got really desperate, there was always the option of begging and wailing, she decided, with a little smile.

The corridor ended with double doors, which were open, leading to an empty room. As she walked in, Jen took a deep breath and tried to go over what she wanted to say. She immediately found herself stifling a yawn— it was only midafternoon but she realized she was exhausted. Still, she wasn't surprised—she'd never known a day like this.

She closed her eyes briefly and leaned against the wall. She should put the flowers down, she decided. It wasn't really helping her, lugging around a huge vase full of water and lily stems.

But before she could move, she felt someone looking at her, and opened her eyes quickly.

There was a man with gray hair frowning at her. "Can I help you?"

"I . . . um . . . I was looking for Daniel. Daniel Peterson."

"Are those for the boardroom?" He was looking at the flowers.

Jen started to shake her head, then decided against it. "Yes. I suppose. I mean, they're for Daniel . . ."

"For the boardroom," the man said. It was a statement, not a question, and Jen found herself walking in and placing the vase in the middle of the table.

"Daniel," the man continued, "what on earth did you order these flowers for? No one will be able to see anyone else."

Jen turned round, startled, to see Daniel appear at the door. He looked over at her and his eyes widened.

"I didn't . . ." he started to say, then stopped, his face utterly flummoxed.

The older man was staring at Jen, who shrugged limply at Daniel.

". . . didn't realize they'd be so big," Daniel finished, looking at Jen curiously now.

She nodded seriously. "No, nor did I," she said. The older man was now staring at her oddly, and she took another breath, turning imploringly to Daniel. She had to let him know why she was here. Had to explain. "The . . . the shop just wanted to inform you . . ." she said hesitantly. "About the mixup a few days ago. Our employee, Gavin—the one who looks like a tramp— he . . . well, he wasn't entirely telling the truth . . ."

There was a hint of a smile playing on Daniel's lips.

"Not *entirely* telling the truth?" he asked.

"Not at all, actually," Jen said, rolling her eyes. "He made it all up."

"I'm so pleased," Daniel said quickly. "I was so desperate to apologize for my dreadful behavior. The last time I was . . ." He looked over at Robert and frowned slightly. ". . . in the shop, I was angry and it had nothing to do with the . . . flowers."

The man was shaking his head now. "Apologize? What sort of contract have we got with these people? And what are you doing spending your time in florists, Daniel? I thought you'd been working on corporate strategies for the board to agree on."

He was smiling thinly, and Jen suddenly realized why they were in the boardroom. Today was the big day, Daniel's make-or-break presentation.

"Actually, no," Daniel said evenly. "And actually, she's not a florist."

Jen reddened guiltily. If Daniel told this guy who she was, he'd never live it down.

"Then who is she?"

Daniel looked at her, then looked at Robert, as if doing a quick mental calculation, while Jen held her breath. This was an important day for Daniel. She wouldn't let him screw it up just because she'd turned up out of the blue.

"I'm from Bell Consulting," she said suddenly. "I've . . . I've been working with Daniel on the ideas for this presentation."

She shrugged helplessly at Daniel, who grinned.

"Robert, meet Jennifer Bell."

Robert turned to look at her curiously, shook his head in wonderment, then wandered over to greet the other people who were arriving for the meeting.

Daniel winked and moved over toward her. "I'm so glad you came," he whispered. "And I'm so, so sorry. You were right—I was a prick."

"No, I'm sorry," Jen whispered. "You present what you like—it's got nothing to do with me."

"Bugger that," Daniel said firmly, then he frowned. "I deleted our presentation," he said dolefully, then looked at Jen hopefully. "Can you remember any of it?"

Jen thought for a moment, then pulled some paper out of her bag. "Most of it's in here," she said, handing him her half-written assignment.

Daniel grinned. "Play along with me, okay?" he said softly as the others came over to say hello.

Jen nodded silently and felt Daniel's hand brush so lightly against hers that she almost thought she imagined it, but the tingling sensation that resulted from it told her otherwise.

"Daniel," said Robert as everyone started to take their seats around the table, "I hope you know what you're doing. I don't remember you mentioning any consultants."

Daniel grinned. "No, I don't think I did. But don't worry—for the first time in a long time I know exactly what I'm doing."

As Robert sat down uncertainly, Daniel turned back round to Jen. "I can't remember half the stuff we talked about," he whispered. "You're going to have to prompt me."

"Stuff?" Jen whispered back. "What do you mean?"

"Bookselling," Daniel whispered, his eyes twinkling. "I want to talk to them about good, old-fashioned bookselling."

"And so," Daniel said, looking around the room, "to sum up, there's no point in us being in the bookselling business if we're going to act like we're selling just anything—potatoes, computers, whatever. The point is that books are different, and if we're going to grow, we need to be different too."

He looked at Jen, who gave him a reassuring smile. Doing a presentation with no notes and no slides was a crazy thing to do, but somehow Daniel had got through it, with Jen scribbling things down on bits of paper as she remembered them, and passing them to him. It had felt quite exhilarating—felt like Daniel and her against the world, fighting their corner. Or, you know, sitting in a boardroom telling a load of businessmen how to run a business. She smiled at Daniel as he looked around the room.

Robert cleared his throat. "All very interesting, Daniel. But we've heard a lot of waffle and very few specifics. Would you like to enlighten us on how you might make Wyman's *different*?"

Jen watched as Daniel put his hands through his hair nervously, three times in a row. "Well," he said hesitantly, obviously thrown off his stride, "we had a number of ideas. There were, um, well, in terms of customer knowledge, we were thinking along the lines of, uh . . ."

"Working in partnership with other companies," Jen prompted. "One of the big travel websites, for instance. A customer books a flight to Spain, and the travel website is linked to Wyman's, so they can buy a Spanish guidebook at the same time, or maybe a couple of novels set in Spain. If it's a beach location, the system suggests beach reads. And then, if you buy a book, it's waiting for you on your seat when you get on the plane so you don't have to carry it around with you."

Jen watched as Robert frowned. Daniel looked at her with a grateful smile and nodded for her to continue.

"Or branding," she said, getting into her stride now. "At the moment, Wyman's is a great shop, but once someone's bought a book, once they've taken it home, it could have come from anywhere, couldn't it? I mean, it's not like Marc Jacobs where you have the label to remind you why you spent that money."

She looked around the boardroom, and was met by a sea of curious eyes.

"Okay, so here's an idea," she said, remembering sitting on Daniel's sofa a couple of weeks before, drinking wine and coming up with all these schemes. "When your buyers choose the books they want to stock each month, they don't just order whatever quantity; they do a joint venture. They guarantee to take a fixed number of books in return for having the Wyman's brand on the back. Books from Wyman's will be instantly recognizable. And people will want to shop there because of it. It's a possibility, right?"

Daniel was grinning now. "We could have a loyalty program," he said, the excitement back in his voice, "with reduced prices for members, invitations to talks by authors, chat rooms to discuss books online. We could publish a magazine with the first chapters of a whole load of books to entice people into the shop. We could even give it out for free on planes and enable people to order books for their return flights . . ."

"Yes, thank you, Daniel, and er . . ." Robert looked at Jen vaguely.

"Jennifer Bell," Daniel said firmly.

"Right. Well, thank you, both of you. But, Daniel, as we've discussed before, I think what the board is really looking for is a, how shall I put this, a more focused plan. A strategic plan that considers our supply chain, cost efficiencies, that sort of thing . . ."

"I disagree," said one of the men round the table. "I think we need a bit of creativity."

"I like the airline idea," said another. "I know the chief exec of American Airlines. I'm sure he'd be interested."

Robert frowned. "Well, of course, we may individually like one or two of the ideas, but in the round, what it amounts to is . . ."

". . . is what I want to do," Daniel concluded for him. "Take it or leave it."

"Well," said Robert, "in that case I really think we need to . . ."

"Take it," said the man who liked the airline idea.

"Absolutely," said the man who was in favor of creativity.

"I agree," said a mousy woman who hadn't spoken for the whole meeting.

Robert looked around, his eyebrows raised to the middle of his forehead.

"But . . . but . . ." he said helplessly.

"Thanks for all your help, Robert," Daniel said, picking up his things. "I think that probably concludes this meeting. I'll see you tomorrow?"

Then he turned to Jen and winked. "If you're not too busy carting bloody great vases of lilies around this evening, do you think I might be able to buy you dinner?"

She smiled broadly. "I'd like that," she said softly. "And Daniel?"

He looked at her expectantly.

"Anita says 'hi.' "

"Anita?" Daniel shook his head. "God, you can't trust anyone to keep their mouths shut these days, can you?"

And with that, he leaned down, picked Jen up, and kissed her, just like she'd been dreaming he would all the way through the meeting.

❧ EPILOGUE

"So did Jack tell you about Brian?"

Jen listened idly to the two men standing nearby as she waited for Daniel outside the church.

"Brian-who-shags-everything-that-moves Brian? No, no I don't think so."

"The very same. Oh, man, you're going to love this then. So, six months ago he's been out at this company bash, a late night, he's maybe overdone it a little on the Bacardi Breezers, if you know what I'm saying. Tried to go home with Carly from Mergers, but she told him where to go. Anyway, he's on his way home when he decides he needs to take a leak. Like, he really needs to. So he convinces the taxi to stop, he jumps out, and he's there, taking a leak down an alley when he's mugged by this group of young guys."

"No!"

"Really! And they don't just take his money—they take all his clothes, too. They leave him with his keys, that's all. Which is nice of them really. I mean, it could be worse, right?"

"I guess . . ."

"Okay, but it doesn't end there. See, he gets home to his apartment building and he finds his wife outside, all packed up ready to go. And when he asks her what she's doing there, she tells him that she doesn't want to see him anymore because she's been sleeping with his best friend for a year."

Jen frowned. She'd heard this story before. If she wasn't very much mistaken, it was the story that had led her to Daniel, all those months ago. And led her into the men's room, of course. Still, hopefully now she'd actually get to find out what happened.

"You're kidding!"

"No, I'm deadly serious. And he's standing there, in his underpants, and fortunately she wants the cab so she agrees to pay his fare too, but when he goes to open the door he finds that she's double locked it. He doesn't have the key. So he decides to go round to see the friend. Only he's got to drive there as he hasn't got any money . . ."

"You look lovely. But what are you doing skulking around here? I've been looking for you."

Jen looked up at Daniel, who was in his morning suit and looked more gorgeous than she'd ever seen him. As he leaned down to kiss her, she heard Jack and his friend wander off toward the church and sighed in irritation.

"Now I'm never going to find out what happened to Brian," she said in exasperation.

Daniel looked at her oddly and she rearranged her tightly boned dress to enable her to breathe.

"Who's Brian?"

Jen grinned. "I have no idea. Look, I'm sorry, I was just eavesdropping. You look pretty nice too, by the way."

He nodded gallantly. "Are you going to be okay walking down the aisle in that thing? It looks hideously uncomfortable."

Jen shrugged. "I don't exactly have much choice, do I? You can't imagine Mum was exactly open to my ideas, can you?"

"Don't be too hard on her," Daniel said as he leaned down to give her another kiss. "It is her wedding day, after all."

"Let's just hope she gets here, shall we?" Jen suggested. Harriet wasn't known for her organizational skills, and as chief bridesmaid, Jen had planned to arrive with her, making sure she got there on time. But, of course, there had been a last minute change of plan—Harriet had had a change of heart about the flowers and had insisted that Jen get there early to check that her instructions had been followed to the letter. She needn't have worried— the whole church was full of white roses and the smell was quite intoxicating.

"She'll be here, don't worry. So are you going to wear that dress to your MBA graduation next week?"

Jen punched Daniel lightly on the arm. "Idiot. Go and do something useful."

He squeezed her hand and wandered off and as he did, Jen saw Angel arrive.

"Angel! Over here!"

Angel wafted over, her beautiful boyfriend in tow. "Hi, Ravi," Jen said, beaming as he kissed her on both cheeks.

"I still can't believe this is the man you're refusing to marry," she whispered to her friend.

Angel gave Jen a little shrug. "I don't want an arranged marriage to him. Doesn't mean he can't ask me nor- mally, though," she said, a little glint in her eye.

Jen rolled her eyes. "Only you, Angel. Look, you should go in and get a good seat—I'm just waiting for my mother."

Angel raised her eyebrows. "Things are getting less complicated for you, at last, aren't they?" she said with the hint of a smile.

Jen winked. "Maybe it's your turn now," she said, grinning.

As Angel and Ravi wandered into the church, Lara and Alan walked over toward Jen.

"Blimey, your tits look big in that dress," Lara said in wonderment. "What have you got in there?"

Jen blushed. "It's the boning. It hoists everything upward," she explained, embarrassed. "And it's bloody painful, to be honest."

Alan grinned sheepishly. "You look lovely," he said. "And please ignore my girlfriend's crude language. She's just jealous that someone else's breasts are more on display than hers."

"You idiot!" Lara said playfully and Jen smiled. She still found it hard to believe the transformation in Alan, for which she took full credit, even though she knew that she'd really had very little to do with it. True to his word, he had applied his business management prowess to himself, and in the process he'd turned himself into an interesting, funny guy, who listened to people and made Lara happier than she'd ever expected to be. Plus, of course, he'd "revamped his brand" by ditching the glasses, buying some very nice clothes, and getting his hair cut. It was like a makeover show, Jen thought to herself regularly, only he'd done it all himself. And all to attract Lara, who he'd secretly been in love with from day one. *Some spy I was,* Jen thought to herself with a little smile. *I didn't see what was going on right under my nose.*

"Come on, Alan," Lara said. "Everyone's in the church

now. We should go in. When's your mum getting here, Jen?"

Jen frowned. "God knows. She's meant to be here any minute . . ."

As she spoke, a car drew up. A white London taxi. And out of it stepped her mother, an apparition in cream silk. Lara and Alan waved at her, then turned to find their places in the church, and Jen ran over to meet her.

"You look . . . perfect," she said, small tears appearing in her eyes. "Just . . . perfect."

Harriet smiled bashfully, and Jen gave her a quick hug. She'd never seen Harriet looking anything that remotely resembled bashful before, and she wanted to make the most of it. As Harriet disentangled herself from Jen's embrace, they made their way to the church door where Geoffrey was waiting for her, his beard back and proud.

"Ready?" he asked.

Harriet turned to Jen. "You think I'm doing the right thing?" she asked. "You don't think it's foolish to marry the same man twice?"

Jen peeked into the church and saw her father waiting nervously at the front, checking his watch and removing imaginary specks from his morning suit. He saw her and smiled, a smile that she'd only discovered recently—the uncertain, humble smile of a man in love. No one had been more surprised than her when they announced that they'd decided to give things another go, and yet now it seemed the most natural thing in the world. George had invested in Green Futures, so they were partners in business again now, and they still argued most of the time, but now it was just friendly bickering. They needed each other, Jen had realized. And had never stopped caring about each other, even if they disguised it as hate for so long.

She smiled back, then looked at her mother carefully. "Do you trust him?" she asked her.

Harriet nodded. "For fifteen years I hated him," she whispered. "And for fifteen years, we spent all our waking moments convincing ourselves we did the right thing, that everything was the other's fault. But it was all because we loved each other so deeply. He isn't a perfect man, Jennifer. He doesn't always do the right thing, doesn't always think of others much. But he loves me, and I love him, and I think that probably we always have."

"Then there's your answer," Jen said with a little smile. "Here, I got you something."

It was a lily.

"Give this to Dad when you get to the altar," Jen told Harriet, pressing it into her hand. "Love is precious, and it's fragile, too. Make sure he knows that."

"Thank you, darling. I think he knows that now. I think we both do. And Jennifer?"

Jen looked up. "Yes, Mum?"

Harriet frowned slightly, and Jen swallowed, steeling herself for an emotional mother-daughter moment, which she hoped her mascara would survive.

"I thought I told you to wear those other shoes," Harriet said. "The ones with the lower heel. I don't want you towering over me down the aisle. You never listen to me, do you?"

Jen smiled. Some things, she realized, would never change.

"Yes, Mum," she said with a smile. "Now get a move on, or you'll be late for your wedding."

Kate Hetherington sighed and put down her drink dramatically.

"I just think there has to be a better way," she said, shaking her head in disbelief. "You'd think they'd have developed some sort of radar by now."

Her friend Sal frowned. "Radar?"

"To find the perfect man. So you don't have to endure things like speed dating. Honestly, Sal, it was the worst night of my life. I hated every minute of it. I hated every man in there. And at the end, I still came out disappointed that I only got one number. I mean, it's wrong on so many levels, I don't even know where to start."

Sal shrugged. "I bet it wasn't that bad. I think it sounds like fun, actually."

Kate looked at her friend levelly. "That's because you're happily married so you know you'll never have to go. Things like speed dating always sound like fun in principle—it's the reality that's so excruciating."

"So why did you go, then?"

"Because you made me."

"I didn't *make* you! I just said you should give it a go, that's all."

Kate sighed. "I know. I think a little voice inside me really thought it might work, too. I mean, I thought I might . . . meet someone's eyes and just know. . . ."

"But it didn't work out that way?"

"No," Kate said despondently. "And the truth is, I'm kind of running out of options here. I'm going to be thirty soon, and I don't see any knights on white steeds turning up to whisk me away, do you?"

Sal shook her head. "Does the steed have to be white?" she asked, a little smile playing on her lips.

Kate grinned. "I'm willing to stretch to cream," she conceded. "If the knight is good-looking enough."

"Ah, here you are. Sorry I'm late. So, how are we all?"

Kate and Sal turned around and saw their friend Tom approaching. "Dreadful, thanks," Kate said lugubriously. "How're you?"

Tom grimaced. "In need of a drink. Can I get either of you a refill?"

Kate handed him her glass, requesting a vodka tonic, and Sal shook her head. As he disappeared off toward the bar, she frowned. "And you're sure there wasn't a single eligible man there? Not even one?"

"Not even one," Kate assured her. "They were all either creepy, letchy, or just plain weird." Sal looked at her dubiously, and Kate's hackles rose. "What?" she demanded. "Don't you believe me?"

Sal widened her eyes. "I didn't say a thing!"

"No, but you looked at me like you wanted to. You think I would have missed some gorgeous guy just waiting to sweep me off my feet?"

Sal hesitated, and then blurted, "I just think that

maybe your aspirations are too high. I mean, all you talk about is sweeping and knights and stuff. Instead of nice-looking, or amenable. I'm just not sure you're looking for the right . . . qualities."

"Right qualities?"

Sal put her drink down. "This is the real world, Kate, that's all. Richard Gere isn't going to turn up in a convertible car to whisk you off into the sunset."

"I don't want Richard Gere to turn up," Kate snapped. "I just want . . ."

Sal raised her eyebrows expectantly.

"Fine," Kate said with a sigh. "I admit it. My aspirations are high. I want fireworks, and I want magic. What's wrong with that? I can't help it if I'd rather chew my own feet off than endure a night of speed dating again."

"Speed dating?" Tom asked, arriving with the drinks. "So you went, did you?"

Kate nodded. "Tried it, hated it, never doing it again." Avoiding Sal's eyes, she took her drink from Tom and shuffled her chair around to make room for him.

They were sitting in the Bush Bar and Grill, a bar-cum-restaurant that was five minutes' walk from each of their homes and which hosted their weekly Sunday-night drinks date. The three of them lived streets away from one another in the area of London that sat between Shepherd's Bush, West Kensington, and Hammersmith. Which particular section they chose to tell people they lived in depended on whether they were at a job interview, trying to impress someone, or hoping not to get mugged. Sal and her husband, Ed, lived on a road that was officially in West Kensington; Kate's zip code said W6, which meant Hammersmith, but she was really closer to Shepherd's Bush. And Tom lived on the Golborne Road, a stone's throw from the Bush Bar and Grill, and two minutes' walking distance from both of the women.

"So it was as ghastly as it sounded?" Tom said dryly.

"Worse," Kate said. "I had to meet twenty people for five minutes, which isn't long, is it?" She gave Tom a hopeful look, and he nodded firmly. "But I still ran out of things to say," she said. "I mean, they asked such stupid stuff. Life if I was an animal, which one would I be and why. What sort of a question is that?"

Tom frowned. "What animal did you say you'd be?" he asked with interest.

"I started off with a dolphin, and then someone made a joke about sperm whales and I lost the will to live. After that, I was a crocodile twice, a rottweiler, and a meerkat." She smirked a little.

"Well, no wonder you didn't meet anyone nice," Sal complained. "They probably thought you were a total Froot Loop."

"But a very sweet Froot Loop," Tom said affectionately.

"I could set you up with one of Ed's friends, if you want," Sal interjected. "I think I can safely guarantee that none of them would ask you any animal-related questions at all."

"Thanks, Sal," Kate said with a shrug. "But I've kind of gone off the whole dating scene for a bit. And anyway, I'm not sure I'd have much in common with many of Ed's friends. . . ."

Sal frowned. "Because you think financiers are all pinstripe shirt–wearing bores?" she asked crossly.

"No!" Kate said. "Not at all. But come on, you and Ed are so . . . grown up."

"Ed's only thirty-five," Sal said defensively. "It's not so old. And I'm no older than you."

"I didn't say 'old.' Grown up is different."

"How?" Sal asked, her eyes narrowing.

Tom grinned. "Sal, darling, don't play the innocent with us. We both know that when you're at home, you and Ed talk about stocks and shares and the impact of the Budget on your pensions. Whereas I doubt Kate here even has a pension. Do you, Kate?"

Kate shifted uncomfortably in her chair. "I'm going to. You know, at some point."

"Kate!" Sal said, shocked. "You don't have a pension? That's so . . . irresponsible."

"I rest my case." Kate sighed. "None of Ed's friends would be interested in me because I don't have a stock portfolio. I don't even know how I'd go about getting one. And the truth is, I don't even care. So I'm going to have to spend the rest of my days at nasty speed-dating events at which hideous pigs leer and stare at my breasts all night. Bloody marvelous."

"Seriously?" Tom asked. "They stared at *your* breasts?"

Kate hit him. Her lack of cleavage was a running gag with Sal and Tom. Had been since high school when she'd been the last girl in their whole class to need a bra. "One guy stared at them for the full five minutes, actually. And then he gave me his card and said he'd love to see me again! Can you believe it? Steve, his name was. I kept his card as a reminder of everything I'm not looking for in a man."

"Nothing wrong with staring at breasts," Tom said, grinning. "I think they're a great indicator of marriage potential, as it happens."

Sal rolled her eyes. "Tom, you are incorrigible. And I

don't know why you're so laid back about the whole thing, either. When's the last time you had a serious girlfriend?"

"I pride myself on steering clear of seriousness in the girlfriend department," Tom replied with dignity. "I have enough seriousness at work, thanks."

"Being a surgeon doesn't preclude you from falling in love," Sal continued. "Don't you ever meet anyone you actually like?"

Tom blanched. "*Like* is an odd word, don't you think?" He looked down at his empty glass. "I *like* lots of things. Doesn't mean I want to move in with them, does it? Doesn't mean I want to sign my life away."

Kate pounced on the opening. To Sal, she said, "See? You say I'm hopeless, but I'm not as hopeless as Tom."

"Ah, that's where you're wrong," Tom said quickly. "You are the epitome of a hopeless romantic. Hopeless, ironically, because you do hope that fairy tale love story will come true for you. I, on the other hand, am comfortable with the fact that it doesn't. Therefore, I, unlike you, am never going to be disappointed."

"You think I'm going to be disappointed?"

Tom raised his eyebrows. "Kate, for a man to live up to your expectations, he would have to be six-foot-four, strapping but sensitive, intelligent but always willing to accept your point of view, continually sweeping you off your feet and basically dedicating his life to you. For a woman to live up to mine, she would need to be . . . well, female. And perhaps not a complete dog."

Kate scowled. "I am not a hopeless romantic. That's rubbish."

"You're not?" Tom said with an ill-concealed grin.

"Do you remember how many universities you had on your shortlist?"

She looked at him curiously. "Two," she said. "No, three."

"You may have had three in the end, but only because you were forced into it. Don't you remember? You were madly in love with that guy in the year above us, Paul James. And you insisted that you had to go to Bristol because that's where he was going, and the two of you were meant to be together."

"So?" Kate knew where this was going. "I liked Bristol. It was a great university."

"Yes, but you split up with Paul at the beginning of the summer holidays! You made a major decision about your life based on some romantic notion that you were meant to be with some spotty teenager, and it could have been a disaster."

"But it wasn't, was it?" Kate said hotly. "And at least I'm open to love. At least I'm open to commitment and marriage and living happily ever after. You've become way too cynical, Tom."

"Maybe. But if I have, then I'm pleased," Tom said with a dismissive wave of his hand. "Anyway, it's not as if anyone has ever expressed any interest in marrying me. I mean, would either of you take someone like me on?"

His eyes met Kate's for a moment, and she frowned. "God, no," she said. "Can't think of anything worse."

Sal sighed. "Me either," she relented, prompting Tom to pull a face of disappointment. "Fine. Well, you both enjoy your lonely existences, and drop in on me and my boring husband from time to time, won't you?"

Kate leant over and squeezed Sal's arm. "Sal, you were

always ahead of the game. You had your university offers before we'd even got round to applying. You had a job before either of us had got over our end-of-university hangovers. We'll get there eventually. At least, I hope we will."

Sal smiled. "Fine, you're right. But I still think you should let me set you up," she said with another sigh.

Kate shook her head. "Thanks, but no. I'll meet my Mr. Right eventually," she said, shooting Tom a meaningful look. "At least I hope I will."